BOOKS BY ELMORE LEONARD

The Bounty Hunters

The Law at Randado

Escape from Five Shadows

Last Stand at Saber River

Hombre

The Big Bounce

The Moonshine War

Valdez Is Coming

Forty Lashes Less One

Mr. Majestyk

Fifty-two Pickup

Swag

Unknown Man No. 89

The Hunted

The Switch

Gunsights

Gold Coast

City Primeval

Split Images

Cat Chaser

Stick

LaBrava

Glitz

Bandits

Touch

Freaky Deaky

Killshot

Get Shorty

Maximum Bob

Rum Punch

Pronto

Riding the Rap

Out of Sight

Cuba Libre

The Tonto Woman and
    Other Western Stories

Elmore Leonard's
    Western Roundup #1

Elmore Leonard's
    Western Roundup #2

Elmore Leonard's
    Western Roundup #3

Be Cool

Pagan Babies

ELMORE LEONARD'S WESTERN ROUNDUP #3

Valdez Is Coming

Hombre

ELMORE LEONARD

Delta
Trade Paperbacks

A Delta Book
Published by
Dell Publishing
a division of
Random House, Inc.
1540 Broadway
New York, New York 10036

The trademark Delta® is registered in the U.S. Patent and Trademark Office and in other countries.
ISBN: 0-385-33324-2
Manufactured in the United States of America
Published simultaneously in Canada

January 1999

10 9 8 7 6 5 4 3 2

BVG

CONTENTS

VALDEZ
IS
COMING

····································

ONE

Picture the ground rising on the east side of the pasture with scrub trees thick on the slope and pines higher up. This is where everybody was. Not all in one place but scattered in small groups, about a dozen men in the scrub, the front line, the shooters who couldn't just stand around. They'd fire at the shack when they felt like it, or when Mr. Tanner passed the word, they would all fire at once.

Others were up in the pines and on the road that ran along the crest of the hill, some three hundred yards from the shack across the pasture. Those watching made bets whether the man in the shack would give himself up or get shot first.

It was Saturday and that's why everybody had the time. They would arrive in Lanoria, hear about what happened, and shortly after, head out to the cattle company pasture. Most of the men went out alone, leaving their families in town, though there were a few women who came. The other women waited. And the people who had business in town and couldn't leave waited. Now and then a few would come back from the pasture to have a drink or their dinner and would tell what was going on. No, they hadn't got him yet. Still inside the line shack and not showing his face. But they'd get him. A few more would go out from town when they heard this. Also a wagon from De Spain's went out with whiskey. That's how the saloon was set up in the pines overlooking the pasture. Somebody said it was like the goddam Fourth of July.

Barely a mile from town those going out would hear the gunfire—like a skirmish way over the other side of the woods, thin specks of sound—and this would hurry them. They were careful though, topping the slope, looking across the pasture, getting their bearings, then peering around to see who was there. They would see a friend and ask about this Mr. Tanner, and the friend would point him out.

The man there in the dark suit: thin and bony, not big especially, but looking like he was made of gristle and hard to kill, with a moustache and a thin nose and a dark dusty hat worn over his eyes. That was him. They had heard about Frank Tanner, but not many had ever seen him. He had a place south in the foothills of the Santa Ritas and almost to the border. They said he had an army riding for him, Americans and Mexicans, and that his place was like a barracks except for the women. They said he traded horses and cattle and guns across into Mexico to the revolutionary forces and he had all the riders in case the Federales came down on him; also in case his customers ever decided not to pay. Sure he had at least twenty-five men and he didn't graze a head of beef himself. Where were they? somebody wanted to know. Driving a herd south. That's what he had come here for, cattle; bought them from Maricopa.

Somebody else said he had brought his wife along—"God-*dam*, a good-looking young woman, I'll tell you, some years younger than he is"—and she was waiting for him at the Republic Hotel right now, staying up in his room, and not many people had seen her.

They would look at Mr. Tanner, then across the cattle pasture to the line shack three hundred yards away. It was a little bake-oven of a hut, wood framed and made of sod and built against a rise where there were pines so the hut would be in shade part of the day. There were no windows in the hut, no gear lying around to show anybody lived there. The hut stood in the sun now with its door closed, the door chipped and splintered by all the bullets that had poured into it and through it.

Off to the right where the pine shapes against the sky rounded and became willows, there in the trees by the creek bed, was the man's wagon and team. In the wagon were the supplies he'd bought that morning in Lanoria before Mr. Tanner spotted him.

Out in front of the hut about ten or fifteen feet there was something on the ground. From the slope three hundred yards away nobody could tell what it was until a man came who had field glasses. He looked up and said, frowning, it was a doll: one made of cloth scraps, a stuffed doll with buttons for eyes.

"The woman must have dropped it," somebody said.

"The *woman*?" the man with the field glasses said.

A Lipan Apache woman who was his wife or his woman or just with him. Mr. Tanner hadn't been clear about that. All they knew was that there was a woman in the hut with him and if the man wanted her to stay and get shot that was his business.

A Mr. Beaudry, the government land agent for the county, was there. Also Mr. Malson, manager of the Maricopa Cattle Company, and a horsebreaker by the name of Diego Luz, who was big for a Mexican but never offensive and who drank pretty well.

Mr. Beaudry, nodding and also squinting so he could picture the man inside the line shack, said, "There was something peculiar about him. I mean having a name like Orlando Rincón."

"He worked for me," Mr. Malson said. He was looking at Mr. Tanner. "I mistrusted him and I believe that was part of it, his name being Orlando Rincón."

"Johnson," Mr. Tanner said.

"I hired him two, three times," Mr. Malson said. "For heavy work. When I had work you couldn't pay a white man to do."

"His name is Johnson," Mr. Tanner said. "There is no fuzzhead by the name of Orlando Rincón. I'm telling you this fuzzhead is from the Fort Hauchuca Tenth fuzzhead Cavalry and his name was Johnson when he killed James C. Erin six months ago and nothing else."

He spoke as you might speak to young children to press something into their minds. This man seemed to have no feeling and he never smiled, but there was no reason to doubt him.

Bob Valdez arrived at the Maricopa pasture about noon. He was riding shotgun on the Hatch and Hodges run from St. David. He swung down from the boot, holding his sawed-off shotgun in the air, as the stage edged past the whiskey wagon.

Somebody standing at the tailgate with a glass in his hand said, "Hey, here's the town constable," and those nearby looked toward Bob Valdez in his dark suit and buttoned-up shirt, wearing a collar button but no tie or bandana; Valdez with his hat straight and slightly forward, the brim flat and the low crown undented.

"We'll get that nigger out of there now," somebody said, and a couple of others gave a little laugh to show they knew the person who said it was kidding.

Bob Valdez smiled, going along with it, though not knowing what they meant. "Out of where?" he said.

They explained it to him and he nodded, listening, his gaze moving over the shooters in the scrub, out to the line shack across the pasture and back to the slope, to the group of men a little way down from him. He saw Mr. Beaudry and Mr. Malson and Diego Luz, and the one they said was Mr. Tanner, there, talking to an R. L. Davis, who rode for Maricopa when he was working.

Bob Valdez watched the two men, both of them cut from the same stringy hide and looking like father and son: Mr. Tanner talking, never smiling, barely moving his mouth; R. L. Davis standing hip-cocked, posing with his revolver and rifle and a cartridge belt hanging over one shoulder, and the funneled, pointed brim of his sweaty hat nodding up and down as he listened to Mr. Tanner, grinning at what Mr. Tanner said, laughing out loud while Mr. Tanner did not show the twitch of a lip. Bob Valdez did not like R. L. Davis or any of the R. L. Davises in the world. He was civil, he listened to them, but God, there were a lot of them to listen to.

Well, all right, Bob Valdez thought. He walked down the slope to the group of men, nodding to Mr. Beaudry and Mr. Malson as they looked up. He waited a moment, not looking directly at Tanner, waiting for one of them to introduce him. Finally he held out his hand. "I'm Bob Valdez," he said, smiling a little.

Mr. Tanner looked at him, but did not shake hands. His gaze shifted as Mr. Malson said, "Bob's a town constable. He works a few nights a week in the Mexican part of town."

"The nights I'm here," Bob Valdez said. "Not on a stage run. See, I work for Hatch and Hodges too."

This time Mr. Tanner turned to say something to R. L. Davis, a couple of words that could have been about anything, and R. L. Davis laughed. Bob Valdez was a grown man; he was forty years old and as big as Mr. Tanner, but he stood there and didn't know what to do. He gripped the shotgun and was glad he had something to hold on to. He would have to stay near Mr. Tanner because he was the center of what was going on here. Soon they would discuss the situation and decide what to do. As the law-enforcement man he, Bob Valdez, should be in on the discussion and the decision. Of course. If someone was going to arrest Orlando Rincón or Johnson or whatever his name was, then he should be the one to do it; he was a town constable. They were out of town maybe, but where did the town end? The town had moved out here now; it was the same thing.

He could wait for Rincón to give up. Then arrest him.

If he wasn't dead already.

"Mr. Malson." Bob Valdez stepped toward the cattle company manager, who glanced over but looked out across the pasture again, indifferent.

"I wondered if maybe he's already dead," Valdez said.

Mr. Malson said, "Why don't you find out?"

"I was thinking," Valdez said, "if he was dead we could stand here a long time."

R. L. Davis adjusted his hat, which he did often, grabbing the funneled brim, loosening it on his head and pulling it down close to his eyes again and shifting from one cocked hip to the other. "Valdez here's got better things to do," R. L. Davis said. "He's busy."

"No," Bob Valdez said. "I was thinking of the one inside there, Rincón. He's dead or he's alive. He's alive, maybe he wants to give himself up. In there he has time to think, uh? Maybe——" He stopped. Not one of them was listening. Not even R. L. Davis.

Mr. Malson was looking at the whiskey wagon; it was on the road above them and over a little ways, with men standing by it being served off the tailgate. "I think we could use something," Mr. Malson said. His gaze went to Diego Luz the horsebreaker and Diego straightened up; not much, but a little. He was heavy and very dark and his shirt was tight across the thickness of his body. They said that Diego Luz hit green horses on the muzzle with his fist and they minded him. He had the hands for it; they hung at his sides, not touching or fooling with anything. They turned open, gestured when Mr. Malson told him to get the whiskey, and as he moved off climbing the slope, one hand held his holstered revolver to his leg.

Mr. Malson looked up at the sky, squinting and taking his hat off and putting it on again. He took off his coat and held it hooked over his shoulder by one finger, said something, gestured, and he and Mr. Beaudry and Mr. Tanner moved a few yards down the slope to a hollow where there was good shade. It was about two or two thirty then, hot, fairly still and quiet considering the number of people there. Only some of them in the pines and down in the scrub could be seen from where Bob Valdez stood wondering whether he should follow the three men down to the hollow or wait for Diego Luz, who was at the whiskey wagon now where most of the sounds that carried came from: a voice, a word or two that was suddenly clear, or laughter, and people would look up to see what was going on. Some of them by the whiskey wagon had lost interest in the line shack. Others were still watching though: those farther along the road sitting in wagons and buggies. This was a day people would remember and talk about. "Sure, I was there," the man in the buggy would be saying a year from now in a saloon over in Benson or St. David or somewhere. "The day they got that Army deserter, he had a Big-Fifty Sharps and an old dragoon pistol, and I'll tell you it was ticklish business."

Down in that worn-out pasture, dusty and spotted with desert growth, prickly pear and brittlebush, there was just the sun. It showed the ground clearly all the way to just in front of the line shack where now, toward midafternoon, there was shadow coming out from the trees and from the mound the hut was set against.

Somebody in the scrub must have seen the door open. The shout came from there, and Bob Valdez and everybody on the slope were looking by the time the Lipan Apache woman had reached the edge of the shade. She walked out from the hut toward the willow trees carrying a bucket, not hurrying or even looking toward the slope.

Nobody fired at her, though this was not so strange. Putting the front sight on a sod hut and on a person are two different things. The men in the scrub and in the pines didn't know this woman. They weren't after her. She had just appeared. There she was; and no one was sure what to do about her.

She was in the trees by the creek awhile, then she was in the open again, walking back toward the hut with the bucket and not hurrying at all, a small figure way across the pasture almost without shape or color, with only the long skirt reaching to the ground to tell it was the woman.

So he's alive, Bob Valdez thought. And he wants to stay alive and he's not giving himself up.

He thought about the woman's nerve and whether Orlando Rincón had sent her out or she had decided this herself. You couldn't tell about an Indian woman. Maybe this was expected of her. The woman didn't count; the man did. You could lose the woman and get another one.

Mr. Tanner didn't look at R. L. Davis. His gaze held on the Lipan Apache woman, inched along with her toward the hut; but he must have known R. L. Davis was right next to him.

"She's saying she didn't give a goddam about you and your rifle," Mr. Tanner said.

R. L. Davis looked at him funny. Then he said, "Shoot her?" like he hoped that's what Mr. Tanner meant.

"You could make her jump some," Mr. Tanner said.

Now R. L. Davis was on stage and he knew it, and Bob Valdez could tell he knew it by the way he levered the Winchester, raised it, and fired all in one motion, and as the dust kicked behind the Indian woman, who kept walking and didn't look up, R. L. Davis fired and fired and fired as fast as he could lever and half aim and with everybody watching him, hurrying him, he put four good ones right behind the woman. His last bullet socked into the door just as she reached it, and now she did pause and look up at the slope, staring up like she was waiting for him to fire again and giving him a good target if he wanted it.

Mr. Beaudry laughed out loud. "She don't give a goddam about your rifle."

It stung R. L. Davis, which it was intended to do.

"I wasn't aiming at her."

"But she doesn't know that." Mr. Beaudry was grinning, twisting his moustache, turning then and reaching out a hand as Diego Luz approached them with the whiskey.

"Hell, I wanted to hit her she'd be laying there, you know it."

"Well now, you tell her that," Mr. Beaudry said, working the cork loose, "and she'll know it." He took a drink from the bottle and passed it to Mr. Malson, who offered the bottle to Mr. Tanner, who shook his head. Mr. Malson took a drink and saw R. L. Davis staring at him, so he handed the bottle to him. R. L. Davis jerked the bottle up, took a long swallow and that part was over.

Mr. Malson said to Mr. Tanner, "You don't want any?"

"Not right now," Mr. Tanner answered. He continued to stare out across the pasture.

Mr. Malson watched him. "You feel strongly about this Army deserter."

"I told you," Mr. Tanner said, "he killed a man was a friend of mine."

"No, I don't believe you did."

"James C. Erin, sutler at Fort Huachuca," Mr. Tanner said. "He came across a tulapai still this nigger soldier was working with some Indians. The nigger thought Erin would tell the Army people, so he shot him and ran off with a woman."

"And you saw him this morning."

"I had come in last night to see this gentleman," Mr. Tanner said, nodding toward Malson. "This morning I was getting ready to leave when I saw him, him and the woman."

"I was right there," R. L. Davis said. "Right, Mr. Tanner? Him and I was on the porch by the Republic Hotel and Rincón goes by in the wagon. Mr. Tanner said, 'You know that man?' I said, 'Only that he's lived up north of town a few months. Him and his woman.' 'Well, I know him,' Mr. Tanner said. 'That man's an Army deserter wanted for murder.' I said, 'Well let's go get him.' He had a start on us and that's how he got to the hut before we could grab on to him. He's been holed up ever since."

Mr. Malson said, "Then you didn't talk to him."

"Listen," Mr. Tanner said, "I've kept that man's face before my eyes this past year."

Bob Valdez, somewhat behind Mr. Tanner and to the side, moved in a little closer. "You know this is the same man?"

Mr. Tanner looked around. He stared at Valdez. That's all he did, just stared.

"I mean, we have to be sure," Bob Valdez said. "It's a serious thing."

Now Mr. Malson and Mr. Beaudry were looking up at him. "We," Mr. Beaudry said. "I'll tell you what, Roberto. We need help we'll call you. All right?"

"You hired me," Bob Valdez said, standing alone above them. He was serious, but he shrugged and smiled a little to take the edge off the words. "What did you hire me for?"

"Well," Mr. Beaudry said, acting it out, looking up past Bob Valdez and along the road both ways. "I was to see some drunk Mexicans, I'd point them out."

After that, for a while, the men with the whiskey bottle forgot Bob Valdez. They stayed in the shade of the hollow watching the line shack, waiting for the Army deserter to realize it was all over for him. He would realize it and open the door and be cut down as he came outside. It was a matter of time only.

Bob Valdez stayed on the open part of the slope that was turning to shade, sitting now like an Apache with a suit on and every once in a while making a cigarette and smoking it slowly and thinking about himself and Mr. Tanner and the others, then thinking about the Army deserter, then thinking about himself again.

He didn't have to stay here. He didn't have to be a town constable. He didn't have to work for the stage company. He didn't have to listen to Mr. Beaudry and Mr. Malson and smile when they said those things. He didn't have a wife or any kids. He didn't have land that he owned. He could go anywhere he wanted.

Diego Luz was coming over. Diego Luz had a wife and a daughter almost grown and some little kids and he had to stay, sure.

Diego Luz squatted next to him, his arms on his knees and his big hands that he used for breaking horses hanging in front of him.

"Stay near if they want you for something," Bob Valdez said. He was watching Beaudry tilt the bottle up. Diego Luz said nothing.

"One of them bends over," Bob Valdez said then, "you kiss it, uh?"

Diego Luz looked at him, patient about it. Not angry or stirred. "Why don't you go home?"

"He says get me a bottle, you run."

"I get it. I don't run."

"Smile and hold your hat, uh?"

"And don't talk so much."

"Not unless they talk to you first."

"You better go home," Diego said.

Bob Valdez said, "That's why you hit the horses."

"Listen," Diego Luz said. "They pay me to break horses. They pay you to talk to drunks and keep them from killing somebody. They don't pay you for what you think or how you feel. So if you take their money keep your mouth shut. All right?"

Bob Valdez smiled. "I'm kidding you."

Diego Luz got up and walked away, down toward the hollow. The hell with him, he was thinking. Maybe he was kidding, but the hell with him. He was also thinking that maybe he could get a drink from that bottle. Maybe there would be a half inch left nobody wanted and Mr. Malson would tell him to kill it.

But it was already finished. R. L. Davis was playing with the bottle, holding it by the neck and flipping it up and catching it as it came down. Beaudry was saying, "What about after dark?" And looking at Mr. Tanner, who was thinking about something else and didn't notice.

R. L. Davis stopped flipping the bottle. He said, "Put some men on the rise right above the hut; he comes out, bust him."

"Well, they should get the men over there," Mr. Beaudry said, looking at the sky. "It won't be long till dark."

"Where's he going?" Mr. Malson said.

The others looked up, stopped in whatever they were doing or thinking by the suddenness of Mr. Malson's voice.

"Hey, Valdez!" R. L. Davis yelled out. "Where you think you're going?"

Bob Valdez had circled them and was already below them on the slope, leaving the pines now and entering the scrub brush. He didn't stop or look back.

"Valdez!"

Mr. Tanner raised one hand to silence R. L. Davis, all the time watching Bob Valdez getting smaller, going straight through the scrub, not just walking or passing the time but going right out to the pasture.

"Look at him," Mr. Malson said. There was some admiration in his voice.

"He's dumber than he looks," R. L. Davis said, then jumped a little as Mr. Tanner touched his arm.

"Come on," Mr. Tanner said. "With the rifle." And he started down the slope, hurrying and not seeming to care if he might stumble on the loose gravel.

Bob Valdez was now halfway across the pasture, the shotgun pointed down at his side, his eyes not leaving the door of the line shack. The door was probably already open enough for a rifle barrel to poke through. He guessed the Army deserter was covering him, letting him get as close as he wanted; the closer he came the easier to hit him.

Now he could see all the bullet marks in the door and the clean inner wood where the door was splintered. Two people in that little bake-oven of a place. He saw the door move.

He saw the rag doll on the ground. It was a strange thing, the woman having a doll. Valdez hardly glanced at it but was aware of the button eyes looking up and the discomforted twist of the red wool mouth. Then, just past the doll, when he was wondering if he would go right up to the door and knock on it and wouldn't that be a crazy thing, like visiting somebody, the door opened and the Negro was in the doorway filling it, standing there in pants and boots but without a shirt in that hot place, and holding a long-barreled dragoon that was already cocked.

They stood twelve feet apart looking at each other, close enough so that no one could fire from the slope.

"I can kill you first," the Negro said, "if you raise it."

With his free hand, the left one, Bob Valdez motioned back over his shoulder. "There's a man there said you killed somebody a year ago."

"What man?"

"Said his name is Tanner."

The Negro shook his head, once each way.

"Said your name is Johnson."

"You know my name."

"I'm telling you what he said."

"Where'd I kill this man?"

"Huachuca."

The Negro hesitated. "That was some time ago I was in the Tenth. More than a year."

"You a deserter?"

"I served it out."

"Then you got something that says so."

"In the wagon, there's a bag there my things are in."

"Will you talk to this man Tanner?"

"If I can hold from busting him."

"Listen, why did you run this morning?"

"They come chasing. I don't know what they want." He lowered the gun a little, his brown-stained tired-looking eyes staring intently at Bob Valdez. "What would you do? They come on the run. Next thing I know they firing at us."

"Will you go with me and talk to him?"

The Negro hesitated again. Then shook his head. "I don't know him."

"Then he won't know you."

"He didn't know me this morning."

"All right," Bob Valdez said. "I'll get your paper says you were discharged. Then we'll show it to this man, uh?"

The Negro thought it over before he nodded, very slowly, as if still thinking. "All right. Bring him here, I'll say a few words to him."

Bob Valdez smiled a little. "You can point that gun some other way."

"Well . . ." the Negro said, "if everybody's friends." He lowered the revolver to his side.

The wagon was in the willow trees by the creek. Off to the right. But Bob Valdez did not turn right away in that direction. He backed away, watching Orlando Rincón for no reason that he knew of. Maybe because the man was holding a gun and that was reason enough.

He had backed off six or seven feet when Orlando Rincón shoved the revolver down into his belt. Bob Valdez turned and started for the trees.

It was at this moment that he looked across the pasture. He saw Mr. Tanner and R. L. Davis at the edge of the scrub trees but wasn't sure it was them. Something tried to tell him it was them, but he did not accept it until he was off to the right, out of the line of fire, and by then the time to yell at them or run toward them was past. R. L. Davis had the Winchester up and was firing.

They say R. L. Davis was drunk or he would have pinned him squarc. As it was, the bullet shaved Rincón and plowed past him into the hut.

Bob Valdez saw Rincón half turn and he saw Rincón's accusing eyes as Rincón pulled the long-barreled dragoon from his belt.

"They weren't supposed to," Bob Valdez said, holding one hand out as if to stop Rincón. "Listen, they weren't supposed to do that!"

The revolver was free, and Rincón was cocking it. "Don't!"

Bob Valdez said. "Don't do it!" Looking right into the Negro's eyes and seeing it was no use, that Rincón was going to shoot him, and suddenly hurrying, he jerked the shotgun up and pulled both triggers so that the explosions came out in one blast and Orlando Rincón was spun and thrown back inside.

They came out across the pasture to have a look, some going inside where they found the woman and brought her out, everybody noticing she would have a child in about a month. Those by the doorway made room as Mr. Tanner and R. L. Davis approached.

Diego Luz came over by Bob Valdez, who had not moved. Valdez stood watching them and he saw Mr. Tanner look down at Rincón and after a moment shake his head.

"It looked like him," Mr. Tanner said. "It sure looked like him."

He saw R. L. Davis squint at Mr. Tanner. "It ain't the one you said?"

Mr. Tanner shook his head again. "I've seen him before though. I know I've seen him somewheres."

Bob Valdez saw R. L. Davis shrug. "You ask me, they all look alike." He was yawning then, fooling with his hat, and then his eyes swiveled over to Bob Valdez standing with the empty shotgun.

"Constable," R. L. Davis said. "You went and killed the wrong coon."

Bob Valdez started for him, raising the shotgun to swing it like a club, but Diego Luz caught him from behind and locked a big arm around his neck, under his chin, until he was still and Mr. Tanner and the others had moved off.

TWO

A man can be in two different places and he will be two different men. Maybe if you think of more places he will be more men, but two is enough for now. This is Bob Valdez washing his hands in the creek and resting in the willows after digging the hole and lowering Orlando Rincón into it and covering him with dirt and stones, resting and watching the Lipan Apache woman who sat in silence by the grave of the man whose child she would have in a month.

This is one Bob Valdez. The forty-year-old town constable and stage-line shotgun rider. A good, hardworking man. And hard looking, with a dark hard face that was creased and leathery; but don't go by looks, they said, Bob Valdez was kindly and respectful. One of the good ones. The whores in Inez's place on Commercial Street would call to him from their windows; even the white-skinned girls who had come from St. Louis, they liked him too. Bob Valdez would wave at them and sometimes he would go in and after being with the girl would have a cup of coffee with Inez. They had known each other when they were children in Tucson. That was all right, going to Inez's place. Mr. Beaudry and Mr. Malson and the others could try to think of a time when Bob Valdez might have drunk too much or swaggered or had a certain smart-aleck look on his face, but they would never recall such a time. Yes, this Bob Valdez was all right.

Another Bob Valdez inside the Bob Valdez in the willows that evening had worked for the Army at one time and had been a contract guide when General Crook chased Geronimo down into the Madres. He was a tracker out of Whipple Barracks first, then out of Fort Thomas, then in charge of the Apache police at Whiteriver. He would sit at night eating with them and talking with them as he learned the Chiricahua dialect. He would keep up with them all day and shoot his Springfield carbine one hell of a lot better than any of them could shoot. He had taken scalps but never showed them to anyone and had thrown them away by the time Geronimo was in Oklahoma and he had gone to work for the stage company, Hatch and Hodges, to live as a civilized man. Shortly after that he was named town constable in Lanoria at twenty-five dollars a month, getting the job because he got along with people, including the Mexicans in town who drank too much on Saturday night, and this was the Bob Valdez that Mr. Beaudry and Mr. Malson and the others knew. They had never met the first Bob Valdez.

And they had forgotten about the second Bob Valdez; they had gone, everyone cleared out of the Maricopa pasture. He was alone with the Lipan Apache woman as evening settled and the grove in the willow trees became dark.

He had not spoken to the woman. He had touched her shoulder before digging the grave—when she had tried to take the shovel from him to do it herself—he had touched her, easing her to the ground, and she had sat unmoving while he formed the hole and dug deep into the soil. He would look at her and smile, but her expression gave him nothing in return. She wasn't an attractive woman. She was a round shape in a dirty gray dress with yellow strands of beads. He did not know how old she was. She was something sitting there watching him but not watching him. She would build a fire and sit here all night and in the morning she would probably be gone.

He had never seen the woman before. He had seen Orlando Rincón in Lanoria. He had recognized him, but had never spoken to him before today. Rincón had a one-loop spread a half day's ride south of Lanoria that he and the woman tended alone. That much was all Bob Valdez knew about them. They had come into town for something and now the man was dead and the woman was alone with her unborn child. Like that, her life, whatever it had been before, good or bad, was gone.

He watched the woman rise from the grave to water the wagon horses in the creek. She returned and made a fire, lighting it with a match. Valdez went over to her then, fashioning a cigarette and leaning in to light it in the fire, taking his time because he wasn't sure of the words he wanted to use.

In Spanish he said, "Where will you go?" and repeated it in the Chiricahua dialect when she continued to stare at him, and now she pointed off beyond the creek.

"This should not have happened," he said. "Your husband had done nothing. It was a mistake." He leaned closer to see her clearly in the firelight. "I did it to him, but I didn't want to. He didn't understand and he was going to kill me."

Christ, if you can't say anything, Valdez thought, quit talking.

He said, "It isn't your fault this has happened. I mean, you are made to suffer and yet you did nothing to cause it. You understand?"

The woman nodded slightly, looking into the fire now. "All right, we can't give him back to you, but we should give you something. You take something from a person, then you have to pay for it. We have to pay. We have to pay you for taking your husband. You see that?"

The woman did not move or speak.

"I don't know how much you pay a woman for killing her husband, but we'll think of something, all right? There were many men there; I don't know them all. But the ones I know I go to and ask them to give me something for you. A hundred dollars. No, *five* hundred dollars we get and give it to you so you can do what you want with it. Have your baby and go home, wherever your home is, or stay here. Buy some, I don't know, something to grow, and a cow and maybe some goats, uh? You know goats?"

Christ, let her buy what she wants. Get it done.

"Look," Valdez said then. "We get in the wagon and go back to town. I see the men and talk to them—you stay in town also. I find a place for you, all right?"

The woman's gaze rose from the fire, her dark face glistening in the light, the shapeless, flat-faced Lipan Apache woman looking at him. A person, but Christ, barely a person.

Why did Rincón choose this one? Valdez thought. He smiled then. "How does that sound? You stay in town, sleep in a bed. You don't have to worry or think about it. We pay for everything."

A Maricopa rider came into De Spain's, where Mr. Beaudry and Mr. Malson were playing poker with another gentleman and the house man, and told them it was the goddamnedest thing he'd seen in a while: Bob Valdez walking into the Republic Hotel with that blown-up Indian woman.

R. L. Davis came over from the bar and said, "What about the Indian woman? Hell, I could have knocked her flat if I'd wanted. Nobody believes that then they never seen me shoot."

Mr. Malson told him to shut up and said to the Maricopa rider, "What's this about Bob Valdez?"

"He's in the Republic registering that nigger's squaw," the rider said. "I saw them come up in the team and go inside, so I stuck my head in."

Mr. Beaudry was squinting in his cigar smoke. "What'd the clerk do?"

"I guess he didn't know what to do," the rider said. "He went and got the manager, and him and Bob Valdez were talking over the counter, but I couldn't hear them."

Mr. Malson, the manager of Maricopa, looked at Mr. Beaudry, the government land agent, and Mr. Beaudry said, "I never heard of anything like that before."

Mr. Malson shook his head. "They won't give her a room. Christ Almighty."

Mr. Beaudry shook his head too. "I don't know," he said. "Bob Valdez. You sure it was Bob?"

"Yes sir," the Maricopa rider said. He waited a minute while the men at the poker table thought about it, then went over to the bar and got himself a glass of whiskey.

Next to him, R. L. Davis said, "Were you out there today?" The rider shook his head, but said he'd heard all about it. R. L. Davis told him how he had taken the Winchester and put four good ones right behind the woman when she came out for water and one smack in the door as she went back inside. "Hell," R. L. Davis said, "I'd wanted to hit her I'd have hit her square."

The Maricopa rider said, "God*dam*, I guess she's a big enough something to shoot at for anybody."

"I was two hundred yards off!" R. L. Davis stiffened up and his face was tight. "I put them shots right where I aimed!"

The Maricopa rider said, "All right, I believe you." He was tired and didn't feel like arguing with some stringy drunk who was liable to make something out of nothing.

For a Saturday night there was only a fair crowd in De Spain's, the riders and a few town merchants lined up and lounged at the bar and some others played poker and faro, with tobacco smoke hanging above them around the brass lamps. They were drinking and talking, but it didn't seem loud enough for a Saturday. There had been more men in here earlier, right after supper, a number of them coming in for a quick glass or a jug to take with them, heading back to their spreads with their families, but now it was only a fair-sized crowd. The moment of excitement had been Mr. Tanner coming in. He had stood at the bar and lit a cigar and sipped two glasses of whiskey while Mr. Malson stood with him. Those who were out at the Maricopa pasture pointed out Mr. Tanner to those who hadn't been there. The reactions to seeing him were mostly the same. So that was Frank Tanner. He didn't look so big. They expected a man with his name and reputation to look different—a man who traded goods to Mexican rebels and had a price on his head across the

border and two dozen guns riding for him. Imagine paying all those men. He must do pretty well. He was a little above average height and was straight as a post, thin, with a thin, sunken-in face and a heavy moustache and eyes in the shadow of his hatbrim. He made a person look at him when he walked in, but once the person had looked, Tanner wasn't that different from anybody else. That was the reaction to Frank Tanner. That he was not so much after all. Still, while he was in De Spain's, it seemed quieter, like everybody was holding back, though most of the men were trying to act natural and somebody would laugh every once in a while. Frank Tanner stayed fifteen minutes and left. He'd gone over to the Republic and shortly after, he and his wife were seen riding out of Lanoria in their buggy with a mounted Mexican trailing them, everyone coming to doors and windows to get a look at them. The men said boy, his wife was something—a nice young thing and not too frail either, and the women admitted yes, she was pretty, but she ought to knot or braid her hair instead of letting it hang down like that; it made her look awful bold.

Frank Tanner had left De Spain's over two hours ago. Now, the next one to come in, just a little while after the Maricopa rider, was Bob Valdez.

The houseman saw him and nudged Mr. Malson under the table. Mr. Malson looked at him funny, frowning—What was the little bald-headed son of a bitch up to?—then saw the houseman looking toward the door. Bob Valdez was coming directly toward their table, his gaze already picking out Mr. Malson, who looked at him and away from him and back again, and Bob Valdez was still looking right at him.

"I buried him," Valdez said.

Mr. Malson nodded. "Good. There were enough witnesses, I didn't see any need for an inquest." He looked up at Bob Valdez. "Everybody knows how he died."

"Unless his wife wants him buried at home," Valdez said.

Mr. Beaudry said, "Let her move him if she wants. Phew,

driving that team in the sun with him on the back. How'd you like to do that?"

R. L. Davis, who had moved over from the bar, said, "I guess that boy stunk enough when he was alive." He looked around and got a couple of the riders to laugh at it.

"I haven't asked her if she wants to," Valdez said. "It's something she'll think about later when she's home. But I told her one thing," he said then. "I told her we'd pay her for killing her husband."

There was a silence at the table. Mr. Beaudry fooled with the end of his moustache, twisting it, and Mr. Malson cleared his throat before he said, "We? Who's we?"

"I thought everybody who was there," Bob Valdez said. "Or everybody who wants to give something."

Mr. Malson said, "You mean take up a collection? Pass the hat around?"

Valdez nodded. "Yes sir."

"Well, I suppose we could do that." He looked at Beaudry. "What do you think, Earl?"

Mr. Beaudry shrugged. "I don't care. I guess it would be all right. Give her a few dollars for a stake."

Mr. Malson nodded. "Enough to get home. Where does she live?"

"Their place is north of here," Valdez said.

"No, I mean where is she from?"

"I don't know."

"Probably across the border," Mr. Beaudry said. "She could collect about ten dollars and it'd be more than any of her kin had ever seen before."

Mr. Malson said, "I suppose we could do it."

"I was thinking of more than ten dollars," Valdez said.

Mr. Malson looked up at him. "How much more?"

Bob Valdez cleared his throat. He said, "I was thinking five hundred dollars."

The silence followed again. This time R. L. Davis broke it. He moved, shifting his weight, and there was a chinging sound of his spurs. He said, "I would like to know something. I would like to know why we're listening to this greaser. It was him killed the nigger. What's he coming to us for?"

"R. L.," Mr. Malson said, "keep your mouth closed, all right?"

"Why can't I say what I want?" R. L. Davis said, drunk enough to tell the manager of Maricopa to his face, "He killed him. Not us."

Mr. Malson said, "Shut up or go to bed." He took his time shifting his gaze to Bob Valdez, then holding it there, staring at him. "That's a lot of money, five hundred dollars."

"Yes sir," Bob Valdez nodded, speaking quietly. "I guess it is, but she needs it. What does she have now? I mean, we take her husband from her and now she doesn't have anything. So I thought five hundred dollars." He smiled a little. "It just came to me. That much."

Mr. Beaudry said, "That's as much as most men make in a year."

"Yes sir," Bob Valdez said. "But her husband won't earn anything anymore. Not this year or any year. So maybe five hundred is not so much."

Mr. Beaudry said, "Giving that much is different than giving her a few dollars. I don't mean the difference in the amount. I mean you give her a sum like five hundred dollars it's like admitting we owe it to her. Like we're to blame."

"Well?" Bob Valdez said. "Who else is to blame?"

Mr. Beaudry said, "Now wait a minute. If you're anxious to fix blame then I'll have to go along with what this man said." He nodded toward R. L. Davis. "You killed him. We didn't. We were there to help flush him out, a suspected murderer. We weren't there to kill anybody unless we had to. But you took it on yourself to go down and talk to him and it was you that killed him. Am I right or wrong?"

Bob Valdez said, "Everybody was shooting——"

Mr. Beaudry held up his hand. "Wait just a minute. Shooting isn't killing. Nobody's shot killed him but yours and there are ninety, a hundred witnesses will testify to it."

"I said it before," R. L. Davis said. "He killed the coon. Nobody else. The wrong coon at that."

A few of them laughed and Bob Valdez looked over at R. L. Davis standing with his funneled hat over his eyes and his thumbs hooked in his belt trying to stand straight but swaying a little. He was good and drunk, his eyes watery looking and the corners of his mouth sticky. But it would be good to hit him anyway, Bob Valdez was thinking. Come in from the side and get his cheek and rip into his nose without hitting those ugly teeth and maybe cut your hand. With gloves on hit the mouth, but not without gloves. He could see R. L. Davis sitting on the floor of De Spain's saloon with his nose bleeding and blood down the front of him. That would be all right.

And who else? No, he should be able to talk to Mr. Malson and Mr. Beaudry, the manager of a cattle company and a government land agent, but he was having one son of a bitch of a hard time because they didn't see it, what he meant, or they didn't want to see it.

He said, "I mean this way. What if she went to court——"

"Jesus Christ," R. L. Davis said, shaking his head.

"What if she went there"—Valdez kept his eyes on Mr. Beaudry now—"with a lawyer and said she wanted to sue everybody that was out there, or this city?"

"Bob," Mr. Beaudry said, "that woman doesn't know what a lawyer is."

"But if she did and they went to court, wouldn't she get some money?"

The houseman said, "I thought we were playing cards."

"Since she's never heard of a lawyer or a county seat," Mr. Beaudry said, "you're talking straight into the wind, aren't you?"

"I mean if she did. Like if you drive cattle over a man's property and damage something," Bob Valdez went on, holding on, "and the man goes to court, then the cattle company has to pay him for the damage. Isn't that right?"

Mr. Malson smiled. He said, "That doesn't sound like much of a cattle company to me," and the others laughed. "I was to get involved in court suits, a man would be out from Chicago and I'd be out of a job."

"But it's happened," Valdez said, staying with it. "The person or persons responsible have had to pay."

Mr. Beaudry said, "I wouldn't worry about it, Bob."

"The person has to stand up and prove damage," Mr. Malson said. "You don't go to court, even if you know where it is, without a case. And by that I mean evidence."

"All right," Valdez said. "That's what I mean. The woman doesn't know anything about court, but we know about the evidence, uh? Because we were there. If we weren't there her husband would be alive."

"Or if he hadn't opened the door," Mr. Beaudry said. "Or if you hadn't pulled the trigger."

"Or," Mr. Malson said, "if he hadn't come to town this morning and if Frank Tanner hadn't seen him."

"Goddam, I was there," R. L. Davis said. "We was on the steps of the Republic."

"There you are," Mr. Beaudry said. "If Frank Tanner hadn't been here this morning it never would have happened. So maybe it's his fault. Tanner's."

Somebody in the group behind Mr. Beaudry said, "Go tell him that," and some of the men laughed, picturing it.

"Now that's not so funny," Mr. Beaudry said. "If this happened because of Frank Tanner, then maybe he's to blame. What do you think, Bob?" he asked him seriously, patiently, as he would ask a stupid, thick-headed person.

"I guess so," Bob Valdez said.

"Well, if you think he's to blame," Mr. Beaudry said, "why

don't you ask him for the money? And I'll tell you what. If he agrees to the five hundred dollars, we will too. How's that?"

Valdez kept his eyes on Mr. Beaudry. "I don't know where he is."

"He's south of town," Mr. Beaudry said. "Probably at the relay station for the night if his cattle got that far. Or he might have gone on."

"He mentioned stopping there," Mr. Malson said.

"All right," Valdez said because there was nothing else he could say. "I'll go talk to him."

"Do that," Mr. Beaudry said.

Mr. Malson waited until Bob Valdez was turning and the men who had crowded in were stepping aside. "Bob," he said, "that Apache woman—somebody said she was over to the hotel trying to get a room."

"No." Valdez shook his head. "The manager said they were full up."

"Uh-huh," Mr. Malson said. "Well, where is she now?"

"I took her to Inez's place," Valdez said. "She's staying there tonight."

Nobody said anything until he was gone. Then R. L. Davis, as drunk as he was, said, "Je-sus H. Christ. Now he's turned that Indin creature into a whore."

He went unarmed, riding south through the darkness, feeling the chill of night settling on the land. He didn't want to go; he was tired. He had come up this road this morning from St. David on the bouncing, bucking, creaking boot of the Hatch and Hodges stage, throwing gravel at the wheelers and yelling, urging the horses on as the driver held the heavy reins and snapped them over the teams. Sun and dust this morning, and sweat soaking his body under the dark suit; now cold darkness over the same ruts that stretched across the mesquite flats and climbed through barrancas to crest a hill and drop curving into the endless flats again, forever, it seemed, on the boot or now in the saddle of a stage company horse.

He said in his mind, Mr. Tanner, I'm Bob Valdez. You remember, I was out at the pasture today when the man was killed.

When the man was killed. When *you* killed him, he said to himself.

We were talking about doing something for his wife and Mr. Beaudry, the land agent, said——

He said go out and try to get it from Frank Tanner, you dumb Mexican son of a bitch. That's what he said. Do you know it?

He knew it. Sure. But what was he supposed to do? Forget about the woman? He had told her they would give her money. God, it would be easy to forget about her. No, it would be good, but it wouldn't be easy. But with all of them watching him he had had to walk out and get a horse and he would have to ride the ten goddam miles or more to the goddam swing station and, getting it over with, smile and be respectful and ask Mr. Tanner if he would please like to give something for this fat squaw who had lived with Rincón and was having his child.

And Frank Tanner, like the rest of them, would say——

No, they said this Tanner had a lot of money. Maybe he would say, "Sure, I'll give you something for her. How much do you want?" Maybe it would be easy to talk to him. Maybe now, at night, after it was over and the man had had time to think about it, maybe he would talk a little and say yes.

A mile or a little more from the stage station he saw low shapes out among the brush patches, cattle grazing, bedded for the night, and among them, the taller shape of a rider. But they were well off from the stage road and none of the cattle he saw or the mounted man came near him. During the last mile he was certain a rider was behind him, but he didn't stop or slow down to let the horse sound catch up with him. It could be somebody on the road, anybody, or one of Tanner's men watching him; but he had nothing to say to whoever it was. His words were for Tanner, even if he didn't know how to put the words to convince the man. It would be easier to say it in Spanish. Or in Chiricahua.

Now, coming over a low rise, he could see the glow of their fires, three of them, where the swing station would be in the darkness. Gradually then, as he approached, he could make out the adobe building, the fires reflecting on pale walls in the night. The front of the building, beneath the mesquite-pole ramada, was in deep shadow. Closer now and he could see the low adobe outer wall across the front yard, shielding the well and the horse corral from open country.

Valdez listened as he approached. He could hear the men by the fire, the thin sound of voices coming across the yard. He could hear horses moving in the corral and a shrill whinnying sound. He was aware of horses closer to him, off in the darkness, but moving in with the heavy muffled sound of hooves on the packed sand. He did not look toward the sound but continued on, coming to the wall and walking his horse through the open gate, feeling the riders out of the darkness close behind him as he entered the yard.

A figure by the wall with a rifle said, "Hold it there," and a voice behind him, in English also but with an accent said, "We have him." The man with the rifle came toward him, raising the barrel of a Henry or a Winchester—Valdez wasn't sure in the dimness.

He said in Spanish, "I have no gun."

And the voice behind him said, also in Spanish, "Get down and show us."

Valdez swung down. He dropped the reins and opened his coat as the man with the rifle, a Winchester, came up to him.

"The saddle," the voice behind him said in English.

Not looking around Valdez said, "You make sure, don't you?" The man behind him didn't answer. He walked his horse forward and dismounted close to Valdez, looking into his face.

"You go where?"

"Here," Valdez said. "To speak to Señor Tanner."

"About what?"

"Money," Valdez said.

The man who had dismounted continued to study him for a moment. He handed his reins to the one with the rifle and walked off toward the adobe. Valdez watched him and saw the men by the fires, on the side of the adobe, looking out toward him. It was quiet now except for the stirring of the horses in the corral. He saw the light in the doorway as the man went inside. The door remained open, but he could see nothing within.

There was a bar inside the room and two long tables. The station man, Gregorio Sanza, would be behind the bar maybe, serving Tanner. He remembered Tanner did not take anything to drink at the pasture.

He said to the one with the rifle, "The company I work for owns that building. The Hatch and Hodges."

The man said nothing. Beyond him now two figures appeared in the doorway, in the light for a moment and out of it into darkness. Not Tanner, neither of them. The one who had gone inside called out, "Bring him over." The two men in shadow came out a few steps and the second one, also with an accent, said, "Against the wall," motioning with a nod of his head to the side.

Some of the men by the fires had stood up or were rising as Valdez walked toward them. Others sat and lounged on their sides—dark faces, dark leather, firelight reflecting on cartridge belts and mess tins—and Valdez had to walk around them to reach the wall. As he turned, the man who had come out of the house walked over to stand across the fire from him, the men standing or sitting there quickly making room for him.

The *segundo*, Valdez thought. They move.

He was a big man, almost as big as Diego Luz, with a straw Sonora hat and a heavy moustache that gave him a solemn expression and a strip of beard beneath his mouth. The segundo, with one cartridge bandolier and two long-barreled .44s on his legs.

Valdez nodded to him and said in Spanish, "Good evening," almost smiling.

"I don't know you," the segundo said.

"Because we have never met."

"I know everyone who does business with Señor Tanner."

"I have no business with him. A private matter."

"You told them business."

"I told them money."

The segundo was silent, watching him. "He doesn't know you," he said then.

"Señor Tanner? Sure, I met him today. I killed a man for him."

The segundo hesitated again, undecided or taking his own time, watching him. He motioned with his hand then, and the Mexican who had gone into the house before moved away, turning the corner. The segundo continued to stare. Valdez shifted his gaze to the left and to the right and saw all of them watching him in the light of the fires. There were Americans and Mexicans, some of them bearded, most of them with their hats on, all of them armed. He counted, looking about idly, and decided there were at least twelve of them here. More of them out in the darkness.

He said in his mind, Mr. Tanner, do you remember me? Bob——

Tanner came around the corner. He took a stub of cigar out of his mouth and stood looking at Valdez.

Now. "Mr. Tanner, do you remember me? Bob Valdez, from the pasture today."

Tanner held the cigar in front of him. He was in his shirt-sleeves and vest and without the dark hat that had hidden his eyes, his hair slanting down across his forehead, the skin pale-looking in the firelight. He seemed thinner now and smaller, but his expression was the same, the tell-nothing expression and the mouth that looked as if it had never smiled.

"What do you want?"

"I just wanted to talk to you for a minute."

"Say it."

"Well, it's about the man today."

"What man?"

"The one that was killed. You know he had a wife with him." Valdez waited.

"Say what you want and get out of here."

"Well, we were talking—Mr. Beaudry and Mr. Malson. You know who I mean?"

"You don't have much time left," Mr. Tanner said.

"We were saying maybe we should give something to the woman now that she doesn't have a husband."

"They sent you out here?"

"No, I thought of it. I thought if we all put in to give her some money"—he hesitated—"about five hundred dollars."

Mr. Tanner had not moved his gaze from Valdez. "You come out here to tell me that?"

"Well, we were talking about it and Mr. Beaudry said why don't I see you about it."

"You want me to pay money," Mr. Tanner said, "to that red nigger he was holed up with?"

"You said it wasn't the right man——"

"What's that got to do with it?"

"It was an accident, not the woman's fault, and she doesn't have anything now. And she's got that child she's going to have. Did you see that?"

Mr. Tanner looked at his segundo. He said, "Get rid of him," and started to turn away.

"Wait a minute!"

Valdez watched him half turn to look at him again.

"What did you say?"

"I mean if you could take time to listen a minute so I can explain it." The hard-working, respectful Bob Valdez speaking again, smiling a little.

"Your minute's up, boy." He glanced at his segundo again. "Teach him something." He turned and was gone.

Valdez called out, "Mr. Tanner——"

"He don't hear you so good," the segundo said. "It's too loud out here." He drew the .44 on his right leg, cocked it and fired as he brought it up, and with the explosion the adobe chipped next to Bob Valdez's face.

"All this shooting," the segundo said. "Man, he can't hear anything." He fired again and the adobe chipped close to the other side of Valdez's face. "You see how easy it would be?" the segundo said.

The Mexican rider who had brought him in said, "Let me have one," his revolver already drawn. "Where do you want it?"

"By the right hand," the segundo said.

Valdez was looking at the Mexican rider. He saw the revolver lift as the man pulled the trigger and saw the muzzle flash with the heavy solid noise and heard the bullet strike close to his side.

"Too high," the segundo said.

Now those who were sitting and lounging by the fires rose and drew their revolvers, looking at the segundo and waiting their turn. One of them, an American, said, "I know where I'm going to shoot the son of a bitch." One of them laughed and another one said, "See if you can shoot his meat off." And another one said, "It would fix this squaw-lover good."

Bob Valdez did not want to move. He wanted to run and he could feel the sweat on his face, but he couldn't move a hand or an elbow or turn his head. He had to stay rigid without appearing to be rigid. He edged his left foot back and the heel of his boot touched the wall close behind him. He did that much, touching something solid and holding on, as the men faced him across the fires, five or six strides away from him, close enough to put the bullets where they wanted to put them—if all of the men knew how to shoot and if they hadn't had too much mescal or tequila since coming to the station. Valdez held on and now kept his eyes on the segundo for a place to keep them, a point to fix on while they played their game with him.

The first few men fired in turn, calling their shots; but now the rest of them were anxious and couldn't wait and they began firing as they decided where to shoot, raising the revolvers in front of them but not seeming to aim, pulling the triggers in the noise and smoke and leaning in to see where their bullets struck. Valdez felt his hat move and felt powder dust from the adobe brick in his eyes and in his nose and felt chips of adobe sting his face and hands and felt a bullet plow into the wall between his knees and a voice say, "A little higher you get him good." Another voice, "Move up a inch at a time and watch him poop his drawers."

He kept his eyes on the segundo in the Sonora straw, not telling the segundo anything with his gaze, looking at him as he would look at any man, if he wanted to look at a man, or as he would look at a horse or a dog or a steer or an object that was something to look at. But as he saw the segundo staring back at him he realized that he was telling the segundo something after all. Good. He had nothing to lose and now was aware of himself staring at the segundo.

What can you do? he was saying to the segundo. You can kill me. Or one of them can kill me not meaning to. But what else can you do to me? You want me to get down on my knees? You don't have enough bullets, man, and you know it. So what can you do to me? Tell me.

The segundo raised his hand and called out, "Enough!" in English and in Spanish and in English again. He walked between the fires to Bob Valdez and said, "You ride out now."

Bob Valdez took his hat off, adjusting it, loosening it on his head. He didn't touch his face to wipe away the brick dust and sweat or look at his hands, though he felt blood on his knuckles and running down between his fingers.

He said, "If you're through," and walked away from the segundo. He mounted the company horse and rode out the gate, the segundo watching him until he was into the darkness and only a faint sound of him remained.

The men were talking and reloading, spinning the cylinders of their revolvers, sitting by the fires to rest and to tell where they had put their bullets. The segundo walked away from them out into the yard, listening to the silence. After a few minutes he went under the ramada to enter the adobe.

The station man, Gregorio Sanza, behind the plank bar and beneath the smoking oil lamp, raised a mescal bottle to the segundo, pale yellow in the light; but the segundo shook his head; he walked over to the long table where Tanner was sitting with the woman. She was sipping a tin cup of coffee.

The woman had gone into a sleeping room shortly after they had arrived in the buggy and had remained there until now. The segundo saw she was still dressed and he wondered what she had been doing in the room. In the months she had been with them—since Tanner had brought her over from Fort Huachuca—the segundo could count the times he had spoken to her on his hands. She seldom asked for anything; she never gave the servants orders as the woman of the house was supposed to do. Still, she had the look of a woman who would be obeyed. She did not seem afraid or uneasy; she looked into your eyes when she spoke to you; she spoke loud enough yet quietly. But something was going on in her head beneath the long gold-brown hair that hung past her shoulders. She was a difficult woman to understand because she did not give herself away. Except that she smiled only a little, and he had never seen her laugh. Maybe she laughed when she was alone with Señor Tanner.

If she was my woman, the segundo was thinking, I could make her laugh and scream and bite.

He said to Tanner. "The man's gone."

"How did he behave?"

"He stood up."

Tanner drew on the fresh cigar he was smoking. "He did, uh?"

"As well as a man can do it."

"He didn't beg?"

The segundo shook his head. "He said nothing."

"He shot the nigger square," Tanner said. "He did that well. But outside, I thought he would crawl."

The segundo shook his head again. "No crawling or begging."

"All right, tell that man to close his bar and go to bed."

The segundo nodded and moved off.

Tanner waited until the segundo had stopped at the bar and had gone outside. "Why don't you go to bed, too," he said to the woman.

"I will in a minute." She kept her finger in the handle of the coffee cup.

"Go in and pretty yourself up," he said then. "I'll take a turn around the yard and be in directly."

"What did the man do?"

"He wasted my time."

"So they put him against the wall?"

"It was the way he spoke to me," Tanner said. "I can't have that in front of them." He sat close to her, staring into her face, at the gray-green eyes and the soft hair close to her cheek. His hand came up to finger the end strands of her hair. Quietly, he said, "Gay, go on in the room."

"I'll finish my coffee."

"No, right now would be better. I'll be there in a minute."

She waited until he was out of the door before rising and going into the sleeping room. In the dim lamplight she began to undress, stepping out of her dress and dropping it on the bed next to her nightgown. The light blue one. Thin and limp and patched beneath one arm. There had been a light blue one and a light green one and a pink one and a yellow one, all with the white-scrolled monogram GBE she had embroidered on the bodice when she was nineteen years old and living in Prescott, a girl about to be married. The girl, Gay Byrnes, had brought the nightgowns and her dresses and linens to Fort Huachuca to become the bride of James C. Erin. During five and a half years as his wife she discarded the nightgowns one by one and used them as dust rags. When her husband was killed six months ago, and she left Huachuca with Frank Tanner, she had only the light blue one left.

Gay Erin slipped the nightgown over her head, brushed her hair and got into the narrow double bed, pulling the blanket up over her shoulder as she rolled to her side, her back to the low-burning lamp.

When Tanner came in and began to undress, she remained with her back to him. She could see him from times before: removing his boots, his shirt and trousers, standing in his long cotton underwear as he unfastened the buttons. He would stand naked scratching his stomach and chest, then go to the wall hook and take his revolver from the holster, making sure the hammer was on an empty chamber as he moved toward the bed.

She felt the mattress yield beneath his weight. The gun would be at his side, under the blanket and next to his hip. He would lie still for a few moments, then roll toward her and put his hand on her shoulder.

"What have you got the nightgown on for?"

"I'm cold."

"Well now, what do you think I'm for?"

"Tell me," Gay Erin said.

"I'll show you."

"As a lover or a husband?"

Tanner groaned. "Jesus Christ, are you going to start that?"

"Six months ago you said we'd be married in a few weeks."

"Most people probably think we already are. What's the difference?"

She started to get up, to throw back the blanket, and his hand tightened on her arm.

"I said we'd be married, we will."

"When?"

"Well not right now, all right?" His hand stroked her arm beneath the flannel. "Come on, take this thing off."

She lay without moving, her eyes open in the darkness, letting her hesitation stretch into silence, a long moment, before she sat up slowly and worked the nightgown out from beneath her. She pulled it over her head, turning to him.

THREE

Inez was fat and took her time coming over from the stove with the coffeepot. Filling the china cup in front of Bob Valdez and then her own, Inez said, "She left early. It must have been before daybreak."

"You hear her?"

"No, maybe one of the girls did. I can ask."

"It doesn't matter."

"I heard what you're doing," Inez said.

"Well, I'm not doing very good. I wanted to tell the woman maybe it would take me a little longer."

"You're crazy."

"Listen, I'm tired," Valdez said. "I'm not going to argue with you, all right?"

"Go upstairs."

"I said I'm tired."

"So are the girls. I mean take a room and go to sleep."

"I have a run to St. David this afternoon and don't come back till the morning."

"Tell them you're sick."

"No, they don't have anybody."

"That Davis was in here last night. I threw him out."

"You can do it," Valdez said.

"He was in no condition. Only talk. I don't need talk," Inez said. She made a noise sipping her coffee and watched Valdez shape a cigarette. He handed it to her and made another one and lit them with a kitchen match.

"Now what do you do, forget the whole thing?"

"I don't know." He rubbed a gnarled brown hand over his hair, pulling it down on his forehead. "I think maybe talk to this Mr. Tanner again."

"You're crazy."

"I didn't explain it to him right. The part that it's like a court where you get money for something done to you. Not like a court, but, you know."

"You're still crazy. He won't listen to you. Nobody will."

"But if he does, the others will, uh?" Valdez sipped his coffee.

"Put a gun in his back if you can get close to him," Inez said. "That's the only way."

"No guns."

"The little shotgun."

Valdez nodded, thinking about it. "That would be good, wouldn't it?"

"Boom!" Inez laughed out and the sound of her voice filled the kitchen.

Valdez smiled. "Has he ever been in here?"

"They say he's got a woman. Maybe he beats her or does strange things to her."

"He's never been here, but you don't like him," Valdez said. "Why?"

"My book."

"Ah, your book. I forgot about it."

"You're in it."

"Sure, I remember now."

Inez called out, "Polly!" and waited a moment and called again.

A dark-haired girl in a robe came through the door from the front room. She smiled at Bob Valdez, holding the robe together in front of her. "Early bird," she said.

"No early bird. Get me the book," Inez said.

"Which, the black one?"

"No, the one before," Inez said. "The green one."

Valdez shook his head. "Black ones and green ones. How many do you have?"

"They go back about twelve years. To your time."

"Like I'm an old man now."

"Sometime you act it."

The girl came into the kitchen again with the scrapbook under her arm. "The green one," she said, winking at Bob Valdez and handing it to Inez, who pushed her coffee cup out of the way to open the book on the table. Inez sat at the end of the kitchen table with Polly standing behind her now, looking over her shoulder. Sitting to the side, Valdez lowered and cocked his head to look at the newspaper clippings and photographs mounted in the book.

"He seems familiar," Valdez said.

Inez looked at him. "I hope so. It's Rutherford Hayes."

"Well, that was twelve, fourteen years ago," Valdez said. He looked up as Polly laughed. She was leaning over Inez and the top of her robe hung partly open.

There were photographs of local businessmen, territorial officials and national figures, including two presidents, Rutherford Hayes and Chester A. Arthur, Profirio Díaz and Carmelita at Niagara Falls, and the Prince of Wales on his visit to Washington.

"Have they been to your place?" Valdez asked.

"No, but if they come I want to recognize them." Inez turned a page. "Earl Beaudry, on his appointment as land agent." Inez moved to the next page, her finger tracing down the column of newspaper clippings.

"Here it is," she said. "The first mention of him. August 13, 1881—Frank Tanner and a Carlisle Baylor were convicted of cattle theft and sent to Yuma Penitentiary."

Valdez seemed as pleased as he was surprised. "He's been to prison."

"For a few years, I think," Inez said. "It doesn't say how long. He was stealing cattle and driving them across the border. There's more about him." Her hand moved down the column and went to the next page. "Here, October, 1886, Frank J. Tanner, cattle broker, arraigned on a charge of murder in Contention, Arizona."

"Cattle broker now," Valdez said.

"The case was dismissed."

"It's getting better."

Inez turned the page. "Ah, here's the picture. You see him there?" Inez turned the book halfway toward Valdez and he leaned in, recognizing Tanner standing with a group of Army officers in front of an adobe building.

Inez read the caption. "It says he has a contract with the government to supply remounts to the Tenth United States Cavalry at Fort Huachuca." She turned a few more pages. "I think that's all."

"Nothing about him now, uh?"

"There's something else sticks in my mind about Huachuca," Inez said, "but I don't see it. Unless—sure, it would be in the other book." She sat back in her chair looking up over her shoulder. "Polly?"

Valdez watched the girl straighten and draw the robe together.

"Should I take this one?" the girl asked.

Inez was turning pages again. "No, I want to show Bob something."

"What have you got now?" he asked her.

Coming to a page, she pressed it flat and turned the book to him. "You remember?"

Valdez smiled a little. "That one."

It was a photograph of Bob Valdez taken at Fort Apache, Arizona, September 7, 1884: Bob Valdez standing among small trees and cactus plants the photographer had placed in his studio shed as a background: Bob Valdez with a Sharps .50 cradled in one arm and a long-barreled Walker Colt on his leg. He was wearing a hat, with a bandana beneath it that covered half of his forehead, a belt of cartridges for the Sharps, and knee-length Apache moccasins. The caption beneath the picture described Roberto Valdez as chief of scouts with Major General George Crook, Department of Arizona, during his expedition into Sonora against hostile Apaches.

"That's the way I still picture you," Inez said. "When someone says Bob Valdez, this is the one I see. Not the one that wears a suit and a collar."

Valdez was concentrating on the book, looking now at a photograph of a young Apache scout in buckskins and holding a rifle, standing against the same background used in the photo of himself. He remembered the photographer, a man named Fly. And the day the pictures were taken at Fort Apache. He remembered the scout washing himself and brushing his hair and putting on the buckskin shirt he had bought and had never worn before.

"Peaches," Valdez said. "General Crook's guide. His real name was Tso-ay, but the soldiers and the general called him Peaches. His skin." Valdez continued to study the photograph. He said, "They'd put a suit and a collar on him too, if they ever took his picture again."

Inez looked up as Polly came in with the other scrapbook. She took it from her and held it over the table.

"I don't know where he is now," Valdez was saying. "Maybe Fort Sill, Oklahoma, with the rest of them. Planting corn." He shook his head. "Man, I would like to see that sometime. Those people growing things in a garden."

Inez opened the book and laid it over the page Valdez was studying. He sat back as she turned a few pages and raised his gaze to Polly, who was looking over Inez's shoulder again, letting her robe come open. She was built very well and had very white skin.

"Here it is," Inez said. "Sutler murdered at Fort Huachuca.

James C. Erin was found shot to death a few miles from the fort today——"

Valdez stopped her. "When was this?"

Inez looked at the date on the clipping. "March. Six months ago."

"That's the one Orlando Rincón was supposed to have killed."

"It says he was found by some soldiers and"—her finger moved down the column—"here's the part. 'Held for questioning was Frank J. Tanner of Mimbreño, said to be the last person to have seen Erin alive. Mr. Tanner stated he had spent the previous evening with Mr. and Mrs. Erin at the fort, but had left for a business appointment in Nogales and had not seen Erin on the day he was reported to have been killed.' "

"He was sure it was Rincón," Valdez said. "And that his name was Johnson."

Inez nodded, looking at the book. "They mention a Johnson, listed as a deserter and also a suspect. A trooper with the Tenth Cavalry."

"Maybe they know this Johnson did it now," Valdez said.

Inez looked over the pages facing her. "I don't see anything more about it."

Valdez raised his eyes from the open robe to the nice-looking face of the dark-haired girl. "It's too bad he doesn't come here," he said.

Inez closed the book. "He never has and I would guess he knows where it is."

"If he did," Valdez said, his gaze still on Polly. "I could wait for him."

Diego Luz had a dream in which he saw himself sitting on a corral fence watching his men working green horses in the enclosure. In the dream, which he would look at during the day as well as at night, Diego Luz was manager of the Maricopa

Cattle Company. He lived with his family in the whitewashed adobe off beyond the corral, where the cedars stood against the sky: a house with trees and a stone well in the yard and a porch to sit on in the evening. Sometimes he would picture himself on the porch with his family about him, his three sons and two daughters, his wife and his wife's mother and whatever relatives might be visiting them. But his favorite dream was to see himself on the corral fence with his eldest son, who was almost a man, sitting next to him.

The hands were very nervous when he watched them with the horses because they knew he was the greatest mustanger and horsebreaker who ever lived. They knew he could subdue the meanest animals and they were afraid to make mistakes in his presence. He had told them how to do it, what they must do and not do, and he liked to watch them at work.

In the dream Diego and his son would watch R. L. Davis hanging on to the crow-hopping bronc until finally they saw him thrown and land hard on his shoulder. His son would shake his head and say, "Should I do it, Papa?" But he would say no, it was good for the man. He made R. L. Davis ride only the rough string, the outlaws and spoiled horses, when they were on roundup or a drive, and made R. L. Davis call him Señor Luz.

R. L. Davis mounted the bronc and was thrown again and this time he went after the horse with a loaded quirt and began beating the animal over the head. At this point in the dream Diego Luz walked over to R. L. Davis and said to him, "Hey," and when R. L. Davis looked around Diego Luz hit him in the face with one of his big fists. R. L. Davis went down and the eldest son poured a bucket of water on him and when the man shook his head and opened his eyes, he said, "What did I do?" Diego Luz said, "You hit the horse." R. L. Davis frowned, holding his jaw. "But you hit them when you broke horses," he said. And Diego Luz smiled and said, "Maybe, but now I hit whoever I want to."

R. L. Davis was a good one to hit. Once in a while though,

he would leave R. L. Davis alone and hit Mr. Malson, not hitting him too hard, but letting him know he was hit. And sometimes he would fire Mr. Malson, call him over and say, "It's too bad, but you're too goddam weak and stupid to do this work anymore so we got to get rid of you. And don't come back."

Diego Luz would think of these things as he worked his land and broke the mustangs he and his eldest son drove down out of the high country. His place was southeast of Lanoria, well off the road to St. David and only a few miles from the village of Mimbreño, though there was no wagon road in that direction, only a few trails if a man knew where to find them.

His place was adobe with straw blinds that rolled down to cover the doorway and windows and an open lean-to built against the house for cooking. There were a few chickens and two goats in the yard with the three youngest children and a brown mongrel dog that slept in the shade of the house most of the day. There was a vegetable garden for growing beans and peppers, and the peppers that were drying hung from the roof of the ramada that shaded the front of the house, which faced north, on high ground. Down the slope from the house was the well, and beyond it, on flat, cleared ground, the mesquite-pole corral where Diego Luz broke and trained the mustangs he flushed out of the hills. He worked here most of the time. Several times a year he drove a horse string down to the Maricopa spread near Lanoria, and he would go down there at roundup time and when they drove the cattle to Willcox.

When Bob Valdez appeared, circling the corral—two days following the incident at the pasture—Diego Luz and his eldest son were at the well, pulling up buckets of water and filling the wooden trough that ran to the corral. They stood watching Bob Valdez walking his horse toward them and waited, after greeting him, as he stepped down from the saddle and took the dipper of water Diego's son offered him.

There was no hurry. If a man rode all the way here he must have something to say, and it was good to wonder about it first

and not ask him questions. Though Diego Luz had already decided Bob Valdez had not come to see them but was passing
through on his way to Mimbreño. And who lived in Mimbreño? Frank Tanner. There it was. Simple.

They left the boy and climbed the slope to the house, Bob
Valdez seeing the children in the yard, Diego's wife and her
mother watching them from the lean-to where they were both
holding corn dough, shaping tortillas. The small children ran
up to them and the eldest daughter appeared now in the doorway of the house. Hey, a good looking girl now, almost a woman. Anita. She would be maybe sixteen years old. Valdez had
not been up here in almost a year.

When they were in the shade and had lighted cigarettes,
Diego Luz said, "There's something different about you. What
is it?"

Valdez shrugged. "I'm the same. What are you talking
about?"

"Your face is the same." Diego Luz squinted, studying him.
Slowly then his face relaxed. "I know what it is. You don't have
your collar on."

Valdez's hand went to his neck where he had tied a bandana.

"Or your suit. What is this, you're not dressed up?"

"It's too hot," Valdez said.

"It's always hot," Diego Luz said. His gaze dropped to
Valdez's waist. "No gun though."

Valdez frowned. "What's the matter with you? I don't have a
coat on, that's all."

"And you're going to see Mr. Tanner."

"Just to say a few things to him."

"My son rode to Lanoria yesterday. He heard about the few
things you said the other night."

Valdez shook his head. "People don't have anything to talk
about."

"Listen, the woman doesn't need any money. She doesn't
know what it is."

"But we know," Valdez said. "I just want to ask you something about Tanner."

Diego Luz drew on his cigarette and squinted out into the sunlight, down the slope to the horse corral. "I know what others know. That's all."

"He lives in Mimbreño?"

"For about two years maybe."

"How do the people like him?"

"There are no people. Most of them left at the time of the Apache. The rest of them left when Frank Tanner come. He's there with his men," Diego Luz said, "and some of their women."

"How many men?"

"At least thirty. Sometimes more."

"Do they ever come here?"

"Sometimes they pass by."

"What do they do, anything?"

"They have a drink of water and go on."

"They never make any trouble?"

"No, they don't bother me. Never."

"Maybe because you work for Maricopa."

Diego Luz shrugged. "What do I have they would want?"

"Horses," Valdez said.

"Once they asked to buy a string. I told them to see Mr. Malson."

"Did Tanner himself come?"

"No, his segundo and some others."

"Do you know any of them?"

"No, I don't think any of them are from around here."

"Do you think that's strange?"

"No, these are guns he hires, not hands. I think they hear of Tanner and what he pays and they come from all over to get a job with him."

"He pays good, uh?"

"You see them sometimes in St. David," Diego Luz said. "They spend the money. But you see different ones each time, so maybe he lose some in Mexico or they get a stomach full of it and quit."

"What, driving cattle?"

"Cattle and guns. He gets the guns somewhere and sneaks them over the border to people who are against Díaz and want to start a revolution. So over there the *rurales* and federal soldiers look for him and try to stop him. Everybody knows that."

"I've been learning the stageline business," Valdez said.

"Keep doing it," Diego Luz said, "and live to be an old man."

"Sometimes I feel old now." He watched the chickens pecking the hard ground and heard Diego Luz's children calling out something and laughing as they played somewhere on the other side of the house. What do you need besides this? he was thinking. To have a place, a family. Very quiet except for the children sometimes, and no trouble. No Apaches. No bandits raiding from across the border. Trees and water and a good house. The house could be fixed up better. A little work, that's all. He said, "I'll trade you. I become the horsebreaker, you work for the stage company."

Diego Luz was looking out at the yard. "You want this?"

"Why not? It's a good place."

"If I had something to do I wouldn't be here."

"You do all right," Valdez said.

"Do it forever," Diego Luz said. "See how you like it."

"Maybe sometime. After I see this Tanner."

Diego Luz was studying Valdez's horse. "You don't have a rifle either."

"What do I need it for?"

'Maybe you meet a couple of them on a trail, they don't like your face."

"I'll talk to them," Valdez said.

"Maybe they don't let you talk."

"Come on, they know who I am. I'm going there to talk, that's all."

"You talk better with a rifle," Diego Luz said. "I give you mine."

From habit, approaching the top of the rise—before he would be outlined for a moment against the sky—Bob Valdez looked back the way he had come, his eyes, half-closed in the sun's glare, holding on the rock shapes and darker patches of brush at the bottom of the draw. He sat motionless until he was sure of the movement, then dismounted and led his claybank mare off the trail to one side, up into young piñon pines.

For a few moments he did not think of the rider coming up behind him; he thought of his own reaction, the caution that had stopped him from topping the rise. There were no more Chiricahuas or White Mountain bands around here. There was nothing to worry about to keep him alert and listening and looking back as well as to the sides and ahead. But he had stopped. Sure, habit, he thought. Something hanging on of no use to him now.

What difference did it make who the man was? The man wasn't following him. The man was riding southeast from the St. David road and must have left the road not far back to cut cross-country toward Mimbreño maybe, or to a village across the border. Sure, it could be one of Tanner's men. You can ride in with him, Valdez thought, and smiled at the idea of it. He would see who it was and maybe he would come out of the pines, giving the man some warning first, or maybe he wouldn't.

Now, as the man drew nearer, for some reason he was sure it was one of the Maricopa riders: the slouched, round-shouldered way the man sat his saddle, the funneled brim of his hat bobbing up and down with the walking movement of the horse.

Maybe he had known all the time who it was going to be. That was a funny thing. Because when he saw it was R. L. Davis, looking at the ground or deep in thought, the stringy, mouthy one who thought he was good with the Winchester, Valdez was not surprised, though he said to himself, Goddam. How do you like that?

He let him go by, up over the rise and out of sight, while he stayed in the pines to shape a cigarette and light it, wondering where the man was going, curious because it was this one and not someone else, and glad now of the habit that had made him look around when he did. He was sure the man had not been following him. The man would have been anxious and looking around and would have stopped before he topped the rise. But the question remained, Where was he going?

When Valdez moved out, keeping to the trees over the crest of the rise, he hung back and let the distance between them stretch to a hundred yards. He followed R. L. Davis this way for several miles until the trail came to open grazing land, and as R. L. Davis crossed toward the scrub trees and hills beyond the flats, a column of dust came down the slope toward him.

You look around, Bob Valdez thought. That habit stays with you. But you don't bring the field glasses.

He remained in the cover of the trees and, in the distance, watched three riders meet R. L. Davis and stand close to him for some time, forming a single shape until the group came apart and the riders, strung out now, one in front of Davis and two behind, rode with him into the deep shadow at the base of the far hills. He saw them briefly again up on the slope and at the crest of the hill.

They wonder about him too, Valdez thought. What do you want? Who do you want to see? They ask questions and take their jobs very seriously because they feel they're important. They should relax more, Valdez thought. He mounted the claybank again and rode out into the sunlight, holding the horse to a walk, keeping his eyes on the slope the riders came down and wondering if they had left someone there to watch.

No, they did it another way. One of them who had been with R. L. Davis came back. When Valdez was little more than halfway up the trail, following the switchbacks that climbed through the brush, he saw the mounted rider waiting for him, his horse standing across the trail.

As Valdez came on, narrowing the distance between them, he recognized the rider, the Mexican who had brought him into the yard of the stage station.

"Far enough," the Mexican said. He held a Winchester across his lap, but did not raise it. He studied Valdez, who reined in a few feet from him. "You come back again."

"I didn't finish talking to him," Valdez said.

"I think he finish with you, though."

"Let's go ask him."

"Maybe he don't want to see you," the Mexican said.

"It's about money again."

"You said that before. For the woman. He don't care anything about the woman."

"Maybe this time when I tell him."

"What do you have on you?"

"Nothing." Valdez raised his hands and dropped one of them to the stock of Diego Luz's rifle in its leather boot. "Only this."

"That could be enough," the Mexican said.

"You want it?" Valdez smiled. "You don't trust me?"

"Sure, I trust you." The Mexican raised the Winchester and motioned Valdez up the grade. "But I ride behind you."

Valdez edged past him up the trail and kept moving until he reached the top of the slope. Now he could see the village of Mimbreño across the valley, a mile from them beyond open land where Tanner's cattle grazed. Valdez had been to this village once before, the day after White Mountain Apaches had raided and killed three men and carried off a woman and burned the mission church. He remembered the blackened walls; the roof had collapsed into the church and the beams were still smoking. He remembered the people in the square when they rode in, the people watching the Apache scouts and company of cavalry and saying to themselves, Why weren't you here yesterday, you soldiers? What good are you?

As they crossed the grazing land Valdez recognized the church, the roofless shell that had never been repaired. It stood at the end of the single street of adobes where the street widened into a square and there was a well with a pump and a stone trough for watering the horses. Beyond the cluster of buildings was a stand of cottonwood trees and a stream that came down out of the high country to the east. Valdez saw the women in the trees, some of them walking this way carrying baskets of clothes. Then he was entering the street, the Mexican next to him now, with the dogs barking and the smell of wood fires, seeing the freight wagons along the adobe fronts and more horses than would ever be in a village this size. It was a village preparing to make war. It was a military camp, the base of a revolutionary army. Or the base of a heavily armed scouting force that would stay here until they were driven out. But at the same time it was not a village. Yes, there were people. There were women among the armed men, women in front of the adobes and a group of them at the well with gourds and wooden pails. But there were no children; no sound of children nor a sign of children anywhere.

"He's there waiting for you," the Mexican said.

Valdez was looking at the church. A gate of mesquite poles had been built across the arched opening of the doorway, and there were horses penned inside the enclosure. He felt the Mexican close to him, moving him to the east side of the square, to the two-story adobe with the loading platform across the front, the building that had been the village's general store and mill and grain warehouse.

Frank Tanner stood at the edge of the loading platform looking down at a group of riders, standing over them with his hands on his hips. A woman was behind him near the open doorway, not a Mexican woman, a blond-haired woman, golden hair in the sunlight hanging below her shoulders to the front of her white dress. Valdez looked at the woman until they were close to the platform and the riders sidestepped their horses to let the Mexican in, Valdez holding back now; and as they moved in among the riders he saw that one of them was the segundo.

He saw R. L. Davis, then, mounted on a sorrel next to the segundo. He didn't look at Davis, who was watching him, but up at Tanner now, the man so close above him that he had to bend his head back, feeling awkward and unprotected and foolish with the woman watching him, to look at Tanner.

Tanner stared down at Valdez as if this would be enough, no words necessary. Valdez did not want to smile because he knew he would feel foolish, but he eased his expression to show he was sincere and had come here as an honest man with nothing to hide.

He said, "I'd like to talk to you once more."

"You've talked," Tanner said. "You get one time and you've had yours."

Maybe he was joking, so Valdez smiled a little bit now, though he didn't want to smile with the woman watching him. "I know you're a busy man," he said, "but you must be a fair man also, uh? I mean you have all these people working for you. You recognize the worth of things and pay a just wage. A man like that would also see when someone is owed something."

Goddam, it didn't sound right, hearing himself speaking with his goddam neck bent back and Tanner looking down at him like God in black boots and a black hat over his eyes.

"I mean if the woman was to go to the courthouse and say some men have killed my husband, by mistake, as an accident. So I think somebody should pay me for that—don't you think the court would say sure and order that we pay her something?"

"Jesus Christ," R. L. Davis said. Valdez did not look at him, but he knew it was Davis. He saw Tanner's eyes shift to the side, slide over and back to him again.

"I'm talking about what's fair," Valdez said. "I'm not trying to cheat anybody—if you think I want to take the money and run off. No, you can give it to the woman yourself. I mean have one of your men do it. I don't care who gives it to her."

Tanner continued to stare at him until finally he said, "You don't learn. I guess I have to keep teaching you."

"Tell me why you don't think she should have something," Valdez said. "You explain it to me, I understand it."

"No, I think there's only one thing you'll understand." Tanner's gaze went to his segundo. "You remember that one tried to run off with the horses?"

Valdez lowered his head to look at the segundo, who was nodding, picturing something. "The one who liked to walk," the segundo said.

Valdez heard Tanner say, "That one," and the segundo continued to nod his head, then raised it and gazed about the square.

"We can use the poles from the gate," the segundo said, looking toward the church, "and have some more cut."

Tanner was saying, "All right," and the segundo was looking at Valdez now. He nodded once.

Valdez felt the hand at his shoulder, fingers clawing into his neck as the hand clutched his bandana, and his own hands went to the horn of his saddle. He felt the Mexican's horse tight against his left leg, then moving away and the Mexican pulling him, choking him, until his hands slipped from the saddle horn and he was dragged from his horse, stumbling but not able to fall, held up by the Mexican's fist twisted in the tight fold of his neckerchief. They were around him and someone hit him in the face with a fist. It didn't hurt him, but it startled him; he was struck again on the back of the neck, then in the stomach, seeing the man close to him swing his fist and not being able to turn away from it. He went down and was kicked in the back, pushed over and pressed flat to the hard-packed ground. His hat was off now. A foot came down on his neck, pinning him, face turned to the side against the ground. Now they pulled his arms straight out to the sides and he felt a sharp pain through his shoulder blades as he was held in this position. Several minutes passed and he rested, breathing slowly to relax and not be tensed if they hit him again. Boots were close to his face.

The boots moved and dust rose into his nostrils, but no one kicked him.

They placed a mesquite pole across his shoulders that extended almost a foot on either side beyond his outstretched hands and tied it with leather thongs to his wrists and neck. They placed another pole down the length of his back, from above his head to his heels, and lashed this one to the crosspole and also around his neck and body. When this was done the segundo told him all right, stand up.

Valdez could not press his hands to the ground. He raised his head, turning it, and pushed his forehead against the hardpack, arching against the pole down his spine, straining the muscles of his neck, and gradually, kicking and scraping the ground, worked his knees up under him.

"The other one didn't get up so quick," the segundo said.

Valdez was on his knees raising his body, and he was kicked hard from behind and slammed onto his face again.

"This one don't get up either," the Mexican said.

Valdez heard Tanner's voice say, "Get him out of here," and this time they let him work his way to his knees and stand up. But as he straightened, the bottom of the vertical pole struck the ground and held him in a hunched position, a man with a weight on his back, his eyes on the ground, unable to raise his head. Someone put his hat on his head, too low and tight on his forehead.

"That way," the segundo said, nodding across the square. "The way you came."

"My horse," Valdez said.

"Don't worry about the horse," the segundo said. "We take care of."

There was nothing more to say. Valdez turned and started off, hunched over, raising his eyes and able to see perhaps twenty feet in front of him, but not able to hold his gaze in this strained position.

The segundo called after him. "Hey, don't fall on your back. You'll be like a turtle." He laughed, and some of the others laughed with him.

Frank Tanner watched the stooped figure circle the water pump and move down the street past the women who had come out of the adobes to look at him.

"You fixed him," R. L. Davis said.

Tanner's eyes shifted to Davis, sliding on him and away from him, as he had looked at him before. "I don't remember asking you here," Tanner said.

"Listen," R. L. Davis began to say.

Tanner stopped him. "Watch your mouth, boy. I don't listen to you. I don't listen to anybody I don't want to listen to."

R. L. Davis squinted up at him. "I didn't mean it that way. I come here to work for you."

Tanner's gaze dropped slowly from the bent figure down the street to Davis. "Why do you think I'd hire you?"

"You need a gun, I'm your man."

"I didn't see you hit anything the other day."

"Jesus Christ, I wasn't aiming at her. You said yourself just make her jump some."

"Are you telling me what I said?"

"I thought that's what it was."

"Don't think," Tanner said. "Ride out."

"Hell, you can always use another man, can't you?"

"Maybe a man," Tanner said. "Ride out."

"Try me out. Put me on for a month."

"We'll put some poles on your back," Tanner said, "if you want to stay here."

"I was just asking," R. L. Davis lifted his reins and flicked them against the neck of his sorrel, bringing the animal around and guiding it through the group of riders, trying to take his time.

Tanner watched Davis until he was beyond the pump and heading down the street. The small stooped figure was now at the far end of the adobes.

The woman, Gay Erin, who had been married to the sutler at Fort Huachuca and had been living with Frank Tanner since her husband's death, waited for Tanner to turn and notice her in the doorway behind him. But he didn't turn; he stood on the edge of the platform over his men.

She said, "Frank?" and waited again.

Now he looked around and came over to her, taking his time. "I didn't know you were there," he said.

She kept her eyes on him, waiting for him to come close. "I don't understand you," she said.

"I don't need that boy. Why should I hire him?"

"The other one. He asks you a simple thing, to help someone."

"We won't talk about it out here," Tanner said. They went into the dimness of the warehouse, past sacks of grain and stacked wooden cases, Tanner holding her arm and guiding her to the stairway. "I let you talk to me the way you want," Tanner said, "but not in front of my men."

Upstairs, in the office that had been made into a sitting room, Gay Erin looked out the window. She could see R. L. Davis at the end of the street; the hunched figure of Bob Valdez was no longer in sight.

"You better keep up here from now on," Tanner said, "unless I call you down."

She turned from the window. "And how long is that?"

"I guess as long as I want." Tanner went into the bedroom. He came out wearing his coat, strapping on a gunbelt. "I'm going to Nogales; I'll be back in the morning." He looked down at his belt, buckling it. "You can come if you want a twenty-mile ride."

"Or sit here," the girl said.

He looked up at her. "What else?"

"If you say sit I'm supposed to sit." Her expression and the sound of her voice were mild, but her eyes held his and hung on. "No one can be that sure," she said. "Not even you."

"Well, you're not going to leave," Tanner said. He moved

toward her, settling the gunbelt on his hips. "You don't have anything at Huachuca. You don't have anything left at Prescott. Whatever you have is here."

"Whatever I have," the girl said, "as your woman."

"Aren't I nice enough to you?"

"Sometimes."

"Take what you get."

"Sometimes you act like a human being."

"When I'm in my drawers," Tanner said. "When I'm in my boots that's a different time."

"You had them on outside."

"You bet I did, lady."

"He was trying to help a woman who'd lost her husband; that's all he was doing."

"And I'm helping one already," Tanner said. "One poor widow woman's enough." He was close to her, looking into her face, and he touched her cheek gently with his hand. He said, "I guess I could stay a few more minutes if you like."

"Frank, send someone to cut him loose."

Tanner shook his head, tired of it. "Lady, you sure can break the spell . . ." He moved away from her toward the door, then looked back as he opened it. "Nobody cuts him loose. I don't want to see that man again."

You've looked at the ground all your life, Valdez thought at one point. But never this close for so long.

The pain reached from the back of his neck down into his shoulders. He would try to arch his back, and the pole, with a knot in it, would press against his head and push his hat forward. The hat was low and stuck to his forehead and sweat stung his eyes. He told himself, The hell with it; don't think about it. Go home. You've walked home before.

God, but he had never walked home like this. The ground across the grazing land was humped and spotted with brush, but he had little trouble with his footing. No, God, he could see where he was going all right. He could hear Tanner's cattle and he thought once, What if some bull with swords on his head sees you and doesn't like you? God, he said to himself, give that bull good grass to eat or a nice cow to do something with.

A mile across the grazing land and then up into the foothills, following a gully and angling out of it, climbing the side of a brush slope, not finding the trail and taking a longer way to the top, trying to look up to see where he was going with the pole pressed against his head. He couldn't go straight up. He couldn't lose his footing and fall backward on the crossed poles. He remembered what the segundo had said about the turtle, and at that time he had pictured himself lying on his back in the sun of midday and through the afternoon. No, he would take longer and he wouldn't fall. It was the pain in his legs that bothered him now; it turned his thighs into cords and pulled so, as he neared the top, that his legs began to tremble.

They're old legs, he said to himself. Be good to them. They have to walk twenty miles. Or over to Diego Luz, he thought then. Ten miles. Twenty miles, ten miles, what was the difference?

He wished he could wipe the sweat and dust from his face. He wished he could loosen his hat and rub his nose and bring his arms down and straighten up just for a minute.

Before he reached the crest of the slope he crouched forward and gradually lowered himself to his knees, bending over and twisting his body as he fell forward so that a tip of the crosspole touched the slope first; but this did little to break his fall, and with his head turned his cheekbone struck the ground with the force of a heavy, solid blow. It stunned him and he lay breathing with his mouth open. His hat, tight to his forehead, had remained on; good. Now he rested for perhaps a quarter of an hour, until the pain through his shoulder blades became unbearable. Valdez got to his feet and continued on.

R. L. Davis waited for him in the trees, across the meadow on the far side of the slope. He had watched Valdez work up through the ravine and down the switchback trail on this side. He had waited because maybe Tanner's men were also watching—the lookouts up on the slope—and he had waited because he wasn't sure what they'd do. He thought they might come out and push Valdez down the trail, have some fun with him; but no one appeared, and Valdez had come all the way down to the meadow now and was coming across, hurrying some as he saw the shade of the trees waiting for him.

R. L. Davis moved his sorrel into heavy foliage. There wasn't any hurry: watch him a while and then play with him.

Goddam, now what was he doing, kicking at the leaves? Clearing a spot, R. L. Davis decided. He could hear Valdez in the silence, the sound of the leaves scuffing, and could see him through the pale birch trunks, the bent-over hunched-back figure in the thin shafts of sunlight. He watched Valdez go to his knees; he winced and then smiled as Valdez fell forward on the side of his face. That was pretty good. But as Valdez lay there not moving, R. L. Davis became restless and started to fidget and tried to think of something. You could trample him some, he thought. Ride over him a few times. He decided maybe that was the thing to do and raised his reins to flick the sorrel.

But now the man was stirring, arching onto his head and getting his knees under him.

Valdez rose and stood there, trying to turn his head to look about him. He moved forward slowly, shuffling in the leaves. He turned sideways to edge between trees that grew close together. Farther on he stopped and placed one end of the crosspole against a birch trunk and waved the other end of the pole toward a tree several feet from him but the pole was too short. R. L. Davis watched him move on, touching a trunk and trying to reach another with the crosspole until finally there it was, and R. L. Davis saw what he was trying to do.

Valdez stood between two trees that were a little less than six feet apart. Now, with the ends of the crosspole planted against the trunks, holding him there, he tried to move forward, straining, digging in with his boots and slipping in the leaves. He bent his wrists so that his hands hung down and were out of the way. Now he moved back several steps and ran between the two trees. The ends of the crosspole struck the trunks and stopped him dead. He strained against the pole, stepping back and slamming the pole ends against the trunks again and again. Finally he moved back eight or ten feet and again ran at the space between the trees and this time as the ends struck, R. L. Davis heard a gasp of breath in the silence.

He moved the sorrel out of the foliage. Valdez must hear him, but the man didn't move; he hung there on the crosspole leaning against the trunks, his arms seeming lower than they were before.

R. L. Davis saw why as he got closer. Sure enough, the pole had splintered. And it looked like a sharp end had pierced his back. R. L. Davis sat in his saddle looking down at the blood spreading over Valdez's back. He reined the sorrel around the near birch tree and came up in front of him.

"I swear," R. L. Davis said, "you are sure one dumb son of a bitch, aren't you? When that pole broke, where did you suppose it was going to go?" He saw Valdez try to raise his head. "It's your old amigo you tried to swing a scatter gun at the other day. You remember that? You went and shot the wrong coon and you was going to come at me for it."

Davis sidestepped the sorrel closer to Valdez, pulling his coiled *reata* loose from the saddle thong and playing out several feet of it. He reached over, looping the vertical pole above Valdez's head and snugged the knot tight. "You're lucky a white man come along," Davis said.

Valdez tried to raise his eyes to him. "Look at my back," he said.

"I saw it. You cut yourself."

"God, I think so," Valdez said. "Cut my wrists loose first, all right?"

"Well, not right yet," Davis said. He moved away, letting out rope, and when he was ten feet away dallied the line to his saddle horn. "Come on," he said.

Valdez had to move to the side to free an end of the crosspole and was almost jerked from his feet, stumbling to get between the trees and keep up with the short length of rope. He was pulled this way, through the birch trees and through the brush that grew along the edge of the grove, and out into the glare of the meadow again.

"You must ache some from stooping over," R. L. Davis said.

"Cut my hands and I'll tell you about it."

"You know I didn't like you trying to hit me with that scatter gun."

"I won't do it anymore," Valdez said. "How's that?"

"It made me sore, I'll tell you."

"Cut me loose and tell me, all right?"

R. L. Davis moved in close in front and lifted the loop from the upright pole. He kept the sorrel close against Valdez as he coiled the rope and thonged it to his saddle again.

"Your animal doesn't smell so good," Valdez said.

"Well, I'll give you some air," R. L. Davis said. "How'll that be?" He moved the sorrel tight against Valdez, kicking the horse's left flank to sidestep it and keep it moving.

Valdez said, "You crazy, you put me over. Hey!" He could feel the bottom of the upright pole pushing into the ground, wedged tight, and his body lifting against R. L. Davis' leg. The sorrel jumped forward, sidestepping, swinging its rump hard against Valdez, and he went over, seeing Davis above him and seeing the sky and tensing and holding the scream inside him and gasping as his spine slammed the ground and the splintered pole gouged into his back.

After a moment he opened his eyes. His hat was off. It was good, the tight band gone from his forehead. But he had to close his eyes again because of the glare and the pain in his body, the sharp thing sticking into his back that made him strain to arch his shoulders. A shadow fell over him and he opened his eyes to see R. L. Davis far above him on the sorrel, the funneled hat brim and narrow face staring down at him.

"A man ought to wear his hat in the sun," R. L. Davis said.

Valdez closed his eyes and in a moment the sun's glare pressed down on his eyelids again. He heard the horse break into a gallop that soon faded to nothing.

FOUR

St. Francis of Assisi was the kindest man who ever lived. Maybe not kinder than Our Lord; that was different. But kinder than any real living man. Sure. St. Francis had been a soldier once and got wounded and after that he wouldn't step on bugs or kill animals. Hell, he talked to the animals; like the time he talked to the wolf—probably a big gray lobo—who was scaring everybody and he told the wolf to stop it. Stop it or I'll skin you, you son of a bitch, and wear you for a coat. You would talk to a wolf different than you would talk to other animals. But he talked to all of them, birds, everything; they were all his friends he said. He even talked to the stars and the sun and the moon. He called the sun Brother Sun.

But not today you couldn't call it Brother Sun, Bob Valdez thought.

It was strange the things he thought about, lying in the meadow on a pole like a man crucified, remembering his older sister reading to him a long time ago about St. Francis of Assisi and his prayer, or whatever it was, The Canticle of the Sun. Yes, because he had pictured the sun moving, spinning and doing things, the sun smiling, as his sister read it to him. Today the sun filled the sky and had no edges. It wasn't smiling; this day the sun was everything over him, white hot pressing down on him and dancing orange, red, and black dots on his closed eyelids.

He remembered a man who had no eyelids, who had been staked out in the sun and his eyelids cut off. And his ears cut off also and his right hand. He remembered finding the man's hand and finding the man's son in the burned-out farmhouse on the Gila River south of San Carlos, after Geronimo had jumped the reservation and raided down into old Mexico. They didn't find the man's wife. No, he didn't remember a woman there. Maybe she had been away visiting relatives. Or they had taken her. No, they had been moving fast and she wouldn't have been able to keep up with them. It was funny, he wondered what the woman looked like.

She could look like the Lipan Apache woman and have a child inside her. She could look like the woman with Tanner standing on the loading platform—he remembered her blond hair and her eyes watching him, a blond-haired woman in that village of guns and horses and freight wagons. Her face was brown and she looked good with the sun on her hair, but she should be inside in a room with furniture and gold statue lamps on the tables.

He remembered the girl Polly at Inez's place and her robe coming open as she leaned over to look at the green book and then the black one. He should have stayed. It would be good to be there. It didn't matter about the girl—later—but to be in a bed with the shades down, lying on one side and then the other and moving his arms, bending them all he wanted while he slept. He would only wake up at night when the sun was down and Brother Moon or Sister Moon or whatever the hell St. Francis called it was in the sky with its soft light, and he would drink cool water from the pitcher next to the bed. When the girl came in he would turn his head and see her face, her eyes in the darkness, close to him. She had dark hair, but he thought of her with light hair, and this didn't make sense to him.

He remembered turning his head against the thong holding him to the upright post, the thong cutting his neck as he strained to twist his face away from the white heat pressing him and the colors dancing in his eyes. He remembered thinking that if the thong was wet with his sweat it would shrink when it dried and perhaps strangle him to death if he was still alive. Then he wouldn't be thirsty anymore and it wouldn't matter if his eyes were burned out. It wouldn't matter if Brother Wolf came to see him; he wouldn't have to talk to any Brother Wolf and ask him to go away.

He remembered the knife pain in his shoulders and back. He remembered feeling sick and trying to calm himself and breathe slowly so he wouldn't vomit and drown in his own bile in a mountain meadow. He remembered the worst, the heat and the pain and the thirst, and he remembered opening his eyes to a blue sky turning gray and streaked with red. He remembered a numbness in his body, looking at his hands and unable to move them.

He remembered darkness, opening his eyes and seeing darkness and hearing night sounds coming from the birch trees. He remembered the breeze moving the grass close to his face. He remembered pieces of the whole, sleeping and opening his eyes: the girl from Inez's place over him, lifting his head and holding a canteen to his lips. Why would she use a canteen when the pitcher was on the table? He remembered getting up, standing and falling and the girl holding his arms, bending them carefully, working the joints and feeling a sweet pain that would have made his eyes water if he had water left in him to come out. He remembered stretching and walking and falling and walking and crawling on his hands and knees. He remembered voices, the voices of children and a voice that he knew well and an arm that he knew helping him.

Diego Luz said, "Are you awake?"

Valdez lay with his eyes open, his eyes moving slowly from the ceiling of the room to Diego Luz, a white figure in the dimness. "I think so," he said. "I woke up before, I think; but I didn't know where I was."

"You were saying some crazy things."

"How did you find me?"

"Find you? You crawled into the yard last night. I heard the dogs; I almost shot you."

"I came here myself?"

Diego Luz moved closer to the bed. "What happened to you?"

"Maybe I'm dead," Valdez said. "Am I dead?" He could see the children of Diego Luz behind their father, in the doorway.

"You looked near to it. Somebody stabbed you in the back."

"No, a tree did that."

Diego Luz nodded. "A tree. What kind of a tree is it does that?"

His daughter came into the room with a gourd and a tin cup, and the small children followed her, crowding up to the bed. Valdez smiled at them and at the girl and got up on his elbow to sip the water. He could see the wife of Diego Luz and his wife's mother in the doorway, staying in the other room but raising their faces to look at him on the bed.

"I don't see your boy," Valdez said.

"He's watching."

"For what?"

"To see if they follow you. Or whoever it was."

"Don't worry," Valdez said. "I'm leaving when I find my pants."

"I don't worry," the horsebreaker said. "I'm careful. I wonder when I see a man crawl in half dead."

Valdez handed the cup to the girl. "Have you got some whiskey?"

"Mescal."

"Mescal then."

"You haven't eaten yet."

"I want to sleep, not eat," Valdez said. "In the back of your wagon when you take me to Lanoria."

"Stay here, you be better."

"No," Valdez said. "You said they come by here. Maybe they come by again."

"Maybe they know where you live too."

"I'm not going where I live." He motioned Diego Luz closer and whispered to him as his children and his wife and his wife's mother watched.

Diego Luz straightened, shaking his head. "Half dead and you want to go to that place."

"Half alive," Valdez said. "There is a difference."

Diego Luz brought him in through the kitchen at almost four in the morning. Valdez had passed out in the wagon, his wound beginning to bleed again. But as they dragged him up the stairs and along the dark hallway, Diego Luz and the large woman, Inez, supporting him between them, he hissed at them. "God*dam*, put my arms down!"

"We carry you and you swear at us," Inez hissed back.

"God and St. Francis, put me down!"

"Now he prays," Inez said. She opened a door, and inside they lowered him gently to the bed, settling him on his stomach and hearing him let out his breath. Inez bent over him, lifting his shirt to look at the bloodstained bandage.

"In the back," she said. "The only way you could kill this one." She looked at Diego Luz. "Who shot him? I didn't hear anything."

"A tree," Diego Luz said. "Listen, get something to clean him and talk after."

Valdez heard the woman close the door. He was comfortable and he knew he would be asleep again in a moment. He said, "Hey," bringing Diego Luz close to the side of the bed. "I'm going to leave you everything I have when I die."

"You're not going to die. You got a little cut."

"I know I'm not going to die now. I mean when I die."

"Don't talk about it," Diego Luz said.

"I leave you everything I have if you do one more thing for me, all right?"

"Go to sleep," Diego Luz said, "and shut up for a while."

"If you get me something from my room at the boarding house."

"You want me to go now?"

"No, this time of night that old lady'll shoot you. During the day. Tomorrow."

"What is it you want?"

"In the bottom drawer of the dresser," Valdez said. "Everything that's there."

Goddam, he wished he could tell somebody about it.

R. L. Davis stood at the bar in the Republic Hotel drinking whiskey. He didn't have anything to do. He'd been fired for not being where he was supposed to be, riding fence and not riding all over the goddam country, Mr. Malson had said. He'd told Mr. Malson he'd gone to see Diego Luz about a new horse, but Mr. Malson didn't believe him, the tight-butt son of a bitch. Sure he had gone off to Tanner's place to see about working for him, figuring the chance of getting caught and fired was worth it. What surprised him was Tanner not hiring him. Christ, he could shoot. Probably good or better than any man Tanner had. He saw himself riding along with Tanner's bunch, riding into Lanoria, stampeding in and swinging down in front of the Republic or De Spain's.

He could go over to De Spain's. At least he'd been paid off. Maybe there was somebody over there he could tell. God, it was hard to keep something that good inside you. But he wasn't sure how everybody would take it, telling how he'd pushed Valdez over like a goddam turtle in the sun. The segundo had mentioned the turtle and it had given him the idea, though he thought one of Tanner's men would do it first.

Maybe if he told Tanner what he did——

No, Tanner would look at him and say, "You come all the way out here to tell me that?"

He was a hard man to talk to. He looked right through you without any expression. But it would be something to ride for him, down into old Mexico with guns and beef and shoot up the federals.

R. L. Davis finished his whiskey and had another and said to himself all right, he'd go over to De Spain's. Maybe there was a way of telling it that it wouldn't sound like he'd done it to him deliberately. Hell, he hadn't killed him, he'd pushed him over, and there were seven hundred miles between pushing and killing. If the son of a bitch was still out there it was his own fault.

Outside, he mounted the sorrel and moved up the street. He came to the corner and looked around, seeing who was about, not for any reason, just looking. He saw Diego Luz coming out of the boardinghouse two doors from the corner: Diego Luz coming toward him, carrying something wrapped up in newspaper, a big bundle that could be his wash. Except a Mexican horsebreaker wasn't going to have any wash done in there. He had his own woman for that.

He waited for him to reach the corner. "Hey, Diego, what you got there, your laundry?"

The Mexican looked funny, surprised, like he'd been caught stealing chickens. Then he gave a big smile and waved, like R. L. Davis was his best friend and he was really glad to see him.

Dumb Mexican. He was all right; just a dumb chilipicker. Christ, R. L. Davis thought, it'd be good to tell him what he'd done to Bob Valdez. And then he thought, Hey, that's the boardinghouse Bob Valdez lives in, isn't it?

Each of the seven doors in the upstairs hall bore the name of a girl in a flowery pink and blue scroll—Anastacia, Rosaria, Evita, Elisaida, Maria, Tranquiliña, and Edith. The names were a nice touch and Inez liked them, though only one of the original seven girls was still here. Because of the turnover during the past two years, and because the Mexican sign painter had moved away, Inez had not bothered to have the doors relettered. Maybe she would sometime, though none of her customers seemed to mind that the name on the door didn't match the girl. They didn't care what the girls' names were, long as they were there.

Inez tiptoed down the hall, but the floor still creaked beneath her weight. It was semidark, with one lamp lit at the end of the hall and a faint light coming from the stairway landing. Polly followed her, carrying a tray of ham and greens and fried potatoes and coffee: Bob Valdez's supper if he was awake and felt like eating. He had been here since yesterday morning: two days and going on the second night, sleeping most of the time and sitting up drinking water out of the pitcher when he wasn't sleeping. She had never seen a man drink so much water. Diego Luz had come yesterday afternoon with a bundle of clothes— at least what looked to be clothing—and hadn't been back since then. Diego Luz never came here ordinarily, unless he was looking for someone for Mr. Malson, so it would seem strange if he were seen coming in and out. This was why Bob Valdez told him to stay away. No one was to know he was here. "As far as anybody thinks, I have disappeared," Bob Valdez had said. He had told Inez what happened to him, but she had the feeling he didn't tell her everything. That was all right; it was his business. He told what he wanted, but he always told the truth.

At Rosaria's door Inez paused, listening, taking a key from the folds of her skirt. She turned it in the lock and opened the door quietly, in case he was asleep.

She was surprised to see light from the overhead lamp; she was even more surprised to see Bob Valdez standing by the dresser. She got Polly into the room and locked the door and saw the look on Polly's face as she stared at Bob Valdez.

"Put it down," Inez said. "Before you drop it."

"Over here," Valdez said. "If you will."

Crossing the room, Polly kept her eyes on him as he moved aside the newspaper and oil can and revolver so she could place the tray on the dresser. He was holding his sawed-off ten-bore Remington shotgun, wiping it with a cloth that two days before had been his shirt.

Inez smiled a little watching him, noticing the shotgun shells now on the dresser, the shells standing upright with their crimped ends peeled open. "Roberto Valdez returned," she said.

He smiled back at her. "Bob is easier."

"Bob wears a starched collar," Inez said. "Roberto makes war."

"Just a little war, if he wants it," Valdez said.

"You get crazier every day."

"I ask him once more; that's all."

"You've asked him twice."

"But this time will be different."

"You expect to fight him?"

"If he wants a little. We'll see."

"*We.* There's one of you."

"The ham smells good. Potatoes, fresh vegetables." He smiled at Polly, then moved his gaze back to Inez. "You got any beef tallow?"

"I'll look," Inez said. "Or maybe you can use ham fat."

"I cut lean slices specially," Polly said. She was frowning, trying to understand why a man would want beef tallow when he had a plate of baked ham in front of him.

"He doesn't want it to eat," Inez said, watching Valdez. "He puts the tallow in the shotgun shell; it holds the charge together so it doesn't fly all over the place. How far would you say, Roberto?"

Bob Valdez shrugged. "Maybe a hundred and fifty feet."

"Boom, like a cannon," Inez said. "His own army. Listen, we'll give you food to take, whatever you want."

"I'm grateful."

"When are you going?"

"When Diego brings the horse."

"You're not taking him, are you?"

"No. One is as good as two."

"But not as good as two dozen."

"Maybe a little whiskey with the coffee, if you got some."

"And some to take for your nerve," Inez said. "When do you plan to be back?"

"Two days, three. I don't know."

"So if you're not back in three days——" Inez said.

Valdez smiled. "Pray for me."

A little while later they watched him leave to begin his war: the Valdez from another time, the Valdez in leather *chivarra* pants and the long-barreled Walker Colt on his right thigh, carrying his shotgun and a Sharps carbine and field glasses and a big canteen and a warbag for the ham and biscuits, the Valdez no one had seen in ten years.

He reached the birch forest before dawn, dismounting and leading his buckskin gelding through the gray shapes of the trees to the far side, to the edge of the meadow that reached to the slope where Tanner's lookouts were stationed. The night was clear and there was no sign of life on the hill. But they would be there, he was sure; how many, he would have to wait and see.

In the first light he moved along the edge of the thicket to the place where R. L. Davis had crowded his horse against him and pushed him over. Valdez did not leave the cover of the trees; he could see the cruciformed poles lying in the open; he could see, at the ends of the crosspole and in the middle, the leather thongs that had been cut by someone in the darkness, a shape close to him, an arm raising his head to give him water, hands helping him to his feet. He must have been out of his head not to remember; he must have been worse off than he imagined. Three days ago he had been lying here in the sun. Already it seemed as if it had happened in another time, years before. He moved back to a place where he would have a good view of the slopes across the meadow, and here he dropped his gear and settled down to wait, propping his field glasses on his warbag and canteen and lying behind them to hold his gaze on the slope.

About six o'clock, not quite an hour after first light, three riders appeared against the sky at the top of the slope. They came down into the deep shadows, and shortly after, a single rider passed over the crest going the other way. One at night, Valdez marked down in his mind, and three during the day. Though maybe not all day.

But it did turn out to be all day. Valdez remained in the thicket watching the slope, seeing very little movement; no one came down the trail or crossed the meadow toward the slope; the lookouts remained in dense brush most of the time, and if he did not know where to look for them through the glasses, he probably wouldn't have noticed them. At about five o'clock in the evening a rider came over the crest of the ridge, and soon after the three lookouts climbed the switchbacks and disappeared.

There you are, Valdez said to himself. How do you like it now? It doesn't get any better.

He had not eaten all day and had taken only a few sips of water. Now he ate some of the ham and biscuits and a handful of red peppers; he took a sip of the whiskey Inez had given him and a good drink from the canteen. Valdez was ready.

Crossing the meadow, he let his hand fall to the Walker Colt and eased the barrel in its holster. The stock of the Sharps carbine rested against the inside of his left knee, in the saddle boot; the sawed-off Remington hung on the right side, looped to the saddle horn by a short length of suspender strap. By now the lookout would have seen him and studied him and would be ready. Three of them yesterday came down to meet R. L. Davis, but one up there now would stay put and plan to take him by surprise. Valdez let the buckskin walk, but nudged his heels into its flanks as they reached the rocks and brush and started up the trail.

Now it comes, Valdez thought. When he's ready. Any time. He let himself slouch in the saddle, his shoulders moving with the gait of the horse, a rider climbing a trail, a man relaxed and off guard, in no hurry. Surprise me, he said in his mind to the lookout. I'm nothing to be afraid of. Come out in the open and stop me. I could be one of your friends.

He was a little more than halfway up the slope when the rider appeared, fifty yards and three switchback levels above him. Valdez pretended not to see him and came on, rounding a switchback and reaching an almost level stretch of the trail before the man called out in Spanish, "Enough!"

The Mexican. Valdez recognized the voice and, as he looked up now, the shape of the man on his horse—brown man and brown horse against the evening shadows of the brush slope. The Mexican came down the trail toward him, stopping and coming on again, the sound of his horse's hooves clear in the stillness, reaching the level above Valdez, then tight-reining, his horse moving loose shale as he came down to the stretch of trail where Bob Valdez waited. The Mexican stopped about fifty feet away, facing him on the narrow ledge of the path.

"I thought it was you, but I said no, that man carries a cross on his back."

"I got tired of it," Valdez said.

"Somebody found you, uh?"

"Somebody."

"You had luck with you that time."

"If people help you," Valdez said, "you don't need luck."

"That's it, uh? I didn't know that."

"Sure, like you and me," Valdez said. "We can be friends if we want. We talk awhile. I give you a drink of whiskey. What do you think about something like that?"

"I think I see a lot of guns," the Mexican said. "You come up here to talk and you bring all those guns?" He was at ease, smiling now.

"This little thing?" Valdez raised the cutoff Remington in his right hand, his fingers around the neck of the stock, the stubby barrels pointing straight up. "You think this could hurt somebody? It's for rabbits."

"For rabbits," the Mexican said, nodding. "Sure, there are plenty of rabbits around here. That's what you come for, uh, to hunt rabbits?"

"If I see any maybe. No, I come to ask you to do something for me."

"Because we're good friends," the Mexican said.

"That's right. As a friend I want you to go see Mr. Tanner and tell him Valdez is coming."

The Mexican was silent for a moment, his head nodding slightly as he studied Valdez and thought about him. "You come to see me," the Mexican said then. "How do you know I'm here?"

"You or somebody else," Valdez said. "It doesn't matter."

"You mean me *and* somebody else. Somebody over in the rocks behind you."

"I'll tell you something," Valdez said. "I've been here all day. I saw three of you come and one of you leave. I saw one of you come and three of you leave. There's no somebody else in the rocks—there's just you in front of me. That's all."

The Mexican watched him, unmoving. "You're certain of that? You'd bet your life on it?"

"It's on the table," Valdez said.

The Mexican grinned. "What is this kind of talk with two friends? You want me to go tell him something? All right, I tell him. Put the rabbit gun down." He lifted his reins and began sidestepping his horse to turn around on the narrow trail. Looking at Valdez again, he said, "You wait here, all right? I go tell him what you say and then I come back and tell you what he say. How is that?"

Valdez nodded. "I'll be here." He lowered the shotgun, resting it across his lap.

"Sure, stay right there. It don't take me any time."

The Mexican turned in his saddle and started away, his back to Valdez until he reached the end of the ledge and kicked his horse up over the shale at the switchback, and now, on the level above Valdez and seventy or eighty feet away, came back toward him.

Valdez's right thumb eased back both hammers, his finger curled inside the guard and felt the tension of the first trigger. The Mexican was spurring his horse now, kicking it to a gallop up the low angle of the trail, holding the reins in his left hand. Valdez saw nothing but the Mexican coming and it was in his mind that the man would go past him and suddenly turn and fire from behind. But thirty feet away closing to twenty, he saw the Mexican's right hand come up with the revolver and there it was, right now, the Mexican hunched low in the saddle, screaming *Aiiiii* for the horse or for himself, the revolver across the horse's mane, the man offering only his left leg and side and shoulder, but it was enough. Valdez brought up the barrels of the Remington from his lap, and with the ten-bore explosion close in front of him, the Mexican came out of his saddle, flung back over the horse's rump, his revolver discharging as he struck the ground, and the buckskin beneath Valdez throwing its head and trying to dance away from the man, and loose shale coming down the slope at them. The Mexican rolled to his back almost beneath the buckskin, his clothes filmed with fine dust, a dark, wet stain spreading from his side down over his thigh. His eyes were open and he had his left arm tight to his side.

"How do you feel?" Valdez asked.

The Mexican said nothing, staring up at him with a dazed expression.

Valdez dismounted and went to his knees over the man, raising his arm gently to look at the wound. The shotgun charge had torn through his side at the waist, ripping away his belt and part of his shirt and leather chaps.

"You should have this taken care of," Valdez said. "You know somebody can sew you up?"

The Mexican's eyes were glazed, wet looking. "What do you put in that thing?"

"I told you, something for rabbits. Listen, I'm going to get your horse and put you on it."

"I can't ride anywhere."

"Sure you can." Valdez lowered the Mexican's arm and gave his shoulder a pat. The Mexican winced and Valdez smiled. "You ride to Mr. Tanner, all right? Tell him Valdez is coming. You hear what I said? Valdez is coming. But listen, friend, I think you better go there quick."

FIVE

"He's dying," the segundo said. "Maybe before tonight."

The Mexican was on his back at the edge of the loading platform where they had taken him off his horse and laid him on his
back. His eyes looked up at the segundo and at Frank Tanner
standing over him. He could hear the people in the street, but he
did not have the strength or the desire to turn his head to look at
them. He heard the segundo say he was dying and he knew
he was dying, now, as the sun went down. He was thinking, I
should have gone past him and turned and shot him. Or I should
have shot him as he came up, before he saw me. Or I could have
gone higher and used the rifle. He wished he could begin it
again, do it over from the time Valdez started up the trail, but it
was too late. He could see Valdez raising the gun, the blunt double barrels looking at him; he could see Mr. Tanner looking at
him, the mouth beneath the moustache barely moving.

"What else did he say?"

The Mexican who was dying stared up at Mr. Tanner, and
the segundo said, "Valdez is coming. That's all."

"How do we know it's the same one?"

"It's his name."

"There are a hundred Valdezes."

"Maybe, but it must be the same one," the segundo said.
"You said he killed the Negro with a shotgun."

"A farmer gun," Tanner said.

"I don't know," the segundo said. "The way he used it."

Tanner looked up from the Mexican, his gaze lifting beyond the square, beyond the adobes to the ridge of hills in the distance, to the cold red slash of sky above the shadowed slopes. This Valdez killed one of his men up there and said he was coming. For what? It couldn't be to help any dead nigger's Indian woman. He couldn't come in and pull a gun to get money. He'd never get in or out. Then what was he doing? Who was he?

The segundo followed Tanner's gaze to the hills. "He's gone. He wouldn't be there waiting."

"Send somebody and make sure."

"He could be anywhere."

"Well, goddam it, you've got people who read signs?"

"We've got some, sure."

"Then send them," Tanner said. "I want people all over those hills, and if he's there I want him brought in, straight up or facedown. I don't care. I want some men sent to Lanoria to look every place he might be and talk to anybody knows him. I want a sign put up on the main street that says Bob Valdez is a dead man and anybody known to be helping him is also dead. You understand me?"

"We start the drive tomorrow," the segundo said.

Tanner looked at him. "We start the drive when I tell you we start it."

The man lying on his back dying, with the wet stain of his blood on the platform now—thinking that this shouldn't have happened to him because of the life in him an hour ago and because of the way he saw himself, aware of himself alive and never thinking of himself dying—looked up at the sky and didn't have to close the light from his eyes. He saw the beard on the segundo's face and the under-brim of his straw hat, and then he didn't see the segundo. He saw Mr. Tanner's face and then he didn't see Mr. Tanner anymore. He saw the open sky above him and that was all there was to see. But the sky wasn't something to look at. If he wasn't on the hill tonight he would be in the adobe that was the cantina, with the oil smoke and the women coming in, lighting a cigar as he looked at them and feeling his belly beneath his gunbelts full of beef and tortillas, bringing a woman close to him and drinking mescal with his hand on the curve of her shoulder, touching her neck and feeling strands of her hair between his fingers. But he had done it the wrong way. He should have looked at the three guns on the man and known something. But he had thought of the man as he had remembered him from before, against the wall and with the cross on his back, and he had listened to the man talk even while he planned to kill the man, being careful not being careful enough, not giving the man enough. He should have thought more about the way the man stood at the wall and watched them shoot at him. He should have remembered the way the man got up with the cross on his back and was kicked down and got up again and walked away. Look—someone should have said to him, or he should have told himself—the man wears three guns and hangs a Remington from his saddle. What kind of man is that? And then he thought, You should know when you're going to die. It should be something in your life you plan. It shouldn't happen but it's happening. He tried to raise his left arm but could not. He had no feeling in his left side, from his chest into his legs. His side was hanging open and draining his life as he looked at the sky. He said to himself, What is the sky to me? He said to himself, What are you doing here alone?

"Ask him if he's sure it's the same one," Tanner said.

The segundo stepped close to the Mexican again. He knew he was dead as he looked at him, though the man's eyes were open, staring at the sky.

The Mexican had reached the village, his head hanging, letting the horse take him, but he seemed to be still alive as he entered the street between the adobes.

You can die any time after you tell them, Valdez had thought, watching through the field glasses at the top of the trail. He had nothing against the man except a kick in the back and the certainty the man had wanted to kill him. He knew the man would die, and it would be better if he did; but he didn't wish the man dead. It would happen, that was all.

Soon they would come out. They would come out in all directions or they would come strung out across the graze toward the trail into the hills. As the Mexican had reached the adobes, Valdez had climbed higher, off the trail now, leading the buckskin up into the rocks. From here he watched the three riders coming first, letting their horses out across the open land. They came up through the ravines and went down the switchbacks on the other side, not stopping. Three more came behind them, but not running their horses, taking their time. They climbed over the trail looking at the ground; coming to the place where Valdez had shot the Mexican they dismounted.

There were others coming out from the village, fanning out, not knowing where they were going. They were nothing. The three looking for his sign were little better than nothing; they had less than an hour of light and no chance of catching up with him. He counted seventeen men who had come out of the village. There would be others with the herd and perhaps others somewhere else. There was no way of knowing how many still in the village. There was no way of knowing if Tanner had come out or was still in the village. He would have to go there to find out. And if Tanner was not in the village he would have to think of another way to do it and come back another time. There was no hurry. It wasn't something that had to be done today or tomorrow or this week. It could be done any time. But you'd better do it tonight, Valdez said to himself, before you think about it too much. Do it or don't do it.

Do it, he thought. He took a sip of the whiskey and put the bottle back in the warbag that hung from his saddle.

Do it before you get too old.

He took the reins of the buckskin and began working down through the rocks toward the village. He would circle and approach from the trees on the far side, coming up behind the burned-out church.

The clerk from the Republic Hotel, as soon as he was off duty, went over to De Spain's and asked if the three Tanner riders had been there.

Hell, yes, they had. They'd been here and to Bob Valdez's boardinghouse and the Hatch and Hodges office and had stuck their heads into almost every store along the street. They moved fast and didn't waste any questions and you could tell they wanted him bad. Bad? Did you see the sign out in front? Nailed to the post?

It was a square of board, and one of them had lettered on it with charcoal: BOB VALDEZ IS A DEAD MAN. ANYONE HELPING HIM IS ALSO DEAD.

That was how bad they wanted him. They were going to kill him.

If they ever found him. Where the hell was Valdez? Nobody knew. Nobody remembered seeing him in days. The last time was Saturday when he rode out to see Tanner. No, somebody said, he had made the run to St. David the next day. How about since then? Nobody could recall. Maybe he'd been around; maybe he hadn't. Bob Valdez wasn't somebody who stuck in your mind and you remembered.

Mr. Malson said to Mr. Beaudry, "If he's got Tanner on him and knows it, he'll be seven hundred miles away by now." "Or farther," Mr. Beaudry said. "If he don't know it," somebody said, "then he's a dead man, like the sign says." "There must be something wrong with his head," Mr. Malson said. "Christ, we should have known it the minute he started talking about the Lipan woman something was wrong with him."

R. L. Davis didn't say anything. He wanted to, but he still wasn't sure what people would say. They might say he was crazy. If he'd pushed Valdez over in the sun, then what had he gone back for?

They'd listen to him tell it. "Sure, I pushed him over. I was teaching him a lesson for coming at me with the scatter gun the other day—after he shot the nigger." They'd look at him and say, "You killed a man like that? Like a Indin would do it?"

And he'd say "No, I was teaching him a lesson is all. Hell, I went back and cut him loose and left him a canteen of water." And they'd say "Well, if you cut him loose, where is he?" Somebody else'd say, "If you wanted to kill him, what did you cut him loose for?"

And he'd say, "Hell, if there's something between me and Bob Valdez, we'll settle it with guns. I'm no goddam Apache."

But he had a feeling they wouldn't believe a word of it.

All right, three days ago he'd left Valdez in the meadow. And this evening Tanner's men come in looking for him and write his death sentence. So Valdez must have gone back and done something to them.

Valdez hadn't been here; at least nobody remembered seeing him. So where would he have been the past three days? Not at his boardinghouse.

But, goddam, Diego Luz had been to his boardinghouse! He could see Diego again coming out of it and the funny look on the man's face when he realized he'd been spotted.

What would Frank Tanner say about that? R. L. Davis said to himself. If you could hand him Bob Valdez he'd hire you the same minute, wouldn't he?

Go up to Tanner and cock the Walker in his face and say, All right, give me the money, Valdez was thinking. Not asking him, telling him this time. A hundred dollars or five hundred or whatever he had. Take it and get out and don't think about later until later. He would have to leave Lanoria and go someplace else and maybe worry about Tanner the rest of his life—because he had wanted to help the woman; because he had started it and gotten into it and now was so far in he couldn't turn around and walk out. You must be crazy, Valdez thought. Like Inez had said. Or an idiot. But he was here and was going through with it and he wasn't going to think about why he was here.

He was behind the church, bringing the buckskin along close to the wall, then into the alley that led to the yard of the church. At the far end of the yard was the building with the loading platform. Past the low wall of the churchyard he could see the square and the water pump and stone trough. There was no one in the square now. Farther down the street, in the dusk, he could make out people in front of the adobes, a few of the women sitting outside to talk; he could hear voices and laughter, the sound clear in the silence.

Valdez left the buckskin in the yard. He went over the wall and through the narrow space between the platform and two freight wagons that stood ready for loading. He mounted the steps at the far end. On the platform he looked out at the square again and at the church doorway and the fence across the opening. There were a few horses inside; he wondered if one of them was his claybank. Maybe after, he would have time to look. He crossed the platform and went into the building, into the room crowded with wooden cases and sacks of grain. Maybe this wasn't Tanner's place. Maybe he would have to work his way down the street, hurrying before it was full dark and they gave up looking for him. It was already dark in the room. He had to feel his way at first, moving between the cases to the stairway. The boards creaked and his boots on the stairs made a hard, sharp sound that Tanner would hear if he was upstairs; he would be ready or he would think it was one of his men. Valdez reached the hall and opened the door in front of him.

The room was still and seemed empty, until the woman moved and he saw her profile and the soft curve of her hair against the window. She watched him cross the room and open the door to the bedroom, waiting for him to look toward her again.

"He's not here."

Valdez walked toward her. He stopped to look out the window at the square below. "He went with them?"

"I guess he did," the woman said. "He didn't say."

"Are you his wife?"

She didn't answer for a moment, and Valdez looked at her.

"I will be his wife, soon."

"Do you know him?"

"That's a strange question. I guess I know him if I'm going to marry him."

"Well, it's up to you."

There was a silence between them until she said, "Are you going to wait for him?"

"I don't know yet—wait or come back another time."

"He won't give you another time. You killed one of his men."

"He died. I thought he would die," Valdez said. "Unless you had a doctor."

She watched him look out the window again. "Did you come here to kill Frank?"

"It would be up to him," Valdez said.

"Then what do you want?"

"The same thing as before. Something for the woman."

"Why? I mean why do you bother?"

"Listen," Valdez said. He hesitated. "If I tell you what I think, it doesn't sound right. It's something I know. You understand that?"

"Maybe you'll kill him," the woman said, "but you won't get anything out of him."

Valdez nodded slowly. "I've been thinking of that. If he doesn't want to give me anything, how do I make him? I push a gun into him and tell him, but if I have to shoot him, then I don't get anything."

"If he doesn't kill you first," the woman said.

"I've been thinking," Valdez said. "If I have something he wants, then maybe we make a trade. If he wants it bad enough."

She watched him and said nothing. He was looking at her now.

"Like I say to him, 'You give me the money and I give you your woman.' "

She continued to look at him, studying him. "And if he doesn't give you the money?" she said finally.

"Then he doesn't get his woman," Valdez said.

"You'd kill me?"

"No, the question would be how much does he like you?"

"He'll outwait you. He'll put his men around the building and sooner or later you'll have to go out."

"Not if I'm already out," Valdez said. His face went to the window before he looked at her again. "Listen, if you want to take something with you, get it now."

A woman who belonged to one of Tanner's men saw them leave. She had gone to the water pump in the square and stood looking at them as they came out to the loading platform: the woman of Mr. Tanner with a blanket roll and the man carrying a grain pack with something in it and an empty water skin. She looked at them and they looked at her, but she didn't call out. She told Mr. Tanner she was afraid the man would do something to her or to the woman of Mr. Tanner.

"Go on," Tanner said. "Then what?" He was still mounted, standing with his segundo and several of his men in the lantern glow of the square—the lantern on the seat of a freight wagon so Tanner could see the woman while she told what had happened.

"They went to the yard of the church," the woman said to Tanner. Then the man came over the wall toward her and told her to get a horse from the church, asking for a particular clay-bank horse if it was there. The woman brought out a horse but was not sure of its color in the darkness of the church and it wasn't the claybank but a brown horse. Then he told her to bring a saddle and bridle and a half sack of dried corn.

While this was taking place, the woman of Mr. Tanner was astride a horse in the churchyard, sitting in the saddle as a man does, though she was wearing a dress. "I think a white or a gray dress," the woman said. When Valdez was ready and had mounted the brown horse, he rode into the churchyard and told the woman of Mr. Tanner to follow him.

"Did she say anything to him?" Tanner asked.

"Not that I heard," the woman said.

They left through the alley next to the church. The woman waited until they were in the alley and followed, but by the time she reached the back of the church they were gone.

"Could you hear them?" Tanner asked.

"I think going toward the river," the woman said.

"To reach cover," the segundo said. He was sitting his horse close to Frank Tanner. "Then maybe south into the mountains."

"How long ago?" asked Tanner.

The woman thought about it and said, "Not long. They would be maybe two or three miles away only. Or a little more if they ran their horses."

"You know what to do," Tanner said to the segundo. "Whoever's here, send them out again."

"In the dark," the segundo said, "how do we see them?"

"You listen," Tanner said. "Somebody could run into them."

The segundo waited, about to speak, but looked at Tanner and then only nodded. It was Tanner's business. No, his business was in the morning with the arms and grain and cattle, taking it all across the border and coming back without being killed. That was his business.

But in the morning the freight wagons stood empty, and Frank Tanner waited on the loading platform for his men to come in. Some of the women stood in the square, watching him, waiting to see what he was going to do. The men came in singly and in small groups and would talk to the segundo while they watered their horses and while the women watched. It was almost midmorning when the three trackers came in. One of them was dead, the other two were wounded.

These three who came along the street single file, one of them facedown over his saddle, were the segundo's best hunters and trackers. They had been in the Army and had lived through the campaigns against the Apache. But now one was dead and another would soon be dead.

Tanner sat in a rocking chair in the morning sunlight and watched them brought in: another dead man on the loading platform and a man coughing blood and a third one, luckier than the first two, shot through the left forearm, the bone shattered, and there was no doubt about that. This one could talk and he told what had happened, his the only voice in the stillness. Tanner listened to the man and did not interrupt. He heard how the three had put themselves in Valdez's place and decided he would follow the river south into the hills of the Santa Ritas, then maybe work his way west around toward Lanoria or maybe not, but they'd take a look.

With the first light this morning they had found tracks, fresh prints of two horses that showed the horses were walking. They weren't sure of this man they were following; he didn't try to keep to rocky ground or cover his tracks, and he walked the horses, maybe thinking he had enough time. Still, when they came to the flat open stretch with the trees in the distance, they were careful, knowing he could be waiting for them in the trees. So they made a plan as they crossed the flat stretch: they would spread out before they got to the cover and come up from three sides and if he was in there they'd have him. But they never got to the trees.

"Listen, it was flat open," the man with the shattered arm said, "out to the sides as far as you could see and a mile in front of us. There was no cover near, hardly any brush to speak of. So it was like he rose up out of the ground behind us. He says, 'Throw down your guns and come around.' This voice out there in the middle of nothing. We stop and come around, keeping our iron though, and there he is standing there. I swear to God there was nothing for him to hide behind, yet we'd come over the ground he was standing on just a moment before.

"He says, 'Go back and tell Mr. Tanner we're waiting for him.' That's what he said, waiting for *him*. Meaning he wasn't talking to anybody else. Then he says, 'Tell Mr. Tanner I got something to trade him.' We looked, but she wasn't anywheres around. Just him, and three of us. I guess we all had it in mind to bust him and he must have saw it. He says again, 'Throw down the guns.' We don't move. He says it again and this time when we don't move he brings up the Colt gun in his right hand and puts one through my arm."

He looked toward the dead man and the man who was lying on the ground shot through the lungs. "They went for theirs with the sound of his piece, and he brings up this little scatter gun in his left hand and lets go both barrels and them two boys take it square. This here boy partly in front of the other, a little closer, and it killed him in his boots.

"Then he says to me, 'You tell him, he wants his woman, come out here with five hundred dollars.'

"I say to him, 'Well, where's Mr. Tanner supposed to come? You going to have signs put up?' And then he points."

The man with the shattered arm, standing by the loading platform, turned half around and raised his right arm, his finger extended; he moved it gradually southwest.

"There, you can see it," the man said, "though it was closer where we were at and you could see it better—twin peaks, the one a little higher than the other. He says for you to point to them and he'll get in touch with you.

"I say to him, 'Well, what if Mr. Tanner don't feel like coming?'

"And he says, standing there with the shotgun and the Colt gun, 'Then I kill his woman.' "

Frank Tanner stared at the twin peaks ten miles in the distance. After a few minutes, when he became aware that he was sitting in a rocking chair on the loading platform and his people were below him in the square, waiting for him to say something, he waved his hand and they cleared out, taking the dead

man and the lung-shot man and the man with the shattered left
arm, who thought Mr. Tanner might say something to him per-
sonally. But he didn't—just the wave of the hand.

The segundo stayed; he was the only one. He waited awhile,
getting the words straight in his mind. When he was ready he
said, "You go after him, we don't make the trip."

He waited, giving Mr. Tanner a chance to say something, but
the only sound was someone working the pump handle, a rattly
metal sound in the heat settling over the village.

"We go out there and look for him," the segundo said. "Sure,
we find him, but maybe it take us a few days, a week, if he
knows what he's doing. We're out there, we're not in Sonora
giving the man the things he's paying for. How much is he paying?" The segundo waited again. He said then, "He pay plenty,
but nobody pay you to go up in those mountains."

The segundo stood in the sun waiting for Mr. Tanner to say
something. He could stand here all day and this son of a bitch
Mr. Tanner might never say anything. The segundo was hot and
thirsty. He'd like a nice glass of mescal and some meat and
peppers, but he was standing here waiting for this son of a
bitch Americano to make up his mind.

So he said, smiling a little, "Hey, what if you don't go out?
You let him kill her." His smile broadened and he gestured as if
to say, Do you see how simple it is? He said, "Then what? You
get another woman."

Frank Tanner, sitting in the rocker, looked at his segundo.
He said, "If you were up here I'd bust your face open. And if
you wanted any more I'd give you that too. Do you see the way
it is?"

The segundo had killed five men in his life that he knew of
and had probably killed more if some of them died later or if he
wanted to count Apaches. He had hanged a man he caught
stealing his horses. He had killed a man with a knife in a cantina. He had shot a man who once worked for him and insulted
him and drew his revolver. He had killed two Federales when

the soldiers set an ambush to take the goods they were delivering in Sonora. And with others he had wiped out an Apache *ranchería*, shooting or knifing every living person they found, including the old people and the children. But the segundo was also a practical man. He had a wife in this village and two or three more wives in villages south of here, in Sonoita and Naco and Nogales. He had nine children that he knew of. Maybe he had eleven or twelve. Maybe he had fifteen. He had not wanted to kill the Apache children, but they were Apache. He also liked mescal and good horses and accurate rifles and revolving pistols. He was number two and Mr. Tanner was number one. He was thinking, *Shit*. But he smiled at Mr. Tanner and said, "Why didn't you say so? You want to get this man, we go get him for you."

Frank Tanner nodded, thinking about the woman.

The time he was in Yuma he thought about women every day. He'd thought about women before that, but not the same way he did in that stone prison overlooking the river. He remembered how the men smelled at Yuma, breaking rocks for twelve hours in the sun, working on the road, and coming back in to eat the slop. That's when they'd start talking about women. Frank Tanner would think, They don't know a real woman if they see one, except for some whore who'd smile and laugh and give them everything and rot their insides. No, when he was at Yuma he pictured a blond-haired girl, real long hair and a pretty face and big round breasts, though she wouldn't be too big in the gut or the hips. The hips could be more than a handful, but she'd have to have a nice sucked-in white gut. That's the one he pictured at Yuma, after he and Carlisle Baylor got caught with the goddam branded cows they were running into old Mexico without any bill of sale. Three years picturing the blond golden-haired woman. Two years more raising money and buying stock to sell across the border, buying and selling horses and cattle and dynamite and about anything he could lay his hands on they didn't have down there. He'd bought twenty-five-year-old Confederate muskets and sold them. He bought a few old Whitworth field pieces and sold them too. He'd made money and met people who knew people and pretty soon he was even selling remounts to the United States Cavalry at Fort Huachuca. And that was where he saw the woman, the girl or woman or however you wanted to think of her, there at Huachuca, married to the drunk-ass sutler, who never went a day without a quart of whiskey or a bottle of mescal or even corn beer if he couldn't get any mescal. There she was, the one he'd seen every day at Yuma and about every day since, the blond golden-haired girl who was built for the kind of man he was, sitting in their place talking to the drunk-ass sutler and looking at the woman every chance he got. A year of that; a little more than a year. Talking to her when he wasn't around and trying to find out things about her, about them. Trying to find out if she felt anything for the drunk or not. She felt something when he beat her—sometimes you could see the bruises on her face she couldn't hide with powder—but maybe she liked it. You could never tell about women.

He would have taken her away from the drunk alive, and once he was dead there wasn't anything else to think over. He took her and she came with him. He would marry her, too, but he had things to do and she'd have to wait on that; but in the meantime there wasn't any reason they couldn't live as husband and wife. She saw that and agreed, and she was better than he ever imagined in Yuma she would be. She was real now and she was his, and there wasn't any goddam broken-down Mexican nigger-loving town constable going to run off with her into the hills and threaten to kill her. Valdez, or whatever his name, was a dead man and he could roll over right now and save everybody a lot of time.

Tanner was looking off at the hills that climbed into the Santa Ritas and the twin peaks, far away against the hot sky.

"What's up there?" he said to the segundo.

"Nothing," the segundo answered.

"Why would he want us to track up there?"

"I don't know," the segundo said. "Maybe he's got a place somewhere."

"What kind of place?"

"An Apache camp he's been to," the segundo said. "He knows the Apache—the thing he did to the three of them in the open country, hiding where there's no place to hide."

"He didn't seem like much," Frank Tanner said.

"Maybe," the segundo said. "But he knows the Apache."

R. L. Davis got drunk trying to work up nerve to tell what he did to Bob Valdez and never did tell it. He went over to Inez's, but they wouldn't let him in. Then he didn't remember anything after that. He woke up in the Maricopa bunkhouse when a hand came in and poured water all over him. God, he felt awful. So it was afternoon by the time he got out to Mimbreño.

There seemed to be more activity than the time he was here before, more men in the village sitting around waiting for something, and more horses and more noise. He rode up the street not looking around too much, but not missing anything either. He hoped Mr. Tanner would be outside, and he was, the same place he was the last time, up on the loading platform. The problem was to tell him before Mr. Tanner gave any orders to have him run off or tied to a cross or whatever he might do; so he kept his eyes on Mr. Tanner and the second he saw Mr. Tanner's gaze land on him, R. L. Davis yelled out, "I know where he is!"

They looked at him, all the people standing around there, and let him ride over toward the platform where Mr. Tanner was waiting.

"I think I know where he is," R. L. Davis said to Mr. Tanner.

"You think so or you know so," Tanner said.

"I'd bet a year's wage on it."

"Where?"

"A place up in the mountains."

"I asked you where."

"I was thinking," R. L. Davis said. "Let me ride along and I can show you. Take you right to it."

Tanner kept looking at him deciding something, but showing nothing in his face. Finally he said, "Step down and water your horse."

SIX

Most of the day the woman, Gay Erin, rode behind Valdez as they climbed out of the flatland and across sloping meadows that stretched toward pine timber, in the open sunlight all morning and into the afternoon, until they reached the deep shade of the forest. She noticed that Valdez seldom looked back now. When they had stopped to rest and he stood waiting as the horses grazed, he would look north sometimes, the way they had come, but he stood relaxed and could be looking at nothing more than the view.

Earlier this morning, once it was light, he had looked back. He stopped and looked back for some time as they were crossing flat, open country. When they reached the trees he made her dismount and tied their horses to a dead trunk that had fallen. She watched him walk out of the trees, out across the flats until he was a small figure in the distance. She watched him squat or kneel by a low brush clump and then she didn't see him again, not for more than an hour, not until the three riders appeared and she heard the gunfire. He came back carrying his shotgun; they mounted again and continued on. She asked him, "Did you kill them?" And he answered, "One. Maybe another." She asked, "Why didn't you tie me? I could have run away." He said to her, "Where would you go?"

They spoke little after that. They stopped to rest in a high meadow and she asked him where they were going. "Up there," he answered, nodding toward the rock slopes above them.

Another time she said to him, "Maybe you don't have a natural call to do certain things, but I do." He smiled a little and told her to go ahead, he wouldn't look. She stayed on the off side of her horse and didn't know if he looked or not.

At first she wondered about him, and there were questions she wanted to ask; but she followed him in silence, watching the slope of his shoulders, the easy way he sat his saddle. In time the pain began to creep down her back and into her thighs; she held on to the saddle horn, following the movement of the horse and not thinking or wondering about him after a while, wanting this to be over but knowing he wasn't going to stop until he was ready.

When they reached the edge of the pine timber he dismounted. Gay Erin went to the ground and stretched out on her back in the shade. She could feel her lips cracked and hard and dirt in the corners of her eyes. She wanted water, to drink and to bathe in, but more than water she wanted to stretch the stiffness from her body and sleep.

She heard Valdez say, "We're going to move. Not far, over a little bit." Looking up at the pine branches she closed her eyes and thought, He'll have to drag me or carry me. She could hear him moving in the pine needles and could hear the horses. She waited for him to come over and tell her to get up or kick her or pull her to her feet, but after a while there was no sound, and in the silence she fell asleep.

When she opened her eyes she wasn't sure where she was and wondered if he had moved her. The trees above were a different color now, darker, and she could barely see the sky through the branches. She stretched, feeling the stiffness, and rolled to her side. Valdez was sitting on the ground a few feet away smoking a cigarette, watching her. She pushed herself to a sitting position. "I thought we were moving."

"It's waiting for you," Valdez said.

He led her on foot along the dark-shadowed edge of the timber. Off from them, in the open, dusk was settling over the hills. They walked for several minutes, until she smelled wood burning and saw the horses picketed close below them in the meadow. The camp was just inside the timber, in a cutbank that came down through the pines like a narrow road, widening where it reached the meadow and dropping into the valley below.

At times she looked at him across the low fire, at this man who had taken her up a mountain and let her sleep for a few hours and then served her pan bread and ham and peppers and strong coffee. When they had finished he took a bottle of whiskey from a canvas bag. She watched him now. She could see Jim Erin with his bottle every evening, saying he was going to have a couple to relax and pouring a glass and then another glass, smoking a cigar and taking another drink, his voice becoming louder as he talked. Sometimes she would go out, visit one of the officers' wives, and if she could stay long enough he would be asleep when she got home. But sometimes he wouldn't allow her to go out and she would have to listen to him as he pretended he was a man, hearing his complaints and his obscenities and his words of abuse; the goddam Army and the goddam fort and the goddam heat and the goddam woman sitting there with her goddam nose up in the air. The first time he hit her she doubled her fist and hit him back, solidly in the mouth, and he beat her until she was unconscious. For months he didn't take a drink and was kind to her. But he started again, gradually, and by the time he had worked up to his bottle an evening he was slapping her and several times hit her with his fist. She never fought back after the first time. She was married to him, a man old enough to be her father, who perhaps might grow up one day. Sometimes she thought she loved him; most of the time she wasn't sure, and there were moments when she hated him. But he didn't change; he beat her for the last time and no man would ever beat her again.

It surprised her when Valdez offered the bottle. "For the

cold," he said. "Or to make you sleep." She hesitated, then took a sip and handed it back to him. Valdez raised the bottle. When he lowered it he popped in the cork and got up to put the bottle away.

"I've never seen a man take one drink," she said.

Valdez sat down again by the fire. "Maybe it has to last."

"I was married to a man who drank." He made no comment and she said, "He was killed."

Valdez nodded. "I see."

"What do you see?"

"I mean you were married and now you're not. What's your name?"

"Gay Erin."

He was looking at her but said nothing for a moment. "That's your marriage name?"

"Mrs. James C. Erin."

"Of Fort Huachuca," Valdez said. "Your husband was killed six months ago."

"You knew him?"

He shook his head.

She waited. "Then you heard about it."

Valdez said, "You were in Lanoria Saturday when the man was killed?"

"Frank said an Army deserter was shot."

"No, he wasn't a deserter. Frank Tanner said it was the man that killed your husband, but when he looked at him dead he said no, it was somebody else."

Gay Erin said, "And the Indian woman, the widow——"

"Was the wife of the man we killed by mistake."

She nodded slowly. "I see." She said then, "Frank didn't tell me that."

Valdez watched her. "But you're going to marry him."

"What difference does it make to you?"

"I like to know how much he wants you—if you're worth coming after."

"He'll come," she said.

"I think so too. I think he wants you pretty bad." Valdez placed a stick on the fire and pushed the ends of the sticks that had not burned into the center of the flame. "You know what else I think. I think maybe he wanted you pretty bad when you were still married."

The flame rose to the fresh wood. He could see her face in the light, her eyes holding on his.

"He knew my husband," she said. "Sometimes he'd come to visit. Anyone who was at the hearing knows that."

"And after it you go to live with him."

She was staring at him in the flickering light. "Why don't you say it right out?"

"It's just something I started to wonder."

"You think Frank killed my husband."

"He could do it."

"He could," the woman said, "but he didn't."

"You're sure of that, uh?"

"I know he didn't."

"How do you know?"

"Because I killed him."

She had come from Prescott with her nightgowns and linens to marry James C. Erin, and five years and six months later she fired three bullets into him from a service revolver and left him dead.

Tell this man about it, she thought. The time in the draw at night, a single moment in her life she would see more clearly than anything she had ever experienced. She had told no one about it and now she was telling this man sitting across the low-burning fire, not telling him everything, but not sure what to tell and what to leave out.

She began telling him about Jim Erin and found she had to tell him about her father and the years of living on Army posts and her mother dying of fever when she was a little girl. She remembered Jim Erin when she was younger, in her early teens, and her father was stationed at Whipple Barracks. She remembered Jim Erin and her father drinking together and remembered them stumbling and knocking the dishes from the table. A few years later she remembered her father—after he retired and they were living in Prescott—mentioning Jim Erin and saying he was coming to see them. And when he came she remembered Jim Erin again, the man with the nice smile and the black hair who had a way of holding her arm as he talked to her, his fingers moving, feeling her skin. She remembered her father drinking and cursing the Army and a system that would pass over a man and leave him a lieutenant after sixteen years on frontier station. Now a sutler was something else; he had a government contract to sell stores to the soldiers and could do well. Like his friend Jim Erin. The girl who gets him is getting something, her father had told her, leading up to it, and within a year had arranged the marriage. A year and a half later her father was dead of a stroke.

A lot of men drink, but their wives don't kill them. Of course. It wasn't his drinking. Yes, it was his drinking, but it was more than that. If he wasn't the kind of man he was and he didn't beat her it wouldn't have happened. This was in her mind, though she didn't try to explain it to Valdez. He put wood on the fire, keeping the flame low, while she told him about the night she killed her husband.

It was after Frank Tanner had left. He had come to see Jim Erin on business, with a proposition to supply the sutler's store with leather and straw goods he could bring up from Mexico.

She stared into the fire, remembering that night. "They were drinking when I left to visit for a while," she said. "When I got back Frank was gone and Jim was out of whiskey. He couldn't borrow any. No one would lend it to him, and that night he didn't have enough money to buy any. So he said he was going out to get corn beer . . ."

"He liked tulapai, uh?"

"He liked anything you could drink. He said someone not

far away would sell him a bucket of it. I told him he was too drunk to go out alone, and he said then I was coming with him if I was so concerned. Jim got his gun and we took the buggy, not past the main gate, because he didn't want anybody questioning him. There was no stockade and it was easy to slip out if you didn't want to be seen.

"I don't know where we went except it was a few miles from the fort and off the main road. When we finally stopped Jim got out and left me there. He said 'here,' handing me his gun, 'so you won't be scared.' He didn't mean it as kindness; he was saying 'here, woman, I'm going off alone, but I don't need any gun.' Do you see what I mean?"

She looked at Valdez. He nodded and asked her then, "Was he drunk at this time?"

"Fairly. He'd had the bottle with Frank. He stumbled some, weaving, as he walked away from the buggy. There wasn't a house around or a sign of light. He walked off toward a draw you could see because of the brush in it.

"It must have been a half hour before I saw him coming back, hearing him first, because it was so dark that night, then seeing him. He was carrying a gourd in front of him with both hands and when he got to the buggy he raised it and said, 'Here, take it.' He put his foot up on the step plate to rest the gourd on his knee, but as he did it his foot slipped and he dropped the gourd on the rocks. He looked down at the broken pieces and the corn beer soaking into the ground, then up at me and said it was my fault, I should have taken it. He started screaming at me, saying he was going to beat me up good. I said, 'Jim, don't do it. Please,' I remember that. He started to step up into the buggy, reaching for me, and I jumped out the other side. I ran toward the draw, but he got ahead of me, turning me. I said to him, 'Jim, I've got your gun. If you touch me I'll use it.' I remember saying that too. He kept coming, working around me as I faced him, until I was against the side of the draw and couldn't turn. I said to Jim, please. He came at me and I pulled the trigger. Jim fell to his knees, though I wasn't sure I had hit him. He picked up something, I guess a rock, and came at me again, and this time I shot him twice and knew I had killed him."

Valdez rolled a cigarette and leaned into the fire to light it, and raising his eyes he saw the woman staring into the light. She sat unmoving; she was in another time, remembering, her hands folded in her lap. She seemed younger at this moment and smaller, this woman who had killed her husband.

Valdez said, "You didn't tell anyone?"

She shook her head slowly.

"Why didn't you?"

"I don't know. I was afraid. I went back to the post. The next day, after they found him, they asked me questions. I told them Jim had gone out late, but I didn't know where. They told me he was dead and I didn't say anything, because I couldn't pretend to be sorry. When I didn't tell them then, I couldn't tell them later, at the hearing. They decided it must have been the man who deserted, a soldier named Johnson who everybody knew was buying corn beer from the Indians and selling it at the post."

Valdez drew on his cigarette, letting the smoke out slowly. "You haven't told Frank Tanner?"

"No. I almost did. But I thought better of it."

"Then why did you tell me?"

Her eyes raised now in the firelight. "I don't know," she said softly. "Maybe it's this place. Maybe it's because I wanted to tell somebody so bad. I just don't know." She paused, and with the soft sound gone from her voice said, "Maybe I told you because you're not going to live long enough to tell anyone else."

"You want to stay alive," Valdez said. "Everybody wants to stay alive."

She was staring at him again. "Do you?"

"Everybody," Valdez said.

"Well, remember that when you close your eyes," she said. "I killed a man to be free of him, to stay alive."

"I'll remember that," Valdez said. "I'll remember something else, too, a man lying on his back tied to a cross and someone cutting him loose and giving him water."

He watched closely but there was no change of expression on her face. He said, "The man believes a woman did this. He thought the woman had dark hair, because he had been thinking of a woman with dark hair. But maybe he thought it was dark hair because it was night. Maybe it was a woman with light hair. A woman who lived near this place and knew where he was and could find him."

She was listening intently now, hunched forward, her long hair hanging close to her face. She said, "It could have been one of the Mexican women."

"No, it wasn't one of them, I know that. They live with those men and they would be afraid."

She waited, thoughtful, but still did not move her eyes from his. She said, almost cautiously, "You believe I'm the woman?"

"There's no one else."

She said then, still thoughtful, watching him, "If you believe I saved you, why are you doing this to me?"

Valdez took a last draw on the cigarette and dropped it in the fire. "I'm not doing it to you. I'm doing it to Frank Tanner."

"But if he doesn't give you the money——"

"Let's see what happens," Valdez said. He got to his knees and spread his blanket so that his feet would be toward the fire.

Gay Erin didn't move. She said, "Why do you think I cut you loose?"

"I don't know. Because you felt sorry for me?"

"Maybe." She watched him. "Or maybe because of Frank. To do something against him."

"You're going to marry him," Valdez said.

"He says I'm going to marry him."

"Well, if you don't want to, why didn't you leave?"

"Because I've no place to go. So I'll marry him whether I want to or not." She looked into the fire, moving her hair from the side of her face gently, with the tips of her fingers. "I have no family to go to. People I used to know are scattered all over the territory. I think even when I was married to Jim I felt alone. I stayed with him, I guess, for the same reason I'm going to marry Frank."

Valdez knelt on his blanket, half turned to look at her. "You want to get married so bad, there are plenty of men."

"Are there?" She got up and smoothed her skirt, standing close to the fire. "Where should I spread my blanket?"

"Where do you want to?"

Looking down at him she said, "Wherever you tell me."

Look at him again as he looked at himself that night. His name was Roberto Eladio Valdez, born July 23, 1854, in an adobe village on the San Pedro, where the valley land climbed into the Galiuros. His father was a farmer until they moved to Tucson and his father went to work for a freight company and sent his children to the mission school. Roberto Eladio Valdez, born of Mexican parents in the United States Territory of Arizona, a boy who lived in the desert and knew of many people who had been killed by the Apaches, boy to man in the desert and in the mountains, finally working for the Army, leading the Apache trackers when the hostiles jumped San Carlos and went raiding, and finally through with that and deciding it was time to work the land or work for a company, as most men did, and do it now if it wasn't already too late. Roberto Eladio Valdez worked for Hatch and Hodges, and they put him on the boot with the shotgun because he was good with it. He asked the municipal committee of Lanoria for a town job and they made him a part-time constable and put a shotgun in his hands because he was good with it and because he was quiet and because everybody liked him or at least abided him, because he was one of the good ones who kept himself clean and neat, even wearing the starched collar and the suit when everybody else was in shirtsleeves, and never drank too much or was abusive. Remember, there is the Bob Valdez who knew his place, and the one looking for a normal life and a home and a family.

Now this one is inside the one at the high camp above the mountain meadow at the edge of the timber. Bob and Roberto both there, both of them looking at the woman across the firelight, but Roberto doing the thinking now, saying to himself but to the woman, "All right, that's what you want."

He was not smiling now or holding open the coach door or touching his hat and saying yes, ma'am. He was on his own ground and he was unbuckling the Walker Colt from his leg.

He said, "Bring it over here."

He rose to his feet as she came around the fire with the rolled blanket, now taller and bigger than she was. She spread the blanket next to his, and when she straightened, he took her shoulders in his hands, not feeling her pull back, feeling only the soft firmness of her arms. He said, "You don't want to be alone, uh?"

She said nothing.

"You want somebody to hold you and take care of you. Is that it?"

Her face was close, her eyes looking at him, her lips slightly parted.

"What else do you want? You want me to let you go?"

Slowly her hands came up in front of her and she began unbuttoning her shirt, her hands working down gradually from her throat to her waist. She said, "I told you I killed my husband. I told you I don't want to marry Frank Tanner. I told you I have nothing. You decide what I want."

"I heard something," Diego Luz said.

His wife lay beside him with her eyes closed. He knew she was awake because sunlight filtered through the straw blind covering the window, the way the early morning sunlight looked each day when they rose to work in the yard and the fields and the horse corral until the sun left for the night. Without opening her eyes his wife said, sleep in her voice and on her face, "What did you hear?"

Diego Luz sat up now. "I heard something."

"Your horses," his wife said.

"Horses, but not my horses."

"The chickens," she said.

"Horses." Diego Luz got out of the bed Bob Valdez had slept in a few days before. He looked at the two children on the mat beneath the window; they were asleep. He went into the front room and looked at his daughter and his youngest child and his wife's mother in the bed. His mother-in-law lay on her back staring at the ceiling. Diego Luz said, "What is it?"

"Outside," his wife's mother said.

"What outside? What did you hear?"

"They killed the dogs," the old woman said.

He turned to look at his oldest son, sleeping, and said to himself, Wake him. But he let the boy sleep. Diego Luz pushed aside the straw mat covering the doorway and went outside, out under the mesquite-pole ramada, and saw them in the yard.

An army of them, a half-circle of armed men in their saddles. No sound now, not even from the horses. A dozen of them or more. A dog lying on its side in the yard with a saddle blanket covering its head. The dog smothered. Twelve riders looking at him, staring at him or at the ramada or at the house, facing him and not moving. He heard hooves on the hardpack and two riders appeared from the side of the house. Diego Luz looked that way and saw more of them at the corral and coming up from the horse pasture. They were all around the place; they had been everywhere; they had closed in from all sides and now they were here.

Diego Luz moved to the edge of the ramada shade looking out. He said nothing because there was nothing for him to say;

he didn't ask them here; they came. But he said to himself, He did something to them and they're looking for him.

He saw Mr. Tanner and his segundo and several people that he recognized who had been by here. He saw R. L. Davis and this puzzled him, R. L. Davis being with them; but the way they were here, not passing by and stopping for water, *here,* made him too afraid to wonder about R. L. Davis.

Diego Luz, the horsebreaker, who they said broke horses with his fists, looked out at them and said in his mind to them, Go out to the corral and eat horseshit, goddam you sitting there. But he thought of his wife and his children and his oldest daughter and he said, Jesus, son of God, help me. Jesus, if you listen to anything or have listened to anything. Jesus, from now on——

The segundo said in Spanish, "How are you, friend? How is your family? Are they awake?"

Goddam him, Diego Luz thought and said, "How does it pass with you? Come down and have something with us. I'll wake up the old woman."

"Good," the segundo said, "Bring the woman out. Bring out your daughter."

Over from him several riders, R. L. Davis said, "Mr. Tanner, you want me to ask him? I'll get it from him."

The segundo looked at R. L. Davis from under the straw brim of his Sonora hat. R. L. Davis saw the look, not moving his eyes to Mr. Tanner, knowing better, and decided to keep his mouth shut for a while.

"Now they come," the segundo said pleasantly, smiling, touching the brim of his hat.

Diego Luz could hear them behind him. He thought, Jesus, make them stay inside. But they were out and coming out: his wife and his son and his daughter, standing close to him now; he could hear one of the smaller children, the high questioning voice, and heard the witch voice of his wife's mother, the too-loud annoying sound telling them to be silent; God bless the toothless hag this time, now, Jesus, give her power to keep them inside.

Diego Luz tried to be calm and let this happen, what was going to happen. He wet his lips and tried not to wet his lips. He did not see the segundo motion or hear him speak, but now a rider dismounted, letting his reins trail, and came toward them.

He was an American, a bony man who had not shaved for several days and wore boots to his knees and spurs that chinged as he came forward. He moved past Diego Luz and took his son by the arm and brought him out several strides into the yard. He positioned the boy, moving him by his shoulders, to face his family as the boy looked up at him. The man glanced at the segundo. His gaze dropped slowly to the boy and when he was looking at him, standing a stride in front of him, he stepped in swinging his gloved right fist and slammed it into the boy's face.

Diego Luz did not move. He looked at his boy on the ground and at the man who had struck him and at the segundo.

The segundo said, "We ask you one time. Where is Valdez?"

Diego Luz did not hesitate or think about it. He said, "I don't know." He added then, "No one here knows." And then, because he had said this much, he said, "He hasn't been here in four days." He saw the segundo looking at him and he wished he had said only that he didn't know.

The American with the bony face and the high boots walked over to the ramada. Diego Luz glanced aside and then half turned as he saw his small children out of the doorway. The American picked up the littlest girl, his three-year-old, and held her up in front of him. The man grinned with no teeth, with his mouth sunken. He said, "How're you, honey?" The little girl smiled as he carried her out into the yard. The American looked out toward the mounted men and he said, "Mr. Tanner, I could swing this young'n by her feet and bash her head agin the wall."

Diego Luz screamed, "I don't know!"

Now several men dismounted and came toward him. One of them pushed him aside and they brought his daughter out into the yard. She was wearing only a nightdress, and in the sunlight he could see the shape of his daughter's hips and legs beneath the cotton cloth and saw the men by the ramada looking at her. The man who brought her out was behind her now. He took her nightdress at the neck and pulled down on it. The girl twisted, wrenching away from him, screaming. Some of the men laughed, staring at her now as she tried to hold up her shredded nightdress to cover herself.

The segundo said to Diego Luz, "Maybe we take her inside and mount her one at a time. Or maybe we do it out here so your family can see."

"I don't know where he is," Diego Luz said.

The segundo looked at Mr. Tanner, who was mounted on a bay horse. The segundo stepped out of his saddle. He took a plug of tobacco and bit off a corner as he walked up to Diego Luz, who watched him, feeling his hands hanging heavily at his sides.

He said to the segundo in Spanish, "Tell him to put my little girl down."

"He's talking," the segundo said.

"Not that one."

"He's a little crazy maybe."

"Tell him to put her down."

"I won't let him do it," the segundo said. "She's too young. Maybe she grow up to be somcthing, like your daughter."

Diego Luz said, "If you touch her you'd better kill me."

"We can do that," the segundo said.

"I don't know where he is. Man, who do you think I put first, him?"

"We only asking you," the segundo said. "Maybe you give us a lot of shit and we believe it. That's a nice-looking girl," he said, looking at the man's daughter. "I like a little more up there, but first one of the day, maybe it's all right."

"Shoot her first," Diego Luz said. "You'd do it to a corpse, you filthy son of a whore."

The segundo said, "Man, hold on to yourself if you can do it. Just tell us."

"I don't know where he is," Diego Luz said.

"Listen, leave Maricopa, you can ride for me."

"I don't know where he is," Diego Luz said.

"I don't care where he is," the segundo said. "I mean it, ride for me."

Diego Luz said, "Come here alone to ask me, I'd try to kill you."

The segundo nodded, smiling. "You'd try it, wouldn't you? That's why I want you."

R. L. Davis came out of his saddle. He walked part way toward Tanner and stopped. He eased his funneled hat up and pulled it down again.

"Mr. Tanner, I'd like to ask him something."

"Go ahead," Tanner said. He brought a cigar out of a vest pocket and bit off the tip.

"I want to ask Diego about seeing him in town with Bob Valdez's clothes three days ago."

Tanner lit his cigar and blew out the smoke. "You hear that?"

Diego Luz nodded his head up and down. "I was taking his clothes to him."

"Where?" Tanner said.

"He was hiding."

"I said where."

"In the line shack. At the Maricopa pasture."

To the segundo Tanner said, "They look in the shack?"

"I'll find out," the segundo said.

"If he wasn't there," Tanner said to Diego Luz, "you're a dead man."

"He brought him his clothes," R. L. Davis said, "and he must've brought him his guns too."

"We've stayed long enough," Tanner said. "Tend to the horsebreaker."

R. L. Davis was standing in the yard. He wanted to say more, but it was passing him by. "Mr. Tanner, I could talk to him some——"

But Tanner wasn't paying any attention to him.

Two men and then a third one brought Diego Luz out in the yard. They bent his arms behind him, forcing him to his knees and this way got him facedown on the hardpack, spreading his arms, a man sitting on him and a man clamping each of his arms flat to the ground with a boot.

The segundo went to one knee at Diego Luz's head. He worked the tobacco from one side of his mouth to the other with his tongue and spit a brown stream close to Diego Luz. He said, "I believe you; you don't know where he is. But maybe you're lying. Or maybe you lie some other time to us. You understand?"

The American with the bony face and the high boots went down to his knees close to Diego Luz's left hand that was palm-flat on the ground. The man drew his Colt revolver and flipped it, catching it by the barrel, and brought the butt down hard on Diego Luz's hand. The hand clenched to protect itself as Diego Luz screamed and the gun butt came down on the tight white knuckles and Diego Luz screamed again. This way they broke both of the horsebreaker's hands while his family watched from the shade of the ramada.

"I mean it," the segundo said, as Diego Luz lay there after the men holding him had moved away. "You come work for me sometime."

They herded the family into the yard to get them out of the way while they destroyed the house and burned everything that would burn, beginning inside, pouring kerosene on the beds and the furniture, while outside two mounted men were fixing their ropes to the support posts of the ramada. The flames took the straw blinds covering the windows; the men inside poured out with smoke, and as they cleared the doorway, the mounted men spurred away to bring the mesquite-pole awning down over the front of the house. They burned the ramada and the outbuildings and the corn crib. They pulled his corral apart, scattering the horses, and came back across the yard, gathering and riding out southeast, leaving their dust hanging in the air and the sound of them fading in the early morning sunlight.

They were a good mile from the place, moving single file down the bank of an arroyo, the riders milling in the dry stream bed as they moved one at a time up the other side.

R. L. Davis looked back, squinting at the gray smoke rising in the near distance—not a lot of smoke now; the house would be burned out and most of the smoke was probably coming from the corn crib. He turned in his saddle. Tanner was already up the cutbank, but he saw the segundo still in the dry stream bed, waiting for the file of riders to move up. R. L. Davis walked his horse over to him.

"You see that smoke?"

The segundo looked at R. L. Davis, not at the sky.

"I reckon you can see that smoke a good piece," R. L. Davis said. "We're about a mile. I reckon you could still see it eight, ten miles."

The segundo said, "If he's no farther than that and if he's looking this way."

R. L. Davis grinned. "You see what I mean, huh? I was sure you would, though I wasn't putting much stock in Tanner getting it."

"Be careful," the segundo said. "He'll eat you up."

"I don't mean that insulting. I mean he might want to think about it a while, seeing things I don't see——"

"Hey," the segundo said. He took time to squirt a stream of tobacco to the dry-caked earth. "Why do you think he'd come if he sees the smoke?"

"Because they're friends. He brought him clothes and his guns."

"Would you go? If you saw your friend's place burning?"

"Sure I would."

"No, you wouldn't," the segundo said. "But he might. If he sees it he might."

"It's worth staying to find out," R. L. Davis said.

The segundo nodded. "Worth leaving you and maybe a few more." He started off, reining his horse toward the far bank, then came around to look at Davis again. "Hey," the segundo said, maybe smiling in the shadow of his Sonora hat. "What are you going to do if he comes?"

SEVEN

"**Y**ou don't have to tie me," the Erin woman said. "I'll wait for you; I won't run."

Valdez said nothing. Maybe he had to tie her and maybe he didn't, but a mile from Diego Luz's place now and the smoke gone from the sky an hour, he tied her and left her in the arroyo, marking the place in his mind: willows on the bank and yellow brittlebrush in the dry bed. He left her in deep shade, not speaking or looking at her face.

Though he looked at her over and over as he made his way to Diego Luz's place, picturing her in the darkness of the high meadow, the woman lying with him under the blanket, holding her and feeling her against him and for a long time, after she was asleep, staring up at the cold night sky, at the clouds that moved past the moon.

In the morning the sky was clear, until he saw the smoke in the distance, seven miles northwest, and knew what it was as he saw it. Valdez packed their gear without a word and they moved out, across the meadow and down through the foothills toward the column of smoke. At one point she said to him, "What if they're waiting for you?" And he answered, "We'll see."

They could be waiting or not waiting. Or he could have not seen the smoke. Or he could have continued with the woman southeast and been near the twin peaks by this evening. Or he never could have asked Diego Luz to help him. Or he never could have started this. Or he never could have been born. But he was here and he was pointing northwest instead of southeast because he had no choice. At first he had thought only about Diego Luz and his family. But when there was no sign of Tanner, no dust rising through the field glasses, he began to think of the woman more. When she was still with him when they reached the arroyo, he knew he wanted to keep her and tied her up to make sure of it.

Following the dry stream bed north, Valdez saw the tracks where Tanner's men had crossed; he noticed the prints of several horses leading south. He continued on a short distance before climbing out of the arroyo to move west. This way he circled Diego Luz's place and approached from a thicket beyond the horse pasture, studying the house and yard for some time before he moved into the open.

It might have been a dozen years ago after an Apache raid, the look of the place, the burned-out house and the dog lying in the yard; but there were people here, alive, and a team hitched to a wagon, and that was the difference. They waited for him by the wagon, Diego Luz and his family.

Valdez dismounted. "What did they do to you?"

"What you see," Diego Luz said. He raised his hands in front of him, his hands open, the swollen, discolored fingers apart.

"Did they harm your family?"

"A little. If they did any more I wouldn't be here."

"I'm sorry," Valdez said.

"We're friends. They would have come with or without Mr. R. L. Davis."

"He was with them?"

"He saw me in Lanoria with your clothes. Jesus, my hands hurt."

"Let me look at them."

"No looking today. Get out of here."

"What did they ask you?"

"Where you are. Man, what did you do to them?"

"Enough," Valdez said.

"They want you bad."

"They could have followed me."

"But Mr. Davis brought them here. Listen," Diego Luz said, "if you see him, give him something for me."

"For myself too," Valdez said. "You're going to Lanoria?"

"My son is taking me to get these fixed." He looked at his hands again.

"Will they be all right?"

"How do I know? We'll see. I just need to get one finger working."

"I'll take you," Valdez said.

"Go to hell. No, go where they can't find you," Diego Luz said. "I have my boy and my family."

R. L. Davis came across the Erin woman because he was hot and tired of riding in the sun.

He had moved south along the arroyo with the three riders who would watch with him. "If he comes he'll come from the southeast," the segundo had said. But after the segundo left, R. L. Davis thought, Who says he'll come in a straight line? He could work around and come from any direction. He told this to the three riders with him and one of them, the bony-faced one who'd picked up the little girl and who'd broken Diego Luz's hands, said sure, it was a waste of time; he'd like to get a shot at this Valdez, but it didn't have to be today; the greaser was in the hills and they'd find him.

That one, God, when he'd picked up the little girl, R. L. Davis wasn't sure he could watch what the man wanted to do. Her being a tiny girl.

After a while he said well, he'd double back and take a swing to the north. The others said they'd get up on the banks and look around and head back pretty soon. Good. He was glad to get away from the bony-faced one, a face like a skeleton face, only with skin.

So R. L. Davis moved back up the arroyo. He wasn't looking for anything in particular; there was nothing out here but the hot sun beating down on him. He saw the willow shade up ahead and the bright yellow blossoms of the brittlebush growing along the cutbank. The shade looked good. He headed for it. And when he found the Erin woman in there, sitting in the brush, tied up, he couldn't believe his eyes.

It was a lot to think about all at once. Valdez was here. Had been here. He'd put the woman here out of the way and gone to see Diego Luz. And if he left her like this, tied hand and foot, with a bandana over her mouth, then he was coming back for her. The woman was looking at him and he had to make up his mind fast.

He could pull her up behind him on the sorrel and deliver her to Tanner and say, "Here you are, Mr. Tanner. What else you need done?"

Or he could wait for Bob Valdez. Throw down on him and bring him in as well as the woman. Or gun him if that's the way Valdez wanted it.

The woman looked good. He'd like to slip the bandana from her mouth and get a close look at her. But he'd better not. There was a little clearing in here and rocks that had come down the cutbank. There was room in here to face him. There was room deeper in the brittlebush for his horse, if the son of a bitch didn't make any noise.

God Almighty, R. L. Davis thought. How about it? Bring them both in.

Once he'd moved the sorrel into the brush, he got his Winchester off the saddle and settled down behind the woman, behind some good rock cover. He saw her twist around to the side to look at him, her eyes looking but not saying anything. Probably scared to death. He motioned her to turn around and put one finger to his mouth. *Shhhh.* Don't worry; it won't be long.

Crossing the pasture from Diego Luz's place, Valdez saw the willows in the distance marking the arroyo. There had been some luck with him so far, coming in and going out, though he didn't know Tanner and he wasn't sure if it was luck or not. He didn't know yet how the man thought, if he was intelligent and could anticipate what the other man might do, or if he ran in all directions trusting only to luck. Luck was all right when you had it, but it couldn't be counted on. It worked good and bad, but it worked more good than bad if you knew what you were doing, if you were careful and watched and listened. He shouldn't be here, but he was here, and if the luck or whatever it was continued, he would be in high country again late this afternoon, letting Tanner find him and follow him, but not letting him get too close until the time was right for that.

When he talked to Tanner again it had to be on his own ground, not Tanner's.

The sawed-off Remington was across his lap as he approached the willows and entered the cavern of shade formed by the hanging branches. Holding the Remington, he dismounted and stood still to listen. There was no sound in the trees. He moved along the bank of the arroyo, beyond the thick brush below, to a place where the bank slanted down in deep slashes to the dry bed. He worked his way down carefully. At the bottom, as he entered the brittlebush, he cocked the right barrel of the Remington.

The Erin woman sat where he had placed her. She did not hear him or look this way. The bandana covered the side of her face and pulled her long hair behind her shoulders, which sagged with the weariness of sitting here for nearly an hour. You hold her all night and tie her in the morning, he thought. You make love to her, but you've never said her name. Now she turned her head this way.

He saw the startled expression jump into her eyes. He moved toward her, watching her eyes, wide open; her head moved very slightly to the side and then her eyes moved in that direction. Off to the right of her or behind her. Valdez shifted his gaze to the rocks and deep brush.

He moved forward again, a half step, and a voice he recognized said, "That's far enough!"

"Hey!" Valdez said. "Is that Mr. R. L. Davis?"

"Put down the scattergun and unfasten your belt."

Valdez's gaze shifted slightly. There. He could see the glint of the Winchester barrel in the brush and part of Davis's hat. He was behind an outcropping of rock, looking out past the left side, which meant he would have to expose half of his body to fire from that place. If he's right-handed, Valdez thought. He remembered Davis firing at the Lipan woman across the Maricopa pasture and he said to himself, Yes, he's right-handed.

"You hear me? I said put it down!"

"Why don't you come out?" Valdez said.

The sawed-off Remington was in his right hand, pointed down, but with his finger curled on the trigger. He looked at the brush and the edge of the rock outcropping, judging the distance. He imagined swinging the shotgun up and firing, deciding how high he would have to swing it. You get one time, Valdez thought. No more.

"I'm going to count to three," R. L. Davis said.

"Listen," Valdez called. "Why don't you cut out this game and use your gun if you want to use it? What're you hiding in the bushes for?"

"I'm warning you to put it down!"

"Come on, boy, use the gun. Hey, pretend I'm an Indian woman, you yellow-ass son of a bitch."

There. His shoulder and the rifle barrel sliding higher on the outcropping, more of him in the brush, and Valdez swung up the Remington, squeezing his hand around the narrow neck and seeing the brush fly apart with the explosion.

"Hey, you still there?" He shifted the gun to his left hand and drew the Walker. There was a silence. He glanced at the woman, seeing her eyes on him, and away from her.

"I'm hit!" Davis called out.

"What do you expect?" Valdez said. "You want to play guns."

"I'm *bleeding*!"

"Wipe it off and try again."

Silence.

"Boy, I'm coming in for you. You ready?"

He saw Davis at the edge of the rock again, seeing him more clearly now with part of the brush torn away. Davis came out a little more, his left hand covering his ear and the side of his face.

"Don't shoot. Listen to me, don't."

"The first one was for Diego," Valdez said. "The next one's from me. I owe you something."

"I didn't leave you, did I? I didn't let you die. I could've, but I didn't."

"Pick up your gun."

"Listen, I cut you loose!"

Valdez paused, letting the silence come over the clearing. He heard another sound, far away, off behind him, but his gaze held on Davis.

"Say it again."

"After I pushed you over. That night I come back and cut you loose, didn't I?"

"I didn't see you that night."

"Well, who do you think did it?"

His gaze dropped to the woman, to her eyes looking at him above the bandana. He heard the sound again and knew it was a horse approaching, coming fast up the arroyo.

"I left you my canteen. I can prove it's mine, it's got my initials scratched in the tin part, inside."

Valdez raised his Walker to shut him up and motion him out of the brush. Davis started out, then stopped. He could hear the horse.

"Come on," Valdez hissed.

But Davis hesitated. The sound was louder down the arroyo, rumbling toward them. Davis waited another moment then yelled out, "He's in here!" throwing himself behind the outcropping. "Get him! He's in here!"

Valdez reached the woman and pushed her over. He turned, moving crouched through the brittlebush, at the edge of it now, and stepping out of it as the first rider came at him from thirty yards away, drawing his revolver as he saw Valdez and the barrels of the Remington, then seeing nothing as the ten-bore charge rocked him from the saddle. The second rider was down the arroyo coming fast, low in the saddle and spurring his horse, his handgun already drawn, firing it from the off side of his horse. Valdez raised the Walker. He thumbed the hammer and fired and thumbed and fired and saw the horse buckle and roll, the rider stiff, with his arms outstretched in the air for a split moment, and Valdez shot him twice before he hit the ground. The horse was on its side, pawing with its forelegs, trying to rise. Valdez looked down the arroyo, waiting, then stepped to the horse and shot it through the head. He walked over to the man, whose death's head face looked up at him with sunken mouth and open eyes.

"I hope you're one of them Diego wanted," Valdez said. He turned toward the yellow brittlebush, loading the Remington.

"Where was he?" the segundo asked.

"He must have been in them bushes and fired on them as they come by," the rider said. "I was back a piece, up on the west side looking for his sign. When I heard the gunfire I lit up this way and they was coming out of the draw."

The segundo held up his hand. "Wait. You don't want to tell

it so many times." He squinted under his straw hat brim toward Tanner, mounted on his bay, looking down at them in the arroyo.

Tanner saw the two bodies sprawled in the dry bed. He saw the dead horse and the yellow-baked ground stained dark at the horse's head. He saw the segundo and a man standing next to him and a half dozen mounted men and a riderless horse nibbling at the brittlebush. Tanner kicked the bay down the bank to the stream bed. He stared at the dead men, then at the segundo, a stub of a cigar clamped in his jaw.

"This man," the segundo said, "is one of the four we left."

"You left," Tanner said.

"I left. He says they went south looking for a sign of him. Then after a while the piss-ant you hired, something Davis, he come back this way."

"Let him tell it," Tanner said, judging the man next to the segundo as he looked at him.

"Well, as he says we worked south a ways," the rider said. "Davis come back first and we spread out some. Then these two here must have started back. I was down there a mile and a half, two miles"—he pointed south, more at ease now, a thumb hooked in his belt—"when I heard the shots and come on back."

"Where were they?" Tanner said.

"When I come back? They were laying there. He must have been in the bushes and fired on them as they come by. As I got close they was coming up out of the draw and going west."

"Who's they?" Tanner asked him.

"Two men and a woman."

"You saw them good?"

"Well, I was off a ways, but I could see her hair, long hair flying in the wind."

"You're saying it was Mrs. Erin?"

"Yes sir, I'd put my hand on the Book it was."

"You see Valdez?"

"Not his face, but it must have been him. One of these boys here was blowed off by a scatter gun."

"That one," the segundo said. "This one, I don't know, forty-four or forty-five, in the chest twice, close together."

"That's five men he's killed," Tanner said. He drew on the cigar stub; it was out, and he threw it to the ground. "What about Davis?"

The rider looked up. "I figured he was the other one with them. Once I saw he wasn't around here."

"That's the strange thing," the segundo said. "Why would the man want to take him? He's worth nothing to him."

"Unless he went with him on his own," Tanner said. "Mark him down as another one, a dead man when we catch up with them."

"We'll get him for you," the rider said.

Tanner looked down at him from the bay horse. "Did you fire at them?"

"Yes sir, I got down and laid against the cutbank for support and let go till they was out of range."

"Did you hit anybody?"

"I don't believe so."

"But you might have."

"Yes sir, I might've."

"That range you couldn't tell."

"They was two hundred yards when I opened up."

"You could have hit one though."

"Yes sir."

"You could have hit the woman," Tanner said to him.

"No sir, I wasn't aiming at her. No, I couldn't have hit her. There wasn't any chance I could've. See, I was aiming just at Valdez and he was a good piece from the woman."

Tanner looked at the segundo. "Put him against the bank and shoot him."

The rider said, "Mr. Tanner, there was no chance I could've hit her! I swear to God that's the truth!"

The segundo felt the tobacco in his cheek, rolling it with his tongue as his eyes moved from the rider to Frank Tanner, looking at Tanner now but aware of the mounted men behind him and those up on the bank watching. The segundo said, "We lost five now. We shoot our own, that's six, but the same as Valdez killed him. How many you want to give for this man?"

"As many as it takes," Tanner said.

"Instead of shoot him," the segundo said, "we make him ride point. The first one Valdez sees if he's up there waiting. What do you think of that?"

The rider was watching Tanner. "I'll ride point. Mister, I'll cut his sign, too, and get him for you."

Tanner stared down from his judgment seat on the bay horse. He let the man hang on the edge for a long moment before he said, "All right, this time," saying no more than that, but holding his eyes on the man to let him know how close he had come.

The segundo said to the rider, "Start now, come on." He was aware of the men on the bank, beyond Tanner, moving in their saddles, a man wiping his hand across his mouth and another loosening his hat and putting it on again. They were glad it was over. They had killed men, most of them had, but they didn't want to put this one against the bank and shoot him. That would be the end of it. In a few days they would all be gone.

So that was done. The segundo walked over to Tanner's bay; he touched the horse's withers, feeling the smooth flesh quiver and patting it gently. "We have him now," the segundo said, in a voice only for Tanner. "Yesterday he could take us where he wants with plenty of time. Today he has maybe an hour. He has to run and now he doesn't have no more time."

"Say it," Tanner said.

The segundo's hand remained on the horse, patting the firm flesh. "I was thinking to myself, we got eighteen men here. We got six at Mimbreño. We could send eight or ten back and they could start south with the drive. Then when we finish with him we catch up, maybe lose only two days."

Tanner waited. "You through?"

"I mean we don't need so many," the segundo said, but he knew by the way the man was looking at him his words had been wasted.

"I'm going up the mountain," Tanner said. "You're going up the mountain, and all my men are going up the mountain. My men, segundo. You savvy that?"

"If you say it."

"I say it," Tanner said.

Through the field glasses he watched them come up the slope: small dots that he could not count yet, spread in a line, all of them moving this way, one dot ahead of the others, far in front, the only one that he could identify through the field glasses as a mounted rider.

It wasn't happening the way it was supposed to happen. There was open country behind him and he needed more time, a bigger space between them, if he expected to reach the twin peaks. But they were driving him now, running him and making sure he wasn't going to move around them.

It was late afternoon, three hours and a little more until sunset. Three hours to hold them here—if he could hold them— before he could take his two people and slip out. He lay on the ground with good rock cover in front of him and all along the ridge. Next to him were his guns and Davis's Winchester. Looking at the dots coming up he thought, The Winchester or the Sharps? And said to himself, The Sharps. You know it better. You know what it can do.

Well, he had better let them know. Pretty soon now.

He rolled slightly to look at the Erin woman and R. L. Davis. Gay Erin, he said in his mind. Aloud he said, "Mr. R. L. Davis, I would like you to come over here, please, and go down there about fifty feet. You see where those rocks are?"

Davis stood up awkwardly, his wrists tied to his belt with pieces of rope. His elbows pointed out and he looked as though he was holding his stomach. There was dried blood on the side of his face and in his hair and down the arm of his jacket, which was torn and shredded.

"What do you want me down there for?"

"I want you in front of me," Valdez said. "So I can see you."

"What if they come?"

"They're already coming."

Davis gazed down the slope, squinting. "I don't see nothing."

"Take my word," Valdez said.

"Well listen now, if they start shooting I'm going to be in the line of fire."

"Behind the rocks, you'll be all right."

Davis stood his ground. "You still don't believe me, do you? I can prove it by my canteen."

"I don't have your canteen."

"You had it. It's somewhere."

"And we're here," Valdez said. "Let's talk some other time."

"If I didn't cut you loose, who did?"

"You can walk down or I can throw you down," Valdez said.

He looked toward the woman. Say it, he thought. He said, "Gay Erin. Gay. That's your name? Come over here." He watched Davis moving hunch-shouldered down the slope to the cover of low rocks. He felt the woman near him. As she sank to the ground, he handed her the field glasses. "Count them for me."

He raised up to take Davis's Colt out of his belt. The barrel was cutting into his hip. He placed it on the ground next to him and took the heavy Sharps, the Big Fifty, and laid it on the flat surface of the rock in front of him. He would load from the cartridge belt across his chest. With the stock against his cheek, aware of the oiled metal smell of the gun, he sighted down the barrel. Nothing. Not without the glasses.

"Seventeen," the Erin woman said.

He took the glasses from her. Putting them to his eyes the lower part of the slope came up to him.

They were still far enough away that he could see all of them without sweeping the glasses. He estimated the distance, the first man, the point rider, at six hundred yards, the rest of them at least two hundred yards behind him. The brave one, Valdez thought. Maybe the segundo. Maybe Tanner. He held the glasses on the man until he knew it was not Tanner. Nor the segundo, because of the man's dark hat.

Valdez lowered the glasses. He said, "Nineteen. You missed two of them, but that's very good." He looked at her, at her hair in the afternoon sunlight, the bandana pulled down from her face, loose around her neck now. He reached over and touched the bandana, feeling the cotton cloth between his fingers. "Put this on your head."

"The sun doesn't bother me," she said. She had not spoken since they left the arroyo.

"I'm not thinking of the sun. I'm thinking how far you can see yellow hair."

As she untied the knot behind her neck she said, "You believed I cut you loose. I didn't tell you I did."

"But you let me believe it."

"How do you know he did?"

"Because he told me. Because if someone else did it, he would think I knew who did it and he wouldn't bother to lie. I think I was dreaming of a woman giving me water," Valdez said. "So when I tried to remember what happened, I thought it was a woman."

"I didn't mean to lie to you," she said. "I was afraid."

"I can see it," Valdez said. "If you saved my life, I'm not going to shoot you. Or if you get under a blanket with me."

"I tried to explain how I felt," she said.

"Sure, you're all alone, you need somebody. Don't worry anymore. I know a place you can work, make a lot of money."

"If you think I'm lying," the woman said, "or if you think I'm a whore, there's nothing I can do about it. Think what you like."

"I've got something else to think about," Valdez said. He studied the slope through the field glasses, past Davis lying behind the rock looking up at him, to the point rider. He raised up then and said to Davis, "If you call out, I give you the first one."

He put the glasses on the point man again, three hundred yards away, and held him in focus until he was less than two hundred yards and he could see the man's face and the way the man was squinting, his gaze inching over the hillside. I don't know you, Valdez said to the man. I have nothing against you. He put down the field glasses and turned the Sharps on the point rider. He could still see the man's face, his eyes looking over the slope, not knowing it was coming. You shouldn't have looked at him. Valdez thought.

Then take another one and show them something. But not Tanner. Anyone else.

Through the field glasses he picked out Tanner almost four hundred yards away and put the glasses down again and placed the front sight of the Sharps on the man next to Tanner, not having seen the man or thinking about him now as a man. He let them come a little more, three hundred and fifty yards, and squeezed the trigger. The sound of the Sharps cracked the still-ness, echoing across the slope, and the man, whoever he was, dropped from the saddle. Valdez looked and fired and saw a horse go down with its rider. He fired again and dropped an-other horse as they wheeled and began to fall back out of range. The Sharps echoed again, but they were moving in confusion and he missed with this shot and the next one. He picked up the Winchester, getting to his knees, and slammed four shots at the point rider, chasing him down the slope, and with the fourth shot the man's horse stumbled, throwing him from the saddle. He fired the Winchester twice again, into the distance, then lowered it, the ringing aftersound of the gunfire in his ears.

"Now think about it," Valdez said to Tanner.

He would think and then he would send a few, well out of range, around behind them. Or he would have some of them try to work their way up the slope without being seen.

Or they would all come again.

As they did a few minutes later, spread out and running their horses up the slope. Valdez used the Sharps again. He hit the first man he aimed at, dumping him out of the saddle, and dropped two horses. Before they had gotten within two hundred yards they were turning and falling back. He looked for the two riders whose horses he had hit. One of them was running, limping down the hill, and the other was pinned beneath his dead animal.

"You'd better move back or work around," Valdez said to Tanner, "before you lose all your horses."

Make him believe you.

He raised the angle of the Sharps and fired. He fired again and saw a horse go down at six hundred yards. They pulled back again.

Now, Valdez thought, get out of here.

They could wait until dark, but that would be too late if Tanner was sending people around. He had to be lucky to win and he had to take chances in order to try his luck.

He could leave R. L. Davis.

But he looked at him down there with his wrists tied to his belt, and for some reason he said to himself, Keep him. Maybe you need him sometime.

He called to Davis, "Come up now. Slowly, along the brush there."

The woman sat on the ground watching him. The woman who was alone and needed someone and wanted to be held and got under the blanket. In this moment before they made their run, Valdez looked at her and said, "What do you want? Tell me."

"I want to get out of here," she said.

"Where? Where do you want to be?"

"I don't know."

"Gay Erin," Valdez said, "think about it and let me know."

■ ■ ■

Tanner and the men with him had gotten to the ridge and were looking at the ground and back down the slope to where they had been, seeing it as Valdez had seen it. Now they heard the gunfire in the distance, to the south.

They stopped and looked that way, all of them, out across the open, low-rolling country to the hills beyond.

"They caught him," one of them said.

Another one said, "How many shots?"

They listened and in the silence a man said, "I counted five, but it could've been more."

"It was more than five," the first man said. "It was all at once, like they were firing together."

"That's it," a man said. "The four of them got him in their sights and all fired at once to finish him."

The segundo was standing at the place where Valdez had positioned himself belly-down behind the rocks to fire at them. He picked up an empty brass cartridge and looked at it—fifty-caliber big bore, from a Sharps or some kind of buffalo gun. He noticed the .44 cartridges that had been fired from the Winchester. A Sharps and a Winchester, a big eight- or ten-bore shotgun and a revolver; this man was armed and he knew how to use his guns. The segundo counted fourteen empty cartridges on the ground and tallied what the bullets had cost them: two dead on the slope, two wounded, five horses shot. Now seven dead in the grand total and, counting the men without horses, who would have to walk to Mimbreño and come back, twelve men he had wiped from the board, leaving twelve to hunt him and kill him.

He said to Mr. Tanner, "This is where he was, if you want to see how he did it."

Tanner walked over, looking at the ground and down the slope. "He had some luck," Tanner said, "but it's run out."

The segundo said nothing. Maybe the man had luck—there was such a thing as luck—but God in heaven, he knew how to shoot his guns. It would be something to face him, the segundo was thinking. It would be good to talk to him sometime, if this had not happened and if he met the man, to have a drink of mescal with him, or if they were together using their guns against someone else.

How would you like to have him? the segundo thought. Start over and talk to him different. He remembered the way Valdez had stood at the adobe wall as they fired at him, shooting close to his head and between his legs. He remembered the man not moving, not tightening or pleading or saying a word as he watched them fire at him. You should have known then, the segundo said to himself.

Tanner had sent four to circle around behind Valdez on the ridge and close his back door. A half hour after they heard the gunfire in the distance, one of them came back.

The man's horse was lathered with sweat, and he took his hat off to feel the evening breeze on the ridge as he told it.

"We caught them, out in the open. They had miles to go yet before they'd reach cover, and we ran them, hard," the man said. "Then we see one of the horses pull up. We know it must be him and we go right at him, getting into range to start shooting. But he goes flat on the ground, out in the open but right flat, and doesn't give us nothing to shoot at. He opened up at about a hunnert yards, and first one boy went down and then he got the horse of this other boy. The boy run toward him and he cut him clean as he was a-running. So two of us left, we come around. We see Valdez mount up and chase off again for the hills. We decide, one of us will follow them and the other will come back here."

Tanner said, "Did you hit him?"

"No sir, he didn't look to be hit."

"You know where he went?"

"Yes sir, Stewart's out there. He's going to track them and leave a plain enough trail for us to follow."

Tanner looked at the segundo. "Is he any good?"

The segundo shrugged. "Maybe he's finding out."

They moved out, south from the ridge, across the open, rolling country. In the dusk, before the darkness settled over the hills, they came across the man's horse grazing, and a few yards farther on the man lying on his back with his arms flung out. He had been shot through the head.

Ten, the segundo thought, looking down at the man. Nine left.

"Take his guns," Tanner said. "Bring his horse along."

It was over for this day. With the darkness coming they would have to wait until morning. He took out a cigar and bit off the end. Unless they spread out and worked up into the hills tonight. Tanner lighted the cigar, staring up at the dim, shadowed slopes and the dark mass of trees above the rocks.

He said to the segundo, "Come here. I'll tell you what we're going to do."

EIGHT

"Christ," R. L. Davis said. "I need more than this to eat." Christ, some bread and peppers and a half cup of stale water. "I didn't have nothing all day."

"Be thankful," Valdez told him.

Davis's saddle was on the ground in front of him, his hands tied to the horn. He was on his stomach and had to hunch his head down to take a bite of the pan bread he was holding. The Erin woman, next to him, held his cup for him when he wanted a sip of water. She listened to them, to their low tones in the darkness, and remained silent.

"I don't even have no blanket," R. L. Davis said. "How'm I going to keep warm?"

"You'll be sweating," Valdez said.

"Sweating, man it gets *cold* up here."

"Not when you're moving."

Davis looked over at him in the darkness, the flat, stiff piece of bread close to his face. "You don't even know where you're going, do you?"

"I know where I want to go," Valdez answered. "That much."

Toward the twin peaks, almost a day's ride from where they were camped now for a few hours, in the high foothills of the Santa Ritas: a dry camp with no fire, no flickering light to give them away if Tanner's men were prowling the hills. They would eat and rest and try to cover a few miles before dawn.

Ten years before, he had camped in these hills with his Apache trackers, following the White Mountain band that had struck Mimbreño and burned the church and killed three men and carried off a woman: renegades, fleeing into Mexico after jumping the reservation at San Carlos, taking what they needed along the way.

Ten years ago, but he remembered the ground well, and the way toward the twin peaks.

Valdez had worked ahead with his trackers and let the cavalry troop try to keep up with them, moving deep into the hills and climbing gradually into rock country, following the trail of the White Mountain band easily, because the band was running, not trying to cover their tracks, and because there were many of them: women and several children in addition to the fifteen or so men in the raiding party. He knew he would catch them, because he could move faster with his trackers and it was only a matter of time. They found cooking pots and jars that had been stolen and now thrown away. They found a lame horse and farther on a White Mountain woman who was sick and had been left behind. They moved on, climbing the slopes and up through the timber until they came out of the trees into a canyon: a gama grass meadow high in the mountains, with an escarpment of rock rising steeply on both sides and narrowing at the far end to a dark, climbing passage that would allow only one man at a time to enter.

The first tracker into the passage was shot from his saddle. They carried him back and dismounted in the meadow to look over the situation.

This was the reason the White Mountain band had made a run for it and had not bothered to cover their tracks. Once they made it through the defile they were safe. One of them could squat up there in the narrows and hold off every U. S. soldier on frontier station, as long as he had shells, giving his people time to run for Mexico. They studied the walls of the canyon and the possible trails around. Yes, a man could climb it maybe, if he had some goat blood in him. But getting up there didn't mean there was a way to get down the other side. On the other hand, to go all the way back down through the rocks and find a trail that led around and brought them out at the right place could take a week if they were lucky. So Valdez and his trackers sat in that meadow and smoked cigarettes and talked and let the White Mountain people run for the border. If they didn't get them this year they'd get them next year.

Valdez could see Tanner's men dismounted in the meadow, looking up at the canyon walls, studying the shadowed crevices and the cliff rose that grew along the rim, way up there against the sky. Anyone want to try it? No thank you, not today. Tanner would send some men to scout a trail that led around. But before he ever heard from them again, after a day or two in the meadow, seeing the bats flicking and screeching around the canyon's wall at night, he'd come to the end of his patience and holler up through the narrow defile, "All right, let's talk!"

That was the way Bob Valdez had pictured it taking place: leading Tanner with plenty of time and setting it up to make the deal. "Give me the money for the Lipan woman or you don't get your woman back."

He had almost forgotten the Lipan woman. He couldn't picture her face now. It wasn't a face to remember, but now the woman had no face at all. She was somewhere, sitting in a hut eating corn or *atole*, feeling the child inside her and not knowing this was happening outside in the night. He would say to Tanner, "You see how it is? The woman doesn't have a man, so she needs money. You have money, but you don't have a woman. All right, you pay for the man and you get your woman."

It seemed simple because in the beginning it was simple, with the Lipan woman sitting at her husband's grave. But now there was more to it. The putting him against the wall and tying him to the cross had made it something else. Still, there was no reason to forget the Lipan woman. No matter if she didn't have a face and no matter what she looked like. And no matter if it was not happening the way it was supposed to happen. The trouble now was, Tanner could stop him before he reached the narrow place, before he reached the good position to talk and make a trade.

No, the trouble was more than that. The trouble was also the woman herself, this woman sitting without speaking anymore, the person he would have to trade. He said in his mind, St. Francis, you were a simple man. Make this goddam thing that's going on simple for me.

"You say you know where you're going," R. L. Davis said. "Tell us so we'll all know."

You don't need him, Valdez thought. He said, "If we get there, you see it. If we don't get there, it doesn't matter, does it?"

"Listen, you know how many men he's got?"

"Not so much anymore."

"He's still got enough," R. L. Davis said. "They're going to take you and string you up, if you aren't shot dead before. But either way, it's the end of old Bob Valdez."

"How's your head?"

"It still hurts."

"Close your mouth or I make it hurt worse, all right?"

"I helped you," R. L. Davis said. "You owe me something. I could have left you out there, but being a white man I went back and cut you loose."

"What do you want?" Valdez asked.

"What do you think? I cut you loose, you cut me loose and let me go."

Valdez nodded slowly. "All right. When we leave."

Davis looked at him hard. "You mean it?"

Valdez felt the Erin woman looking at him also. "As you say, I owe it to you."

"It's not some kind of trick?"

"How could it be a trick?"

"I don't know. I just don't trust you."

Valdez shrugged. "If you're free, what difference does it make?"

"You're cooking something up," R. L. Davis said.

"No." Valdez shook his head. "I only want you to do me a favor."

"What's that?"

"Give Mr. Tanner a message from me. Tell him he has to pay the Lipan, but now I'm not sure I give him back his woman."

He felt her staring at him again, but he looked out into the darkness thinking about what he had said, realizing that it was all much simpler in his mind now.

It was two o'clock in the morning when Valdez and the Erin woman moved out leading Davis's bareback sorrel horse. They left Davis tied to his saddle with his own bandana knotted around his mouth. As Valdez tied it behind his head, Davis twisted his neck, pushing out his jaw.

"You gag me I won't be able to yell for help!"

"Very good," Valdez said.

"They might not find me!"

"What's certain in life?" Valdez asked. He got the bandana between Davis's teeth and tightened it, making the knot. "There. When it's light stand up and carry your saddle down the hill. They'll find you."

He would have liked to hit Davis once with his fist. Maybe twice. Two good ones in the mouth. But he'd let it go; he'd cut him fairly good with the Remington. Mr. R. L. Davis was lucky.

Now a little luck of your own, Valdez thought.

They walked the horses through the darkness with ridges and shadowed rock formations above them, Valdez leading the way and taking his time, moving with the clear sound of the horses on broken rock and stopping to listen in the night silence. Once, in the hours they traveled before dawn, they heard a single gunshot, a thin sound in the distance, somewhere to the east; then an answering shot far behind them. Tanner's men firing at shadows, or locating one another. But they heard no sounds close to them that could have been Tanner's riders. Maybe you're having some more luck and you'll get through, Valdez thought. Maybe St. Francis listened and he's making it easier. Hey, Valdez said. Keep Sister Moon behind the clouds so they don't see us. They moved through the night until a faint glow began to wash the sky and the ground shadows became diffused and the shapes of the rock formations and trees were more difficult to see. The moment before dawn when the Apache came through the brush with bear grass in his headband and you didn't see him until he was on you. The time when it was no longer night, but not yet morning. A time to rest, Valdez thought.

They moved into a canyon, between walls that rose steeply and were darkly shadowed with brush. Valdez knew the place and the horses snorted and threw their heads when they smelled the water, the pool of it lying still, undercutting one side of the canyon.

The Erin woman moved around the pool while Valdez stripped off the bridles and saddles to let the horses drink and graze freely. He watched her, looking past the horses, watched her kneel down at the edge of the water and drink from her cupped hands. Valdez took off his hat and slipped the heavy Sharps cartridge belt over his head. A time to rest at dawn, before the day brought whatever it would bring. He moved around the pool toward her.

"Are you hungry?"

She looked up at him, shaking her head, then brushing her hair from her face. "No, not really. Are you?"

"I can wait."

"Are you going to sit down?"

"If you're not going to stand up," Valdez said. He went down next to her, touching her hair, feeling his finger brush her cheek and seeing her eyes on him.

He said, "Gay Erin. That's your name, uh? What was it before?"

"Gay Byrnes."

He took her face gently, his palm covering her chin, and kissed her on the mouth. "Gay Erin. That's a good name. You like it?"

"It's my name because I was married to him."

"What do you want to talk about that for?"

"I don't want to talk about it."

"Then don't. Do you know my name?"

"Valdez."

"Roberto Valdez. How do you like Roberto?"

"I think it's fine."

"Or Bob. Which do you like better?"

"Roberto."

"It's Mexican."

"I know it is."

"Listen, I've been thinking about something."

She waited.

"You heard me tell him I don't know if I'm going to give you back or not."

"I told you before," the Erin woman said. "I don't want to go back."

"That's what you told me." Valdez nodded. "All right, I believe you. Do you know why? Because it's easier if I believe you. If I think about you too much, then I don't have time to think about other things."

"What do you think about me?"

"I think I'd like to live with you and be married to you."

She waited. "We've been together two days."

"And two nights," Valdez said. "How long does it take?" He could see her face more clearly now in the dawn light.

Her eyes did not leave his. "You'd marry me?"

"I think I know you well enough."

"I killed my husband."

"I believe you."

"I've been living with Frank Tanner."

"I know that."

"But you want to marry me."

"I think so, yes."

"Tell me why."

"Listen, I don't like this. I don't feel right, but I don't know what else to say. I believe you because I want to believe you. I say to myself, You want her? I say, Yes. Then I say, What if she's lying? And then I say, Goddam, believe her and don't think anymore. Listen, I couldn't do anything to you. I mean if he says, I won't give you the money, shoot her, you think I'd shoot you?"

She shook her head. "No, I didn't think you would."

"So don't worry about that."

"I never have," the Erin woman said. "I may have been feeling sorry for myself, but I didn't lie down with you just because I wanted to be held."

"Why did you then?"

She hesitated again. "I don't know. I wanted to be with you. I still want to be with you. If I'm in love with you then I'm in love with you. I don't know, I've never loved a man before."

"I've never been married," Valdez said.

She took his hand and brought it up to her face. "I haven't either, really."

"Maybe we can talk about it again. When there's time, uh?"

"I hope so," she said.

Believe that, Valdez thought, and don't think about it. He gave her R. L. Davis's Colt revolver and that sealed it. If she was lying to him she could shoot him in the back. She had already killed one man.

Still, it was easier in his mind now. Much easier.

■ ■ ■

They found R. L. Davis a little after sunup, a hunched-over figure on the brush slope, dragging a saddle and a thin trail of dust. The two men who found him cut him loose. One of them took the saddle and the other pulled R. L. Davis up behind him and they rode double over to where Mr. Tanner had spent the night. He was alone; all the others were still out on scout.

He looked different. Mr. Tanner had not shaved for two or three days, and the collar of his shirt was dirty and curled up. His moustache looked bigger and his face thinner.

R. L. Davis noticed this, though God Almighty, his back ached from dragging the goddam saddle all over the countryside.

"I wouldn't mind a drink of water from somebody."

The rider who'd brought him in was about to hand him a canteen, but Tanner stopped him.

"Wait'll we're through."

"I haven't had no water since last night."

"You won't die," Tanner said. "Less I see I should kill you."

"Mr. Tanner, look at me. He drew down with that scattergun, like to took my head off."

"Where are they?"

"He let me go about four hours ago and headed south."

"Mrs. Erin was with him?"

"Yes sir."

"How is she?"

"She looks fine to me. I mean I don't think he's mistreated her any."

"God help him," Tanner said. "Did you speak to her?"

"No, he was right there all the time. There wasn't nothing I could say he wouldn't've heard."

"Then she didn't say anything to you."

"No sir. He said something he wanted me to tell you, though."

Tanner waited. "Well, goddam it, go ahead."

"He said, 'Tell him he still has to pay the Indin, but I'm not sure now I'm giving him his woman back.' "

Frank Tanner hit him. He clubbed Davis in the face with his right fist and the man sprawled on his back in the dust.

"I didn't say it—he said it! Them are his words."

"Tell it again."

"I swear it's what he said."

"Tell it!"

"He said you're to pay the Indin, but he wasn't so sure he was going to give you your woman back. Them words exactly."

"Did she say anything?"

"No sir, not a word, the whole time I was there."

"He keep her tied?"

"When she was in the draw, but not when he's around. I mean riding or when he's made camp."

"Why'd he let you go?" Davis hesitated and Tanner said, "I asked you a question."

"Well, I reckon to tell you what he said. There's no other reason I know of."

"God help you if there is," Tanner said.

He was mounting his bay horse, when two riders came in with a string of fresh horses. They had walked all night back to Mimbreño from the place where they had left their dead mounts on the slope.

Tanner looked at R. L. Davis. "Put your saddle on one of them," he said. "I want you present when we run him down."

During the early morning the segundo, whose name was Emilio Avilar but who had been called only segundo for the past six years, found three of his men in the mountain wilderness and signaled them, gathering them in. The men were tired and their horses were worn and needed water. They were ready to head back, and Frank Almighty Tanner could whistle out his ass if he didn't like it. They were paid to drive cattle and freight wagons and shoot *rurales*; they had not signed on to chase a man who'd run off with Tanner's woman. That was his lookout if he couldn't keep her home. After all night in the saddle, it was time to unroll the blankets.

The segundo said, "You think he doesn't want to sleep? Man, he has to stay awake, doesn't he? He got to watch the woman, he got to watch for us. Man, ask him what it's like to be tired."

Two of the riders were American and one Mexican, the Mexican a young man who had been hired only a few months before by the segundo.

One of the Americans said it was none of their business. And the segundo said maybe not, but look, the sooner they caught this crazy man the sooner they could ride to Mexico and have a good time.

"You want some fresh water, uh?" the segundo said. "Don't you think he want some fresh water?"

"If he know where it was," one of the Americans said.

"Listen, when are you going to understand what kind of man he is?" the segundo said. "Sure he's crazy, but he knows what he's doing. You think he come down this way if he don't know there's water? Where it is? He's not that crazy."

"Well, him knowing doesn't help us," the other American said.

The segundo took his hat off and wiped his forehead with his sleeve and set the Sonora hat over his eyes again. He shook his head and said to the man, "Where do I get people like you? You think I work around here six years I don't know where the goddam water is? What kind of segundo doesn't know where the water is?"

"Well, let's go get it," the rider said.

Emilio Avilar, the segundo, smiled. "Sure, I thought that was what you want."

A little later that morning, watering their horses at the pool, the cliffs and sloping canyon walls reflected in the still water, the three riders looked at the segundo and the segundo smiled again. God, there were fresh tracks all over the place close to the bank, two horses and two people: no doubt about it, a man and a woman. They filled their canteens and wiped down their horses and at this moment were willing to follow the segundo anyplace he wanted to go. Hell, let's get him!

"Which way would you go?" the segundo asked.

"Follow their tracks."

"But that take too long," the segundo said. "What if we know where they going?"

"How could you figure that?"

"Two days ago," the segundo said, "he told Señor Tanner to approach the two peaks. You remember?" He lifted his gaze. "We come from a different way now, but there are the two peaks. Why should he change his mind and not go there? The only difference is now he don't have so much time."

The two American riders thought about it and nodded and one of them said, "What's up there?"

The segundo answered, "We find out."

This is all, he thought, watching the three men move out, slouched in their saddles, heads bobbing, sweat staining a column down their spines. No more. He watched them another moment before calling out, "Hey, Tomás!" The riders looked around and the young Mexican he had hired a few months before reined in to wait for him.

In Spanish the segundo said, "You have a ride the other way. Bring Señor Tanner."

The young Mexican picked up his reins, getting ready. "How will I know where to bring him?"

"You'll hear us," the segundo said.

NINE

The twin peaks reached above them, beyond the slope that was swept with owl clover and cholla brush, beyond the scrub oak and dark mass of timber, stone pinnacles against the sky, close enough to touch in the clean, clear air.

"Up there," Valdez said. "We go through the trees and come out in a canyon. At the end of the canyon is a little trail that goes up through the rocks and passes between the two peaks and down the other side. You stand in there and look straight up and the peaks look like they're moving in the wind."

The Erin woman's eyes were half closed in the glare; she shielded her eyes with her hand.

"Once we go through there, we see if we can make a slide to block the trail," Valdez said. "Then we don't hurry anymore. We take our time because it takes them a few days to find a way around."

Her gaze lowered and she looked at him now. "A few days. Is that all we'll have?"

"It's up to us," Valdez said. "Or it's up to him. We can go to Mexico. We can go to China if there's a way to go there. Or we can go to Lanoria."

"Where do you want to go?" she asked him.

"To Lanoria."

"He'll come for us."

"If he wants to," Valdez said. "I run today, but not forever. Today is enough."

"Whatever you want to do," the Erin woman said, "I want to do."

Valdez looked at her and wanted to reach over to touch her hair and feel the skin of her sun-darkened cheek and move the tips of his fingers gently over her cracked lips. But he kept his hand in his lap, around the slender neck of the Remington.

He said, "If you want to go back now, you can. I let you go, you're free. Go wherever you want. Tell him you got away from me."

Next to him, sitting in their saddles, their legs almost touching, she said again, "Whatever you want to do."

"We'll go," he said, reaching back and flicking the rope that trailed from his saddle to R. L. Davis's sorrel horse.

They left the trail and started up across the slope on an angle, moving through the owl clover and around the cholla bushes that were like dwarf trees, Valdez leading, aware of the woman behind him, wanting to turn to look at her, but only glancing at her as his gaze swept the hillside and back the way they had come.

Roberto Valdez kept watch up the slope and Bob Valdez, inside him, pictured the woman coming out of an adobe into the front yard: a place like Diego Luz's, alone in the high country, but larger than Diego's, with glass in the windows and a plank front porch beneath the ramada. The woman in a white dress open at the throat and her hair hanging below her shoulders, her hair shining in the sunlight. He would be coming up from the horse pasture and see her and she would raise her arm to wave. God, he would like to ride up to her, twisting out of the saddle, and take hold of her with her arm still raised, his hands moving under her arms and around her and hold her as tightly as a man can hold a woman without injuring her. But he would stop at the pump and have a drink of water and wash himself and then go to the yard, walking his horse, because he would have the rest of his life to do this.

As Bob Valdez pictured this, finally reaching the yard and the woman, Roberto Valdez saw the riders far below them starting across the slope in single file. Six of them and three horses in a string.

Valdez took the field glasses from his saddlebag. He picked out Frank Tanner and R. L. Davis. He saw them looking up this way and saw one of the men pointing, saying something.

Come on, Valdez thought, as they spread apart now and spurred their horses up through the brush. When you get here we'll be gone. But still watching them, counting them again, he thought, If Tanner is here, where is his segundo?

Emilio Avilar watched from above, from the shadowed edge of the timber.

They had the man almost in their sights, Valdez coming across the slope through the scrub oak, leading the horse and the woman behind him, coming at a walk and angling directly toward them, walking into their guns, and now Tanner the Almighty, the white barbarian, had ruined the ambush and was running him again.

God, the man would have been dead in a moment, shot out of his saddle, but now with the woman behind him, kicking their mounts straight up the grade, Valdez had reached the top of the slope and was entering the timber. Not here, where the segundo had waited with his two Americans for almost an hour, but more than a hundred yards away: a last glimpse of Valdez and the woman disappearing into the trees.

The segundo had scouted the timber and the canyon beyond, studying the canyon and the narrow defile at the end of it, and known at once Valdez was coming here. Where else? This man knew the ground and the water sinks and fought like an Apache. Sure Valdez was coming here: to escape through the defile or to stand in it and shoot them one at a time as they came for him.

Don't let him get in the canyon, the segundo had thought. Don't take a chance with him. Wait for him at the canyon mouth and shoot him as he enters. But Valdez would be coming through the cover of the trees and maybe his nose or his ears would tell him something, warn him, and he would run off another way. You have to think of him as you would a mountain lion, the segundo thought. Trap him in the open, away from cover.

So the segundo had gone back through the timber to the edge overlooking the slope and had told his two men very carefully what they would do: how they would watch for him, then study his angle of approach from the cover of the trees, and be waiting for him to walk into it, waiting until he was close to the trees but still in the open, and kill him before he saw them.

But now Valdez was already in the timber. The segundo had told his men to be quiet and keep their horses quiet and listen.

One of them said, "You know he's going for the canyon."

"He reached it, that's all," the other one said. "Once he gets in the hole ain't nobody going in after him."

"Not this child," the first man said. "Tanner can go in himself he wants him so bad."

Christ Jesus, the segundo said to himself. "Will you be quiet!" They listened.

"I don't hear him," one of them said. "I don't hear a sound."

The segundo drew the two men closer to him, listening, and they listened with him. "Do you know why?" he said. "Because he's not moving, he's listening. He knows we're in here with him."

"He didn't see us."

"When are you going to know him?" the segundo said. "He doesn't have to see you."

"He's got to move sometime," one of them said.

The segundo nodded. "Before Tanner and the others come up. All right, we separate, spread out a little. But all of us move toward the canyon." His voice dropped to a hushed tone. "Very quietly."

There were open patches where sunlight streaked through the pine branches a hundred feet above, and there were thickets of scrub oak and dense brush. There was an occasional sound close to them, a small scurrying sound in the brush, and there were the shrill faraway cries of unseen birds in the treetops. The birds would stop and in the shadowed forest, high in the Santa Ritas, a silence would settle.

They moved deep into the trees from the open slope before Valdez brought them up to listen. And as he listened he thought, You should have kept going and taken the chance. You don't have time to wait.

He heard the sound through the trees, a twig snapping, then silence. In a moment he heard it again and the sound of movement in dead leaves.

He was right, some of them were already in the trees. But it did no good to be right this time. They should have kept going and not stopped. They weren't going to sneak through and keep running, and now he wondered if the woman should go first or follow him. Follow him through the trees and in the open, if they reached the canyon, then first into the defile while he held them off. He couldn't remember the distance to the canyon. Perhaps fifty yards, a little more. He was certain of the general direction, the way they would point and keep going.

He said to the woman, "The last time we run. Are you ready?"

She nodded once, up and down. Both of her hands were on her saddle horn, but she didn't seem tense or to be holding on.

"I go first," Valdez said. He nodded in the direction. "That way. You come behind me. Don't go another way around the trees, keep behind me. If you see them in front of us, stay close to me, as close as you can. At the end of the canyon you'll see the opening. You go in first. Don't get off, ride in—it's wide enough—and I'll come in after you."

She nodded again. "All right."

He smiled at her. "Just a little ride, it's over."

She nodded again and tried to smile and now he saw she was afraid.

Valdez dismounted. He untied the sorrel, moving it aside, holding the bridle under the horse's muzzle. As soon as Tanner's men entered the trees he would send the sorrel galloping off and hope they would take off after its sound. He waited, telling Tanner's men to hurry so he would hear them soon; and when it came, moments later, the sound of their horses rushing into the timber, he hissed into the sorrel's ear, yanking the bridle and slapping the Remington hard across the horse's rump as it jumped to a start and ran off through the trees.

"Now," Valdez said.

They were moving, running through the shafts of sunlight and darkness with the beating, breathing sound of the horses and the tree branches cutting at their faces, running through the brush, through the wall of leaves and snapping branches and through a clearing into trees again, now hearing Tanner's men calling out somewhere behind and somewhere off in the timber. Valdez could see the canyon ahead through the foliage, the open mouth of the meadow, the rock escarpment slanting to the sky.

He saw the opening and he saw a rider slash out of the trees in front of him and come around, his horse rearing with the sudden motion. Valdez broke out of the trees straight for the rider, seeing him broadside now and kicking his mount. He bore down on the man, raising the Remington in front of him, and at point-blank range blew the man off the back of his horse.

He was aware of horses behind him and felt the next man before he saw him or heard him coming up on the left. He switched the Remington to that hand, extending it at arm's length, and when he looked, he fired as the rider fired and saw the man go out of his saddle. The man's horse kept running, racing him, and now he felt the wind in the open and saw the sun balanced on the west rim of the escarpment and heard the Erin woman's horse holding close behind him.

A high whine sang through the narrows as a rifle opened up on him. He remembered the sound of gunfire in the canyon from a time before. He remembered the shadowed crevices high on the walls and the thick gama grass. But he remembered the meadow longer than this, a half mile long in his mind. Now it was not half that distance and he was almost to the end.

Another rifle shot sang out as he reached the defile and came around.

The woman would be there, behind him, and ride in and he would follow her.

But the horse that came behind him was riderless.

The horse veered off, seeing the canyon wall. As it moved out of the way, Valdez saw her: she was about thirty yards from him, her horse was down, and she was rising to her feet, holding her head with both hands and looking at the dead horse.

He saw the segundo close beyond her, dismounting and coming up with a rifle in his hands. Valdez wanted to call out to her, "Run! Come on, do it!" But it was too late. The segundo came on, walking through the gama grass with the rifle in his right hand, his finger through the trigger guard. He stopped before reaching the Erin woman.

Valdez loaded the Remington—not thinking about it, but loading it because it was empty and saying to the segundo with his gaze, You want to do something, come on, do it. He was tired, God, at the end of it, but this is what he was saying to the segundo. With the Remington loaded and cocked he walked out to the woman.

She stood with one hand covering the side of her face, dirt and pieces of grass on her dress and in her hair, as she watched Valdez coming. She looked tired and still afraid, her eyes dull and without question or hope.

"Almost, uh?" Valdez said.

"Almost," the Erin woman said.

"Are you all right?" She nodded and he said then, "You don't have to go back with him. Remember that."

A look of awareness came into her eyes, as if she had been suddenly awakened from sleep. "Don't say that."

"It has to be said."

"I go with you. I don't go with him."

"Frank Tanner doesn't know that." Valdez paused. He said then, "Frank," smiling with the weariness etched in his face. "Francisco. Francis. I had a friend named Francis. I don't know what happened to him."

He laughed out loud and saw the startled look come over her and saw the segundo looking at him.

He heard his own laughter again in the canyon and at the far end saw Frank Tanner and men on both sides of him coming out into the meadow. He saw Tanner stop, looking this way.

Gay Erin touched his arm, holding on to it. He said to her, "I don't know why I thought it was funny. This Frank and my friend having the same name. They're not much alike." He smiled, still thinking of it, and watched the segundo approach, the segundo staring at him, trying to understand what would make him laugh.

With his left hand Emilio Avilar raised his hat and wiped his forehead with the same hand and put his hat on again. He said to Valdez, "You have tobacco? For chewing?"

"Cigarette," Valdez said.

The segundo nodded. "All right."

Valdez brought the sack and paper out of his pocket and moved toward the segundo, who stepped forward to meet him. The segundo rolled a cigarette and returned the sack to Valdez, who made one for himself, and the segundo lighted the cigarettes. Valdez stepped back, the cigarette in his mouth, the Remington in his right hand, pointed down.

The segundo said, blowing out smoke and shaking the match, "Tell me something—who you are."

"What difference does it make?" Valdez answered. He looked beyond the segundo to Tanner coming up with his men spread behind him.

"You hit one yesterday," the segundo said. "I think five hundred yards."

"Six hundred," Valdez said.

"What was it you use?"

"Sharps."

"I thought some goddam buffalo gun. You hunt buffalo?"

"Apache," Valdez said.

"Man, I know it. When?"

"When they were here."

"You leave any alive?"

"Some. In Oklahoma now."

"Goddam, you do it," the segundo said. "You know how many of mine you kill?"

"Twelve," Valdez said.

"You count them."

"You better, uh?" Valdez said.

The segundo drew deeply on the cigarette and exhaled slowly. He was looking at Valdez and thinking, How would you like about four of him? All the rest of them could go home. Four of him and no Tanner and they could drive cattle to Mexico and become rich. And then he was thinking, Who would you rather shoot, him or Tanner? It was too bad the two of them couldn't trade places. Tanner liked to put people against the wall. This one knew how to do it. He didn't need a wall. He could kill a man at six hundred yards, and the son of a bitch kept count.

"It's too bad it turns out like this," the segundo said.

"Well," Valdez shrugged. "It will be settled now. It will be finished."

The segundo continued to study him. "Why don't you give him his woman? Tell him you won't do it again."

"It's not his woman now."

The segundo smiled. "Like that."

"Sure, it's up to him. He wants her back, he has to take her."

"You think he can't do it?"

Valdez shrugged again. "If he tries, he's dead. Somebody will get me, there are enough of you. But he still will be dead."

"He don't think that way," the segundo said.

Valdez held his gaze. "What do you think?"

"I believe it." The segundo saw Valdez's gaze lift and he moved to the side, looking over his shoulder to see Frank Tanner coming toward them. The segundo backed away several more steps, but Tanner stopped before reaching him. He was holding a Colt revolver at his side. A man behind Tanner took his horse, and the rest of the men, five of them, spread out, moving to both sides, keeping their eyes on Valdez. R. L. Davis was next to Tanner, a few feet to his right.

Tanner was looking at the Erin woman, who had not moved as he approached. He stared at her and his expression showed nothing, but he was making up his mind.

He said finally, "Come over here next to me."

The woman made no move. "I'm all right where I am."

"You better start thinking straight," Tanner said. "You better have something to tell me when we get home."

"I'm not going home with you."

Tanner took his time. "That's how it is, huh?" His gaze shifted to Valdez. "She better than a Mexican bitch?"

Valdez said nothing.

"If that's how it is, you better tell that whore next to you go get out of the way."

Quietly, Valdez said to her, "Move over a little. Just a little."

Tanner waited. "Have you got something you want to say to me?"

"I've said it," Valdez answered.

Tanner's eyes held on Valdez. He said, "Put this man against the wall over there and shoot him."

He waited and said then, "Emilio!"

"I hear you," the segundo said.

"Take him."

The segundo did not make a move or seem about to speak.

"Number two"—Tanner's voice rose—"I'm telling you something!"

The segundo looked at Tanner now, directly at him. He said, "It's not my woman."

Valdez's eyes shifted to the man, hung there, and returned to Tanner. His hand gripped the Remington lightly, feeling the weight of the gun, the sawed-off barrel hanging at his knee.

Tanner turned his head slowly to the left, to the three men standing off from him, then to the right, to R. L. Davis and the two men beyond him.

"I'm going to give the word," Tanner said.

"Wait a minute!" R. L. Davis said. "I'm no part of this." He saw Tanner looking at him as he edged back a few steps, bumping against his horse and pushing it. "I don't even have a gun."

"I give you mine," the segundo said.

"I don't want one!" Davis was edging back, taking himself out of the group, his eyes holding on the Remington at Valdez's side. "I don't have any fight with him."

In Spanish, the segundo said to the young Mexican on Tanner's left, "Tomás, go home. This isn't yours."

The young man wasn't sure. "I work for him," he said.

"Not anymore. I let you go."

Tanner's head jerked toward the segundo. "What're you telling him?"

"That she's your woman," the segundo said easily. "A man holds his woman or he doesn't. It's up to him, a personal thing between him and the man who took the woman. All these men are thinking, What have we got to do with it?"

"You do what I tell you. That's what you've got to do with it." Tanner glanced both ways and said, "I'm talking to everybody present. Everybody hears me and I'm telling you now to shoot him. Now!"

He looked at his men again, not believing it, seeing them standing watching him, none of them ready to make a move.

"You hear me—I said shoot him!"

Valdez waited in the silence that followed. He waited as

Tanner looked at his men, from one to the next. He drew on the cigarette, finishing it, and dropped it and said, "Hey."

As Tanner turned to him, Valdez said, "I got an idea, Frank," and waited another moment. "You have a gun in your hand. Why don't you shoot me?"

Tanner faced him, the Colt revolver at his side. He stared at Valdez and said nothing, eyes sunken in the shadow of his hat brim, dusty and beard stubbled, still looking like he was made of gristle and hard to kill.

But he's not looking at himself, Valdez was thinking, and it isn't an easy thing to raise and fire a Colt at someone. So he jabbed at Tanner saying, "See if your gun is as good as mine. What do you think of something like that? You and I, that's all, uh? What do you need anybody else for?"

Tanner stood stiffly, no part of him moving.

"Let me say it to you this way," Valdez said. "You give me money for the Lipan woman whose husband was killed or you use the gun. One or the other, right now. Make up your mind."

Tanner's hand tightened on the Colt and his thumb lifted to the hammer. He could feel the move he would make and he was looking squarely at Valdez twenty feet away from him, looking at him dead center where the cartridge belt crossed his chest. The moment was there, *now,* but his gaze flickered to the stubby barrel of the Remington and lingered there and the moment was past. His thumb came off the hammer.

"Not today," Tanner said. "Another time."

Valdez shook his head slowly. "No, that was your time. You get one time, mister, to prove who you are."

"I should have killed you three days ago," Tanner said. "I should have killed you, but I let you go."

"No"—the segundo started past him toward the horses, pausing to take the Colt from Tanner's hand—"three days ago you should have started for Mexico."

"Or paid the Lipan woman," Valdez said. "It wouldn't have cost you so much."

HOMBRE

....

At first I wasn't sure at all where to begin. When I asked advice, this man from the *Florence Enterprise* said begin at the beginning, the day the coach departed from Sweetmary with everybody aboard. Which sounded fine until I got to doing it. Then I saw it wasn't the beginning at all. There was too much to explain at one time. Who the people were, where they were going and all. Also, starting there didn't tell enough about John Russell.

He is the person this story is mainly about. If it had not been for him, we would all be dead and there wouldn't be anybody telling this. So I will begin with the first time I ever saw John Russell. I think you will see why after you learn a few things about him. Three weeks went by before I saw him again and that was the day the coach left Sweetmary. It was in the afternoon, right after they had brought the McLaren girl over from Fort Thomas.

Some things, especially concerning the McLaren girl and also some of my ideas about John Russell at the time, are embarrassing to put on paper. But I was advised to imagine I was telling it to a good friend and not worry about what other people might think. Which is what I have done. If there's anything anybody wants to skip, like innermost thoughts in places, just go ahead.

As for the title, it could be called any one of John Russell's names; he had more than one as you will see. But I think *Hombre*, which Henry Mendez and others called him sometimes and just means *man*, is maybe the best.

For the record, the day the coach left Sweetmary was Tuesday, August 12, 1884. Figure back three weeks if you want to know what day I first met John Russell. It was not at Sweetmary, but at Delgado's Station.

Carl Everett Allen
Contention, Arizona

ONE

Here is where I think it begins—with Mr. Henry Mendez, the Hatch & Hodges Division Manager at Sweetmary and still my boss at the time, asking me to ride the sixteen miles down to Delgado's with him in the mud wagon. I suspected the trip had to do with the company shutting down this section of the stage line; Mr. Mendez would see Delgado about closing his station and take an inventory of company property. But that was only part of the reason.

It turned out I was the one had to take the inventory. Mr. Mendez had something else on his mind. As soon as we got to the station, he sent one of Delgado's boys out to John Russell's place to get him.

Until that day John Russell was just a name I had written in the Division account book a few times during the past year. So many dollars paid to John Russell for so many stage horses. He was a mustanger. He would chase down green horses and harness-break them; then Mr. Mendez would buy what he wanted, and Russell and two White Mountain Apaches who rode for him would deliver the horses to Delgado's or one of the other relay stations on the way south to Benson.

Mr. Mendez had bought maybe twenty-five or thirty from him during the past year. Now, I suspected, he wanted to tell

Russell not to bring in any more since we were shutting down. I
asked Mr. Mendez if that was so. He said no, he had already
done that. This was about something else.

Like it was a secret. That was the trouble with Mr. Mendez when I worked for him. From a distance you could never
tell he was Mexican. He never dressed like one, everything
white like their clothes were made out of bedsheets. He didn't
usually act like one. Except that his face, with those tobacco-
stained looking eyes and drooping mustache, was always the
same and you never knew what he was thinking. When he
looked at you, it was like he knew something he wasn't telling,
or was laughing at you, no matter what it was he said. That's
when you could tell Henry Mendez was Mexican. He wasn't
old. Not fifty anyway.

Delgado's boy got back while we were having some coffee
and said Russell would be here. A little while later we heard
horses, so we went outside.

As we stood there seeing these three riders coming toward
the adobe with the dust rising behind them, Mr. Mendez said to
me, "Take a good look at Russell. You will never see another
one like him as long as you live."

I will swear to the truth of that right now. Though it was not
just his appearance.

The three riders came on, but giving the feeling that they
were holding back some, not anxious to ride right up until they
made sure everything was keno. When Russell pulled up, the
two White Mountain Apaches with him slowed to a walk and
came up on either side of him. Not close, out a ways, as if giving themselves room to move around in. All three of them were
armed; I mean *armed*, with revolvers, with cartridge belts over
their shoulder and carbines, which looked like Springfields at
first.

As he sat there, that's when I got my first real look at John
Russell.

Picture the belt down across his chest with the sun glinting on the bullets that filled most of the loops. Picture a stained, dirty looking straight-brim hat worn almost Indian-fashion, that is, uncreased and not cocked to either side, except his brim was curled some and there was a little dent down the crown.

Picture his face half shadowed by the hat. First you just saw how dark it was. Dark as his arms with the sleeves rolled above his elbows. Dark—I swear—as the faces of the two White Mountain boys. Then you saw how long his hair was, almost covering his ears, and how clean-shaved looking his face was. Right then you suspected he was more to those Apaches than a friend or a boss. I mean he could be a blood relation, no matter what his name was, and nobody in the world would bet he wasn't.

When Mr. Mendez spoke to him you believed it all the more. He stepped closer to John Russell's roan horse, and I remember the first thing he said.

He said, *"Hombre."*

Russell didn't say anything. He just looked at Mr. Mendez, though you couldn't see his eyes in the shadow of his hat brim.

"Which name today?" Mr. Mendez said. "Which do you want?"

Russell answered Mr. Mendez in Spanish then, just a few words, and Mr. Mendez said, in English, "We use John Russell. No symbol names. No Apache names. All right?" When Russell just nodded, Mr. Mendez said, "I was wondering what you decided. You said you would come to Sweetmary in two days."

Russell used Spanish again, more this time, evidently explaining something.

"Maybe it would look different to you if you thought about it in English," Mr. Mendez said and watched him closely. "Or if you spoke about it now in English."

"It's the same," Russell said, all of a sudden in English. In good English that had only a speck of accent, just a faint edge that you would wonder every time you heard him if it really was some kind of accent.

"But it's a big something to think about," Mr. Mendez said. "Going to Contention. Going there to live among white men. To live as a white man on land a white man has given you. To have to speak English to people no matter what language you think in."

"There it is," Russell said. "I'm still thinking all the different ways."

"Sure," Mr. Mendez said. "You could sell the land. Buy a horse and a new gun with some of the money. Give the rest to the hungry ones at the San Carlos Indian agency. Then you got nothing."

Russell shrugged. "Maybe so."

"Or you sell only the herd and grow corn on the land and make *tizwin*, enough to keep you drunk for seven years."

"Even that," Russell said.

"Or you can work the herd and watch it grow," Mr. Mendez said. "You can marry and raise a family. You can live there the rest of your life." He waited a little. "You want some more ways to picture it?"

"I have too many ways now," Russell said. But he didn't sound worried about it.

That didn't satisfy Mr. Mendez. He was trying to convince him of something and kept at it. He said then, "I hear it's a good house."

Russell nodded. "If living there is worth it to you."

"Man," Mendez said, like something good was staring at Russell and he didn't know enough to take it. "What do you want?"

Russell looked down at him. In that unhurried easy way he said, "Maybe a *mescal* if there's some inside, uh?"

Delgado laughed and said something in Spanish. Mr. Mendez shrugged and both of them turned to the adobe.

I was watching Russell though. He dismounted, still holding his carbine, which I now saw was an old .56-56 Spencer, and came right toward me looking at the ground, then looking up quick as he must have sensed me. For a second we were close and I saw his eyes. They had that same tell-nothing-but-know-everything expression as Henry Mendez's eyes. That same Mexican, Indian look. Only John Russell's eyes were blue, light-blue looking in his Indian-dark face. Maybe that doesn't sound like anything, but I'll tell you it gave me the strangest feeling.

The two Apaches carried Springfields, as I had guessed. They held them cradled across one arm and even with the bullet belts and all, they looked kind of funny. Mainly because of their vests and straw hats that were very narrow and turned up all around. They went inside too and I followed.

Only I didn't stay long. Mr. Mendez sent me out to the equipment shed to start the inventory. Then over to see about the feed stores. So it was maybe a half hour before I got back to the main adobe. Five saddle horses along with the mud wagon were standing in front now instead of three.

Inside, I saw Mr. Mendez and John Russell at one end of the long table the stage passengers sat at. Russell's carbine lay on the table, like he never went far without it; another thing that was just like an Apache.

At the bar along the right wall stood his two Apache riders. Down from them were two more men. I didn't look at them good till I sat down next to Mr. Mendez. Right away then I got the feeling something was going on. It was too quiet. Mendez was looking over at the bar; Russell down at his drink, as if thinking or listening.

So I looked at the two men again. I recognized them as hands who rode for a Mr. Wolgast who supplied beef to the reservation up at San Carlos. I would see them in Sweetmary every once in a while and they would most always be drunk. But it was a minute or two before I remembered their names.

One was Lamarr Dean, who was about my age, maybe a year older. The other one's name was Early; he was said to have served time at Yuma Prison.

Delgado poured them a whisky like he'd rather be doing something else. Early, who wore his hat funneled down over his eyes and ordinarily didn't talk much, said, "I guess anybody can come in here."

"If they allow Indians," this Lamarr Dean said. He was looking at the two Apaches. They heard him, you could tell, but didn't pay any attention. Of course not, I realized; they didn't know any English.

The one named Early asked Delgado, "When did they start letting Indians drink?" I didn't hear what Delgado answered.

Lamarr Dean stood with his side against the bar so that he was facing the first Apache. "Maybe they have been drinking *tizwin*," he said. "Maybe that's where they bought the nerve to come in here."

Early said, "It would take a week with *tizwin*."

"They got time," Dean said. "What else do they do?"

"That's *mescal*," Early said then.

Lamarr Dean went on staring. "I guess," he said. He moved toward the first Apache, holding his drink, his elbow sliding along the edge of the bar until he was right next to the Apache. Early stayed where he was.

"Mescal," Lamarr Dean said. "But it's still not allowed. Not even sticky-sweet Mex drinks."

The first Apache, not even knowing what was going on, raised his glass. It was right up to his mouth when Lamarr Dean nudged him, reaching out and pushing him a little, and the *mescal* spilled over the Apache's chin and down the front of his vest. He looked at Lamarr Dean then, not understanding, I guess not sure if it was an accident or what.

"They just can't hold it," Lamarr Dean said. "Nobody knows why, but it's a fact of nature." He raised his whisky right in front of the Apache, as if daring the Apache to try the same thing on him.

That was when Russell stood up. His eyes never left Lamarr Dean, but his right hand closed on the Spencer and it was down at his side as he walked over the few steps to the bar.

Lamarr Dean was facing the Apache, starting to drink, sipping at the whisky to give the Apache all the chance he needed. Like saying come on, nudge my arm and see what happens. Then his chin raised as he started to down the whisky.

Russell was right there. But he didn't nudge him. He didn't ask or tell him to leave the Apache alone. Or say anything like, "If you want to pick on somebody, try me." He didn't give Lamarr a chance to know he was there.

He just swung the barrel of the Spencer up clean and quick and before you had a chance to believe it was happening the barrel shattered the glass right against Lamarr Dean's mouth. Lamarr jumped back, dropping the broken pieces and with blood all over his hand and face.

I think he would have tore into Russell the next second, with his fists or his revolver, but now the Spencer was leveled at his belly, almost touching it. Early had his hand on his gun, but it had happened so fast even he couldn't do anything.

Russell said, "No more, uh?"

Lamarr Dean didn't say anything. I don't think he could talk.

Russell said, "Before you leave, put money down for a *mescal*."

That was John Russell, no older than I was at twenty-one and no more Apache than I was. Except he had lived with them—the wild free ones in the mountains and the wild caught ones up at San Carlos—about half his life and that made the difference. He was perhaps one-part Mexican, according to Mr. Mendez, and three-parts white. But I will go into more of that a little later. Right here I just wanted to tell about the first time I ever saw him.

■ ■ ■

Now, three weeks later, here is where I was advised to begin—
with them bringing the McLaren girl over from Fort Thomas in
an ambulance wagon and the lieutenant taking her right into
the Alamosa Hotel.

I was out in front of the Hatch & Hodges office at the time,
directly across the street, and I got a clear look at the girl even
with all the people around. She was seventeen or eighteen and
certainly pretty. Though maybe pretty wasn't the word, the way
her hair was cut almost as short as a boy's and her face dark
from the sun. But she looked good anyway. Even after living
with Apaches over a month and after all the things they must
have done to her.

Somebody said the girl had been taken by Chiricahuas on a
raid and held four or five weeks before a patrol out of Fort
Thomas surprised their *rancheria* and found her. She had
stayed at Thomas a while and now this officer was to put her on
a stage for home. Some place around St. David.

Only by now there weren't any more southbound stages, and
there hadn't been for over a week. There were notices all over,
but that was like the Army to bring her all the way over to
Sweetmary not knowing Hatch & Hodges had shut down its
stage service. They told the lieutenant over at the hotel, but he
wanted to hear it directly from the company. So he sent one of
the escort soldiers for Henry Mendez who went right over.

I stayed out front hoping to get another look at the girl if she
came out. That's why I was still there when John Russell appeared, which was some fifteen minutes later.

Somebody might laugh, but just for something to do I was
picturing the McLaren girl and I sitting alone in the hotel café.
We were talking and I heard myself say, "It must have been a
very terrible experience, being with those Apaches." Her eyes
stayed on her coffee, and she didn't say anything to that.

So we talked about other things. I heard myself speaking

calmly in a low tone, telling her how I would be looking into some other business now that this office was closing. Go some place else. With no family here there was nothing to keep me. Then I pictured us traveling together. (Do you see how one thing led to another?) But what would we travel in?

That's when I thought of the mud wagon, the light spring coach Mr. Mendez and I had taken to Delgado's that day. It was still here.

I said to the McLaren girl, "Since you're anxious to leave and there's no regular stage, I wonder if you would like to ride along with me?" (Which proves that using the mud wagon was my idea; whether Mr. Mendez agrees or not.)

Then I skipped the part where she says yes and goes and gets her things and all and pictured the two of us in the coach again. It was night and we were traveling south. Above the wind and the rattle sounds I'd hear her start to cry and put my arm around her and lift her chin and say something that would calm her. She'd sniffle and nestle closer, and even with the peculiar haircut I'd know she wasn't any boy.

We might have rode along in that coach the whole night while I just stood there in front of the office. But both the McLaren girl and the coach disappeared the second I saw John Russell. The new John Russell.

He was sitting his roan horse on this side of the street but down a ways. He was watching the hotel, sitting there like he'd always been there. Smoking a cigarette, I remember that too. But the only thing I recognized about him right away was his hat, worn straight and the brim just curled a little.

Now he had on a suit. It was a pretty worn dark gray one, but it fit him all right. You could see that his hair had been cut. Without the hair covering the ears and that shell belt and all he wasn't someone you would stare at. At least not till you saw him close.

That was not till a few minutes later. Until Mr. Mendez

came out of the hotel and Russell nudged his roan up to in front of the office. As he dismounted he looked at me over the saddle and there was that tell-nothing expression, looking at me no different than the way he had looked at Lamarr Dean the moment before he broke a whisky glass against his mouth.

Mr. Mendez was standing there now. He said, "You're going to do it?"

"I'm going there to sell the place," Russell said.

Mr. Mendez seemed to stare at him for awhile, thinking or just looking, I don't know which. Finally he said, "It's up to you. You can be white or Mexican or Indian. But now it pays you to be a white man. To look like a white man for awhile. When you go to Contention, you say, How are you? I'm John Russell. I own the Russell place. Some people will remember you from before; some won't. But they will all know you as John Russell who owns the Russell place. You look at it. If you don't like it, sell it. If you like it, keep it, and see what happens and then decide." Mr. Mendez almost seemed to smile. "Did you know life was that simple?"

"I've learned some things," John Russell said. "That's why I sell it."

He left his roan horse in front and went with Mr. Mendez back across the street to the Alamosa Hotel. Mr. Mendez hadn't bothered to introduce us. In fact he had not bothered to look at me at all. Which was all right.

A little later this Mexican boy who worked for us took Russell's horse around to the stable. I was in the office then, having given up on seeing the McLaren girl again. The boy came in through the back carrying Russell's blanket roll and carbine and put them down on the passenger bench. I remember thinking, What will he do without the Spencer if Lamarr Dean or Early are over there at the Alamosa?

I also remember thinking at the time that dressing like a white man and taking a white man's name wasn't ever going to hide the Apache in him. I don't mean Apache blood. I just mean after the way he had lived, how was he even going to convince anybody he was a white man? He didn't even prefer to speak English. It was things like that gave you the feeling he had no use for white men or our ways.

According to Mr. Mendez he was most likely three-parts white, as I have said, and the rest Mexican on his mother's side. John Russell himself had no memory of his father and only some memory of living in a Mexican village. Probably in Sonora. At that time they say the Apaches were forever raiding the little pueblos and carrying off whatever they needed, clothes, weapons, some women, and sometimes boys young enough to be brought up Apache-style. Which is what must have happened to John Russell. Piecing things together, he must have lived with them about from the time he was six to about age twelve.

Here is where a James Russell, late of Contention, comes in. At that time he owned supply wagons contracted to the Army, and he was at Fort Thomas when this boy who was called *Ishkay-nay* was brought in with some prisoners. The boy was assigned to a work detail under James Russell and that was how the two became friends. Just a month later, when James Russell sold his business and went to settle in Contention, he took the boy with him and gave him his American name, John Russell. Five years or so passed and the boy even went to school there. Then all of a sudden he left and went up to San Carlos and joined the reservation police as if to become Apache again. (Here they called him *Tres Hombres*, which I will try to tell you about later.)

Now we are almost up to the present. He was with the police about three years, mostly up at Turkey Creek and Whiteriver. Then he moved again. Off on his own now as a mustanger. (I guess to break horses you don't have to be halter-broke yourself, because he was pretty good at it Mr. Mendez said.)

A month ago, then, when Mr. James Russell died, the word was passed to John Russell through Mr. Mendez that he had

been left Russell's place outside Contention. Mr. Mendez wanted to put him on a coach and send him down there in style, but
Russell kept backing off. Finally, when he did show up willing,
there were no more stagecoaches. As I have explained.

Hatch & Hodges was leaving Sweetmary partly because
there wasn't enough business from here south; partly because the
railroad was taking too much business other places. But that
day, all of a sudden, you'd never know we were hard up for
business.

First the McLaren girl had come. Then John Russell. Then,
right after he and Mr. Mendez left, a mustered-out soldier from
Thomas came in looking for passage to Bisbee. He was going
to get married in a week and anxious to get there. I told him
how it was and he left, walking over to the hotel.

It wasn't long after that Dr. Favor came.

I had never seen him before, but I had heard of him. So
when he came in and introduced himself, I knew this was Dr.
Alexander Favor, the Indian Agent at San Carlos.

His name was heard because San Carlos was so close, but
not too much. You heard of Indian Agents if they were very
good, like John Clum, or if they were bad and got caught deal-
ing poorly with the Indians for their own personal gain. You
heard when they weren't at the reservation anymore and you
heard of the new man arriving. So I didn't know much about
Dr. Favor. Only that he had been up at San Carlos about two
years and had a wife that was supposed to be very pretty and
about fifteen years younger than he was.

He came in so unexpectedly I probably acted dumb at first.
He stood with his hands and his hat on the counter which sepa-
rated the waiting room from the office part, looking straight at
me and never away. He was a big man, not so tall but heavy,
with kind of reddish-brown hair—what there was of it—and a
finely-kept half-moon beard on his chin. But no mustache. You
have probably seen the style I am talking about.

He knew the stage line had stopped running. But what about hiring a rig and driver? I told him we were out of business, even for hiring. He said, but what was the possibility? We talked about that for a while and that was when I got the idea of using the mud wagon. Not just for him but for the McLaren girl too, and just like before I could see myself sitting in it with her.

That's when I started to get excited about the idea. I wanted to get away from here. Why not in the mud wagon? I could talk to Dr. Favor on the way to Bisbee, which was where he wanted to go, and ask his advice about what business to get into. A man like Dr. Favor would know, and maybe he would even have some good connections. Between that and the idea of seeing the McLaren girl, it sounded better and better and finally I got the Mexican boy, who was out front again, and sent him after Mr. Mendez.

About fifteen minutes passed. Dr. Favor came through the gate at the end of the counter and sat at Mr. Mendez's desk. We didn't talk much and I felt dumb again. Finally Mr. Mendez came in.

He came right through the gate. I introduced them and Mr. Mendez nodded. Dr. Favor didn't rise or even reach out his hand.

He said, "We're talking about hiring a coach."

Mr. Mendez looked at me. "Didn't Carl tell you? This office is closed."

"But you still have a coach here," Dr. Favor said. "He called it a mud wagon."

"That." Mr. Mendez leaned back against the counter. "We move our office records in it when we leave."

"Come back to get them," Dr. Favor said.

I said, "They have to be in Bisbee Friday." That was in three days. I even added, "If they don't get there, it'll be too late."

Mr. Mendez just shrugged. "If I could do something—"

I said, "Why not use the mud wagon and come back? We could do that without any trouble."

Mr. Mendez was probably already mad because I was talking up, but he still looked patient. He said, "And who would drive it?"

"I could do it," I said. Which just came to me that moment.

"Do you think the company would put an inexperienced driver on a run like that?"

"Well," I said, "how do you get experience?"

"All of a sudden you want to be a driver."

"I'm trying to help Dr. Favor. If he has to be in Bisbee, I think the company should see he gets there."

"Within the company's power," Mr. Mendez said, still patient. "I think you and I can discuss this another time, uh?"

"That doesn't help Dr. Favor any."

Dr. Favor said, "What if I'm willing to let him drive?"

"You might also be willing to bring suit if something happens," Mr. Mendez said.

"If I bought the rig?" Dr. Favor said.

But Mr. Mendez shook his head. "It's not mine to sell."

"Then if I paid more than just our fares."

"You're anxious to get there," Mr. Mendez said.

"I thought you understood that."

Mr. Mendez nodded his head to the side. "Isn't that your buggy by the hotel? Use that."

"It's government property," Dr. Favor said. "There's a regulation about using it for private matters."

"We have regulations too."

"How much do you want?" Dr. Favor seemed just as patient as Mr. Mendez.

"Well, if there was a driver here."

"Then it comes down to a driver."

"And horses. We would have to get four, six horses."

"All right, get them."

"But I couldn't take responsibility for them," Mr. Mendez said. "Now there are no change stations working. The same horses would have to go all the way." Mr. Mendez shrugged. "If they don't make it, who pays for them?"

"I buy the horses," Dr. Favor said.

Mr. Mendez started to nod, very slowly, as if he was just understanding something. "You want to get there pretty bad, uh?"

"I have a feeling," Dr. Favor said, "you're going to find a driver." He pushed up out of the chair, his eyes on Mr. Mendez. "If I went over to the hotel now and had supper, that would give you about an hour to find a man and get ready. Say six-thirty."

"Tonight?"

"Why not?"

"I'll see," Mr. Mendez said.

"Do that," Dr. Favor said. He moved through the gate, taking his hat from the counter.

"But I won't promise you," Mr. Mendez said after him. The Indian agent just walked out, like it was settled.

I said, soon as he was gone, "Mr. Mendez, I know I can drive it."

"Driving a stage isn't something you know you can do," Mr. Mendez said.

"I've pulled the teams around from the yard plenty of times. And that mud wagon's lighter than a Concord."

"The horses pull it," he said. "Not you."

We argued some more, and finally I said, "Well, who else do you have?"

"Don't worry about it," he said.

"Well, I am worrying, because I want to go too."

He looked at me closely with those brown-stained eyes not telling anything, and I hoped my face was just as calm and natural.

"To talk to this Favor, uh? Get to know him?"

"Why not?"

"It's all right, Carl."

"I was thinking of some others too," I said. "An ex-soldier who was in here. And there's the McLaren girl."

Mr. Mendez nodded again as if he was thinking. "The McLaren girl. Sure," he said. "And maybe John Russell."

It was all right with me. "That would be five inside," I said.

"Six," Mr. Mendez said.

"Not if I'm driving."

Mr. Mendez shook his head. "You're inside like a passenger. How does that sound?"

"Well," I said, "could I ask who's going to drive it then?"

"I am," Mr. Mendez said. "Who else?"

The way Mr. Mendez decided to go all of a sudden didn't make any sense at all until I thought about it a while. And then I realized it might not have been so all of a sudden at that. He could have seen money in this right off and been leading Dr. Favor on, seeing to make about a month's wages in three days if he kept all the fares; and why wouldn't he? That was one thing.

The other was John Russell being here. I think Mr. Mendez wanted to get him on his way before he had time to change his mind; before he spent another night staring at the ceiling and counting all the reasons why he shouldn't go to Contention. Put him in a coach now and by morning Russell might be used to being close to white people again. But why Mr. Mendez bothered or cared was something else. Maybe because he was Mexican and John Russell was part Mexican. Does that make sense?

There was a lot to do before six-thirty. I had the Mexican boy get his father; they'd take care of the coach and horses. Mr. Mendez said he would go to the hotel for John Russell and the McLaren girl and also try and find the ex-soldier. So he would see me later.

Before he went though I reminded him I was going too, and he paid me my last wages. From then on I was no longer with

Hatch & Hodges. It was a pretty good feeling, even not knowing what I was going to do in life now.

First thing, I went to the boarding house where I lived and
put on my suit. It was pretty old and too small now, making me
look skinnier than I was, but it would be all right for the trip. I
didn't want to buy a new one in Sweetmary. I thought about
buying a gun, but decided against that too; I'd be out of money
before I left. I wrote to my mother who lived up at Manzanita
with her sister, Mrs. R. V. Hungerford, telling her how I was
leaving my position and would write again when I had found
some place I liked. Then I rolled up my things in a blanket and
went out and had something to eat. By the time I got back to
the office it was almost six-thirty.

John Russell was waiting. He was sitting on the bench along
the wall on the left. His blanket roll, with the cartridge belt
wrapped around it and the Spencer inside with part of the barrel and stock showing, was next to him.

I'll admit he gave me a start, because it was dim in the office
and I didn't expect to see anybody. I left my blanket roll by the
door and went around behind the counter and started making
out a passenger list and tickets. Might as well do it right, I
thought. Then it started to feel funny, just the two of us there
and nobody talking.

So I said, "You ready for your stagecoach ride?"

His eyes raised and he nodded. That was all.

"What about your horse?"

"Henry Mendez bought it."

"How much he give you?"

"Ask him," Russell said.

"I just wondered, that's all."

"Ask him," Russell said again.

Why bother? I thought, and went on making out the list. I
put all the names down but the ex-soldier's because I didn't
know his. I just put down Ex-Soldier and never did change it,

even when he came in a couple of minutes later with this canvas bag on his shoulder. He swung it down, bouncing it off the counter, and reached into his coat pocket.

"What's the fare?"

"I guess you saw Mendez," I said, and told him how much.

"I don't know the whyfor," he said. "But I'm for it."

He waited while I tore off one of the orange-colored tickets, then another one. "If any stops are open on the way, show this for meals. Drinks are extra. You hand it in when you reach your destination. The other one's for him." I nodded to Russell. "You want to hand it to him?"

The ex-soldier looked at the ticket as he walked over to the bench. He was a heavy man and his coat was tight-smooth across the back. I would judge him to have been about thirty-seven or -eight. "I see you're going to Contention," he said, handing the ticket to Russell. "I change there for Bisbee. Yesterday I was in the Army. Next week I'm a mining man and the week after I'll have a wife, one already arranged for and waiting. What do you think of that?"

John Russell pulled the blanket roll toward him as the man sat down, propping his feet on his canvas bag. "You saving your lamp oil?" the ex-soldier said to me.

"I guess we can spare some." I came around and put a match to the Rochester lamp that hung from the ceiling. Just then I heard the coach and I said, "Here it comes, boys."

You could hear the jingling, rattling sound coming from the equipment yard next door. Then through the window you could see it—smaller than a Concord and almost completely open with its canvas side-curtains rolled up and fastened—just turning out of the yard, and the next moment the jingling, rattling sound was right out front. Four horses were pulling the mud wagon; two spares were on twenty-foot lines tied to the back end.

The ex-soldier said, "I wouldn't complain if it was an ore wagon all loaded."

"It's mainly just for rainy spells," I explained. "Sometimes a heavy Concord gets mired down; but three teams can pull a mud wagon through about anything."

The Mexican boy and his father were both up on the boot. Then Mendez, who must have just crossed the street, was standing there. "Everybody's going," he said. Then looked at John Russell. "Your saddle is on the coach. Now I go up and get myself ready."

I waited till we heard him on the stairs, then told them how I had offered to drive this run, but now that I was a passenger it would be against the rules. "There's rules about who can ride up with the driver," I said, looking at John Russell and wondering if he had any ideas. But that was all the farther I got.

The man who came in was wearing range clothes and carrying a saddle which he let go of just inside the door and came on, looking straight at me, but not smiling like he was ready to say something friendly.

He was tall by the time he reached the counter, with that thin, stringy look of a rider and the *ching-ching* sound of spurs. Even the dust and horse-smell seemed to be still with him, and he reminded you of Lamarr Dean and Early and almost every one of them you ever saw: all made of the same leather and hardly ever smiling unless they were with their own look-alike brothers. Then they were always loud, loud talking and loud laughing. This one had a .44 Colt on his hip and his hat tipped forward with the brim curled almost to a point, the hat loose on his head but seeming to be part of him.

"Frank Braden," he said. His hands spread out along the edge of the counter.

I said, "Yessir?" as if I still worked for Hatch & Hodges.

"Write it down for that coach out front."

"That's a special run."

"I heard. That's why I'm going on it."

I looked down at the four orange cards on the counter, lining them up evenly. "I'm afraid that one's full-up. Four here and those two. That is all the coach holds."

"You can get another on," he said. Telling me, not asking.

"Well, I don't see how."

"On top."

"No one's allowed to ride with the driver. That's a company rule. I was just telling these boys here, certain people can ride inside, certain people outside."

"You say they're going?" He nodded toward the bench.

"Yessir. Both of them."

He turned without another word and walked over to John Russell with that soft *ching*-ing spur sound.

He said, "That boy at the counter said you got a stage ticket."

John Russell opened his hand on his lap. "This?"

"That's it. You give it to me and you can take the next stage."

"I have to take this one," Russell said.

"No, you want to is all. But it would be better if you waited. You can get drunk tonight. How does that sound?"

"I have to take this one," John Russell said. "I have to take it and I want to take it."

"Leave him alone," the ex-soldier said then. "You come late, you find your own way."

Frank Braden looked at him. "What did you say?"

"I said why don't you leave him alone." His tone changed. All of a sudden it sounded friendlier, more reasonable. "He wants to take this stage, let him take it," the ex-soldier said.

You heard that *ching* sound again as Frank Braden shifted around to face the ex-soldier. He stared at him and said, "I guess I'll use your ticket instead."

The ex-soldier hadn't moved, his big hands resting on his knees, his feet still propped on the canvas bag. "You just walk in," he said, "and take somebody else's seat?"

Braden's pointed hat brim moved up and down. "That's the way it is."

The ex-soldier glanced at John Russell, then over at me. "Somebody's pulling a joke on somebody," he said.

Russell didn't say anything. He had made a cigarette and now he lit it, looking at Braden as he blew the smoke up in the air.

"You think I come in here to kid?" Braden asked the ex-soldier.

"Look here, this boy is going to Contention," the ex-soldier explained, "and I'm going to Bisbee to get married after twelve years of Army. We got places to go and no reason to give up our seats."

"All this *we*," Braden said. "I'm talking to you."

The ex-soldier didn't know what to say. And, even with his size, he didn't know what to do with Braden standing over him and not giving an inch. He glanced at John Russell again, then over to me like he'd thought of something. "What kind of a business you run?" he said. "You let a man walk in here and say he's taking your seat—after paying your fare and all—and the company doesn't do a thing about it?"

"Maybe I better get Mr. Mendez," I said. "He's upstairs."

"I think he ought to know about this," the ex-soldier said and started to rise. Braden stepped in closer and the ex-soldier looked up, almost straight up, and you could see then that he was afraid but trying hard not to show it.

"This is our business," Braden said. "You don't want somebody else's nose stuck in."

The ex-soldier seemed to get his nerve back—I guess because he realized he had to do something—and he said, "We better settle this right now."

Braden didn't budge. He said, "Are you wearing a gun?"

"Now wait a minute."

"If you aren't," Braden said, "you better get one."

"You can't just threaten a man like that," the ex-soldier said. "There are witnesses here seeing you threaten me."

Braden shook his head. "No, they heard you call me a dirty name."

"I never called you anything."

"Even if they didn't hear it," Braden said, "I did."

"I never said a word!"

"I'm going to walk out on the street," Braden said. "If you don't come out inside a minute, I'll have to come back in."

That's all there was to it. The ex-soldier stared up at Braden, the cords in his neck standing out, his hands spread and clamped on his knees. And even as he gave up, as he let himself lean back against the wall, he was holding on, knowing he had backed down and it was over, but doing it gradually so we wouldn't see the change come over him. Braden held out his hand. The ex-soldier gave him his ticket. Then he picked up his bag and walked out.

Braden didn't even offer to pay him for the ticket. He watched the ex-soldier till he was gone, then walked over to his saddle and carried it out to the coach. I could feel him right outside, but it bothered me that I hadn't done anything. Or Russell hadn't. I motioned him over to the counter and he came, taking his time and stepping out his cigarette.

"Listen," I said, "shouldn't we have done something?"

"It wasn't my business," Russell said.

"But what if he had taken your ticket?" I stared at him and this close you could see that he was young. His face was thin and you saw those strange blue-colored eyes set in the darkness of his skin.

Russell said, "You would have to be sure he was making it something to kill over."

"He made it plain enough," I said.

"If you were sure," Russell said, "and if the ticket was worth it to you, then you'd do something to keep it."

"But I don't think that soldier even had a gun."

Russell said, "That's up to him if he doesn't carry one." Even the way he said it made me mad; so calm about it.

"He would have helped you and you know it," I said.

"I don't know it," Russell said. "If he did, it would be up to him. But it wouldn't be any of his business."

Just like that. He walked back to the bench and just then Mendez came in. Now he was wearing a coat and hat and carrying a maleta bag and a sawed-off shotgun.

"Time," Mendez said, sounding almost happy about it. He came through the gate to get something from his desk. That gave me the chance to tell what Braden had done, sounding disgusted as I told it so Mendez would have no doubt what I thought about Braden's trick.

"Then we still have six," Mendez said. That was all.

And that was the six—seven counting Mendez—who left Sweetmary that Tuesday, August 12.

Nothing much happened just before we left. Russell asked to ride up with Mendez, saying they could talk about things.

"Talk," Mendez said. "You can't hear yourself." He pushed Russell toward the coach. "Go on. See what it's like."

Then there was a talk between Mendez and Dr. Favor. Probably about all the other people in what was supposed to be a hired coach. I heard Mendez say, "I haven't seen any money yet." They talked a while and finally must have settled it.

The seating inside was as follows: Russell, the McLaren girl, and I riding backwards, across from Braden, Mrs. Favor, and Dr. Favor. Which was perfect. We sat there a while, almost dark inside after Mendez dropped the side curtains, not saying anything, feeling the coach move up and down on its leather thorough braces as the boy who worked for us put the traveling bags in the rear end boot and covered them with a canvas.

I tried to think of something to say to the McLaren girl, hardly believing she was next to me. But I decided to wait a while before speaking. Let her get comfortable and used to everybody.

So I just started picturing her. She was too close to look right at. But I could feel her there. You had the feeling, when you pictured her, that she looked like a boy more than a woman. Not her face. It was a girl's face with a girl's eyes. It was her body and the way she moved; the thinness of her body and the way she had walked up the hotel steps. You had the feeling she would run and swim. I could almost see her come out of the water with her short hair glistening wet and pressed to her forehead. I could see her smiling too, for some reason.

Mrs. Favor was watching the McLaren girl, staring right at her, so I had a chance to look at Mrs. Favor. Audra was her name, and she was nice looking all right: thin, but still very womanly looking, if you understand me. That was the thing about her. If anybody ever says *woman* to me, like "You should have seen that woman," or, "Now there was a woman for you," I would think of Audra Favor, thinking of her as Audra, too, not as Mrs. Favor, the Indian Agent's wife.

That was because one got the feeling she was not with her husband. Dr. Favor was older than she was, at least fifteen years older, which put her about thirty, and he could have been just another man sitting there. That would be something to watch, I decided. To see if she paid any attention to him.

Frank Braden, I noticed, looked right at Mrs. Favor. With his head turned his face was close to hers and he stared right at her, maybe thinking nobody could see him in the dimness, or maybe not caring if they did.

Just before we left, I raised up to straighten my coat and sneaked a look at the McLaren girl. Her eyes were lowered, not closed, but looking down at her hands. Russell, his hat tilted forward a little, was looking at his hands too. They were folded on his lap.

What would these people think, I wondered, if they knew he'd been living like an Apache most of his life, right up until a little while ago? Would it make a difference to them? I had a feeling it would. I didn't think of myself as one of them, then; now I don't see why I should have left myself out. To tell the truth, I wasn't at all pleased about Russell sitting in the same coach with us.

When the coach started to roll I said, "Well, I guess we'll be together for a while."

TWO

There wasn't much talking at all until Mrs. Favor started after the McLaren girl. I saw her watching the girl for the longest time and finally she said, "Are those Indian beads?"

The McLaren girl looked up. "It's a rosary."

"I don't know why I thought they were Indian beads," Mrs. Favor said. Her voice soft and sort of lazy sounding, the kind of voice that most of the time you aren't sure if the person is kidding or being serious.

"You might say they are Indian beads," the girl said. "I made them."

"During your experience?"

Dr. Favor said, "Audra," very low, meaning for her to keep quiet.

"I hope I didn't remind you of something unpleasant," Mrs. Favor said.

Braden, I noticed, was looking at the McLaren girl too. "What happened?" he said.

The McLaren girl did not answer right away, and Mrs. Favor leaned toward the girl. "If you don't want to talk about it, I can understand."

"I don't mind," the McLaren girl said.

Braden was still looking at her. He said again, "What happened?"

"I thought everybody knew," the McLaren girl said.

"Well," Braden said. "I guess I've been away."

"She was taken by Apaches," Mrs. Favor said. "With them, how long, a month?"

The McLaren girl nodded. "It seemed longer."

"I can imagine," Mrs. Favor said. "Did they treat you all right?"

"As well as you could expect, I guess."

"I suppose they kept you with the women."

"Well, we were on the move most of the time."

"I mean when you camped."

"No, not all the time."

"Did they—bother you?"

"Well," the McLaren girl said, "I guess the whole thing was kind of a bother, but I hadn't thought of it that way. One of the women cut my hair off. I don't know why. It's just now starting to grow back."

"I meant did they *bother* you?" Mrs. Favor said.

Braden was looking right at her. "You can talk plainer than that," he said.

Mrs. Favor pretended she didn't hear him. She kept her eyes on the McLaren girl and you could see what she was trying to get at. Finally she said, "You hear so many stories about what Indians do to white women."

"They do the same thing to them they do to Indian women," Braden said, and after that no one spoke for a minute. All the sounds, the rattling and the wind hissing by, were outside. Inside it was quiet.

I kept thinking that somebody ought to say something to change the subject. In the first place I felt uneasy with the talk about Apaches and John Russell sitting there. Second, I thought Braden certainly shouldn't have said what he did with ladies present, even if Mrs. Favor had started it. I thought Dr. Favor would say something to her again, but he didn't. He could have been seven hundred miles away, his hand holding the side curtain open a little and staring out at the darkness.

I would like to have said that I thought Mr. Braden should be reminded that there were ladies present, but instead I said, "I don't know if the ladies enjoy this kind of talk very much." That was a mistake.

Braden said, "What kind of talk?"

"I mean about Apache Indians and all."

"That's not what you meant," Braden said.

"Mr. Braden." The McLaren girl, her hands folded in her lap, was looking directly at him. "Why don't you just be quiet for a while?"

Braden was surprised, as all of us were, I suppose. He said, "You speak right up, don't you?"

"I don't see any other way," she said.

"I was talking to that boy next to you."

"But it concerned me," the McLaren girl said. "So if you'd be so kind as to shut up, I'd appreciate it."

That was something for her to say. The only trouble was, it egged Braden on. "A nice girl talking like that," he said, watching her. "Maybe you lived with them too long. Maybe that's it. You live with them a while and you forget how a white person talks."

I couldn't see Russell's face or his reaction to all this. But a minute later I could see what was going to happen, and I began thinking every which way of how to change the subject.

"A white woman," Mrs. Favor said, "couldn't live the way they do. The Apache women rubbing skins and grinding corn, their hair greasy and full of vermin. The men no better. All of them standing around or squatting, picking at themselves and the dogs sniffing them. They even eat the dogs sometimes."

She was watching the McLaren girl again, leading up to something, but I wasn't sure what. "I wonder," she said, "if a woman could fall into their ways and after a while it wouldn't bother her. Like eating with your fingers. Or do you suppose you could eat a dog and not think anything of it?"

Here's where you could see it coming.

John Russell said, "What if you didn't have anything else to eat?" This was the first time he'd spoken since we left Sweetmary. His voice was calm, but still there was an edge to it.

Mrs. Favor looked from the McLaren girl to Russell.

"I don't care how hungry I got. I know I wouldn't eat one of those camp dogs."

"I think," John Russell said, "you have to know the hunger they feel before you can be sure."

"The government supplies them with meat," Mrs. Favor said. "Every week or so I'd see them come in for their beef ration. And they're allowed to hunt. They can hunt whenever their rations are low."

"But they are always low," Russell said. "Or used up, and there's not game enough to take care of everybody."

"You hear all kinds of stories of how the Indian is oppressed by the white man," Dr. Favor said. I was surprised that he had been listening and seemed interested now.

He said, "I suppose you will always hear those stories as long as there is sympathy for the Indian's plight, and that's a good thing. But you have to live on a reservation for a time, like San Carlos, to see that caring for Indians is not a simple matter of giving them food and clothing."

He was watching John Russell all the while and seemed to be picking his words carefully. "You see all the problems then that the Interior Department is faced with," he said. "The natural resentment on the part of the Indians, their distrust, their reluctance to cultivate the soil."

"Having to live where they don't want to live," John Russell said.

"That too," Dr. Favor agreed. "Which can't be helped for the time being." His eyes were still on Russell. "Do you happen to know someone at San Carlos?"

"Many of them," Russell said.

"You've visited the agency?"

"I lived there. For three years."

"I didn't think I recognized you," Dr. Favor said. "Did you work for one of the suppliers?"

"On the police," Russell said.

Dr. Favor didn't say anything. I couldn't see his expression in the dimness, only that he was still looking at Russell.

Then his wife said, "But the police are all Apaches."

She stopped there, and all you heard was the rattling and creaking and wind rushing past and the muffled pounding of the horses.

I thought, Now he'll explain it. Whether he thinks they'll believe him or not, at least he'll say something.

But John Russell didn't say a word. Not one single word. Maybe he's thinking how to explain it, I thought. There was no way of knowing that. But he must have been thinking something and I would have given anything to know what it was. How he could just sit there in that silence was the hardest thing I have ever tried to figure out.

Finally Mrs. Favor said, "Well, I guess you never know."

You never know what? I thought. You never know a lot of things. Still, it was pretty plain what she meant.

Braden was looking at me. He said, "You let anybody on your stage?"

"I don't work for the company anymore," I answered. I'll admit, it was a weak-sister thing to say, but why should I stick up for Russell?

This wasn't any of my business. He couldn't help the ex-soldier, saying it was none of his business. All right, this was none of my business. If he wanted to act like an uncivilized person—which is what he must be and you could see it clearer all the time—then let him alone. Let him act any way he wanted.

I wasn't his father. He was full grown. So let him talk for himself if he had anything to say.

But maybe he even thought he really was Apache. That had never occurred to me before. It would have been something to look into his mind. Not for long. Not for more than a few minutes; just time enough to look around with his eyes, around and back at things that had happened to him. That would tell you a few things.

I started to think of the stories Henry Mendez had told about Russell, piecing little bits of it together now.

How he had been Juan something living in a Mexican pueblo before the Apaches came raiding and took some of the women and children. How he had been named *Ish-kay-nay* and brought up by these Chiricahuas and made the son of Sonsichay, one of the sub-chiefs of the band. Five years with them and he must have learned an awful lot.

Then, after that, living in Contention with Mr. James Russell until he was about sixteen. He had gone to school there. And he had almost killed a boy in a fight. Maybe there was a good reason he did it. But he had left soon after, so maybe there wasn't a good reason; maybe he just couldn't be taught anything.

Then the most interesting part. How John Russell got his next name, *Tres Hombres*.

He had been with the mule packers on that campaign of the Third Cavalry's, chasing down into Mexico after the bands of Chato and Chihuahua, and he got his new name in a meadow high in the Sierra Madre, two days west of the village of Tesorababi.

He had gone out looking for these mule packers who had wandered off the trail, hunting them all day and finding them, three *mozos* and eighteen mules, an hour before dark and a moment before the sudden gunfire came out of the canyon walls and caught them and ended four of the mules.

John Russell, who was sometimes Juan or Juanito, but more often *Ish-kay-nay* to the older ones of the Apache Police, shot six more of the mules in the moments that followed and he and the *mozos* laid behind the dead mules all night and all the next day. The Apaches, nine or ten of them, came twice. Running and screaming the first time they left two dead before they could creep back out of range of John Russell's Spencer. That was the evening of the first day. They came again at dawn, silently through the rocks with their bodies mud-streaked and branches of mesquite in their headbands. They said that John Russell, with the Spencer steadied on the neck of a dead mule, waited until he was sure. He fired seven times with the Spencer, taking his time as they came at him, and emptied his Colt revolver at them as they ran. Maybe two more were hit.

The packers, their eyes closed and their bodies tight against the mules while the firing was going on, smiled at John Russell and laughed with relief at their fear when it was over. And, when they returned to the main column, they told how this one had fought like three men against ten times as many of the barbarians. From then on, among the Apache Police at San Carlos, the trackers at Fort Apache and Cibucu, John Russell was known as *Tres Hombres.*

But knowing all this wasn't the same as seeing things through his eyes. Maybe his past relations with white people explained why he acted the way he did, why he didn't speak up now, but I'm not sure. Maybe you can see it.

It was colder later on, so I got the two robes from the floor and handed one of them to Dr. Favor. He took it and his wife spread it out so it would cover Frank Braden too. I unfolded the other robe for our seat. There was the soft clicking sound of the McLaren girl's beads as she raised her hands. She gathered the end of the robe close to her, wedging it against her leg and not offering any of it to John Russell. I even had the feeling she had moved closer to me, but I wasn't sure.

I heard Dr. Favor say something to his wife; the sound not the words. She told him not to be silly. I asked the McLaren girl if she was comfortable. She said, yes, thank you. Mostly though, no one spoke. It was a lot colder and the canvas curtains, that were all the way down now, would be flat one minute, then snap and billow out with the wind and through the opening you could see the darkness and shapes now and then going by alongside the road.

Frank Braden had eased lower in the seat and his head was very close to Mrs. Favor's. He said something to her, a low murmur. She laughed, not out loud, almost to herself, but you could hear it. Her head moved to his and she said one word or maybe a couple. Their faces were close together for a long time, maybe even touching, and yet her husband was right there. Figure that one out.

We came in to Delgado's Station with the slowing, braking sound of the coach coming off the slope that stretched out toward a wall of trees and the adobes that showed faintly against the trees. The coach kept rolling slower and slower and slower, with the sound of the horses getting clear and heavy, and finally we stopped. We sat there in silence and when Mrs. Favor said, "Where are we?" in just a whisper, it sounded loud inside that coach in the darkness. No one answered until we heard Henry Mendez outside.

"Delgado!" he yelled.

Then close on it came the sound of his steps and the door opened. "Delgado's Station," Mendez said. He stood there holding his leather bag. Beyond him, a man was coming out of the adobe carrying a lantern.

"Mendez?" The man raised the lantern.

"Who else?" Mendez said. "You still got horses?"

"For a few more days," Delgado, the stationmaster, answered.

"Change them for these."

"You got a stage?"

"A long story," Mendez said. "Get your woman to make coffee."

Delgado was frowning. He wore pants with striped suspenders over his underwear. "How do I know you're coming?"

"Just move your people," Mendez said. He turned to the

coach again. "You wash at the bench by the door. You follow the path around back for other things." He offered his hand and Mrs. Favor got out. Then the McLaren girl.

"Twice in one night," Delgado said. "An hour ago we are in bed and three men come by."

"You should have stayed up," Mendez said.

Mr. Favor was just getting out of the coach. "Did you know them?" he asked.

"Some riders."

"But did you know them?"

Delgado looked thoughtful. "I don't know. I think they work for Mr. Wolgast."

"Is that usual," Dr. Favor said, "them coming by this time of night?"

"Man, it happens," Delgado said. "People go by here."

By the time I went around back and came out again, just Mendez and Russell were standing there. Mendez took a bottle that looked like brandy out of his leather bag and both of them had a long drink.

Two boys, in shirts and pants but barefooted, came out of the adobe. Both of them smiled at Mendez and one of them called, "Hey, Tio, what have you got?"

"Something for your grease pails," Mendez said, "and the need of clean horses." The boys ran off again, around the adobe, and Mendez turned to John Russell again.

"How do you like a mud wagon?"

Russell said something in Spanish.

"How do you like it in English?" Mendez said.

"That again," Russell said.

"Practice, uh? Then you get good."

"Maybe if I don't speak it's better."

"And what does that mean?" Mendez asked.

Russell didn't say anything. One of the boys came running out again with a bucket and Mendez said, "Paint them good, *chico*."

"This costs more at night," the boy said, still smiling, as if still smiling from before.

"I'll pay you with something," Mendez said. He took a swipe at the boy with the leather bag, but the boy got past him. Then he offered the brandy to Russell again. "For the dust," he said. "Or whatever reason you want."

While Russell was taking a drink, Mendez saw me and offered me one, so I joined them and had a swallow. It was all right, except it was so hot. I don't know how they took the big swigs they did. Mendez took his turn then handed the bottle to Russell and went into the adobe.

The Mexican boy with the grease pail was working on the front wheels now. The other boy had unhitched the lead team and was taking the horses off. We watched them a while. Then I said, "How come you didn't tell them?"

He looked at me, holding the bottle. "Tell them what?"

"That you're not what they think."

His eyes looked at me another second. Then he took a drink of the brandy.

"You want to go in?" I said. He just shrugged.

We went in then—into a low-ceilinged room that was lighted by one lantern hanging from a beam; the lantern had smoked and there was still the oil smell of it in the room.

The Favors and the McLaren girl and Braden were sitting at the main table, a long plank one in the middle of the room. Mendez stood there like he had been talking to them. But he moved away as we came in and motioned us over to a table by the kitchen door. Delgado's wife came out with a pot of coffee, but went over to the main table before pouring us some. Mendez waited, looking at Russell all the while, until she went out to the kitchen again.

"They think you're Apache," he said.

Russell didn't say anything. He was looking at the brandy bottle as if reading the small print. Mendez picked up the brandy and poured some of it in his coffee.

"You hear what I said?"

"Does it make a difference?" Russell said then.

"Dr. Favor says you shouldn't ride in the coach," Mendez said. "That's the difference."

Russell's eyes raised to Mendez. "They all say that?"

"Listen, you wanted to ride with me before."

"Do they all say I shouldn't be in the coach?"

Mendez nodded. "Dr. Favor said they agreed to it. I said this boy isn't Apache, did you ask if he was? Did you ask him anything? But this Favor says he isn't going to argue about it."

Russell kept looking at Mendez. "What did you say?"

"Well—I don't know," Mendez said. "Why have people unhappy? Why not just"—he shrugged—"let them have their way? It isn't a big thing. I mean I don't know if it's something worth making trouble about. He's got this in his mind now and we don't have time to convince him of the truth. So why should we let it worry us, uh?"

"What if I want to ride in the coach?" Russell said.

"Listen, you wanted to ride with me before. Why all of a sudden you like it inside now?"

It was the first time I ever saw Mendez look worried, like something was happening that he couldn't handle or have an answer for. He drank some of his coffee, but looked up quickly, holding the cup, as Braden and Dr. Favor rose from the table. Braden went outside. Dr. Favor went over to the bar where Delgado was, and Mendez seemed to relax a little and sip his coffee.

"Is it worth arguing about?" Mendez said. "Getting people upset and angry? Sure, they're wrong. But is it easier to convince them of it or just forget about it? You understand that?"

"I'm learning," Russell said.

Right there, again, I'd like to have seen what was going on in his mind, because you certainly couldn't tell from his tone. He had such a quiet way of speaking you got the feeling nothing in the world would ever bother him.

While we were still sitting there, Dr. Favor motioned Mendez over to the bar where he and Delgado were. Mendez stood there talking to them for a long time, while we finished our coffee and had another. Finally Mendez came back. He didn't sit down but took a drink of the brandy.

"Dr. Favor wants to go another way," Mendez said. "The road down past the old San Pete Mine."

It was a road Hatch & Hodges had used years before when the mine was still in operation. It ran fifteen or so miles east of the main road, through foothills and on up into high country past the mine, then it joined the present main road again on the way to Benson. But I had never heard of anyone taking it these days. The country through there was wild and climbing, harder to travel over. That's why the new road had been put through after the mine shut down. The only thing you could say about the old road was it was shorter.

But was that reason to take it?

Mendez said why not? Delgado was sure the rest of the stations along the main road had already shut down. At least all their change horses had been moved south by now. Delgado was the only one left with any and his would be gone in a few days. If we have only six horses and there are no more stations, Mendez said. Why not go the short way?

That made sense. We'd have to bring extra food and water, though. Mendez agreed to that. He said as long as Dr. Favor was paying for most of this, why not keep him happy? (Henry Mendez seemed very anxious to keep people happy.)

"Maybe he's a little worried too," Mendez said. "He was talking to Delgado again about those people who came by here. What did they look like? Did they say where they were going? Things like that."

"If he thinks they plan to hold us up," I said, "they couldn't. They wouldn't know a stage was coming by here tonight."

"I told him that," Mendez said. "He said, 'If there is a possibility of being stopped, we should take precautions.' I said,

'Maybe, but, if this was the regular stage, we wouldn't even be talking about it.' "

"Maybe he is really worried," I said.

Mendez nodded. "Like something's after him. And he knows it."

A little later, after Mendez had seen about the provisions and water bags, we got moving again. Frank Braden was already in the coach asleep with his feet on the seat across from him. We just let him be. There was room enough with John Russell up on the boot now.

Soon we were alone in the night with the rumbling and creaking sounds. We turned off the road about two miles south of Delgado's and went through a mesquite thicket with the branches scraping both sides of the coach. Then this trail opened up and you could feel it beginning to climb. We would move through trees, in and out of close darkness, all the time following the winding, climbing road that led on and on, two rutted tracks that were overgrown but I guess still visible to Mendez.

About three hours out of Delgado's, Mendez and Russell changed the teams, giving the two spares a turn in the harness, and watering them. I was the only one who got out of the coach, though I'm sure Dr. Favor was awake too. I had a drink of water from Mendez's canteen (this was kept in the driver's boot; three hide bags of water on the back end were for the passengers and the horses) and then we were off again.

I went to sleep after that, wondering for the longest time if the McLaren girl would say anything if I was to put my arm around her. I never did find out.

With the first signs of daylight and down out of a winding, steep-sided canyon, we came to the abandoned San Pete mine. Mendez and Russell were standing there as we got out, everybody stretching, feeling the stiffness from being cramped up so long, and looking around at the company buildings.

The ones near us were built against the slope so that the front verandas were on stilts and high as a second floor. Out across the canyon the mine works were about two hundred yards off: the crushing mill part way up the slope, the ore tailings that humped in hogbacks down from the mine shaft way up higher. Braden was looking at Mendez. "This isn't the stage road," he said.

"We took a different way," Mendez answered. He was at the back untying one of the waterskins.

"What do you mean a different way?"

I noticed John Russell step away from the horses. He watched Braden move toward Mendez who was lifting the waterskin to his shoulder.

"You take any road you feel like?"

"Talk to Dr. Favor," Mendez said.

"I'm talking to you."

Mendez had started for the building, but he stopped. "The others agreed on it," he said. "You were asleep. But I thought, if he wants to come with us so bad then this is all right with him."

Braden kept watching him. "Where does it lead?"

"Same places," Mendez answered. He took the waterskin under the veranda and came out again stretching, looking up at the sky that was still dull though streaked with traces of sunlight above the far end of the canyon. "We eat now," Mendez said. "Then rest for two hours."

Dr. Favor said, "If you're thinking of us—"

"More of the horses," Mendez said. "And me."

We ate breakfast under the veranda of the main company building, some of the bread and cold meat and coffee Mendez had brought. And after Mendez took his blanket roll to the next house, the only one besides the main one that still had a roof. John Russell went with him and they slept for a couple of hours.

So there was nothing to do but wait during that time. The

mud wagon stood alone with the horses grazing farther down the canyon where there was grass and some owl clover. After a while Frank Braden walked out past the coach, gazing at the slope above the mine works, then looking up-canyon, the way he had come. He went on getting smaller and smaller as he crossed the canyon and got up by the crushing mill. He kept going, finally reaching what looked like an assay shack high up by the mine shaft and you couldn't see him any more. I wondered if he was waiting for Mrs. Favor to come up. That or he was just restless.

Whichever, Braden was back in plenty of time. He had calmed down and he asked Mendez how long it would take to reach Benson. Mendez told him this way was shorter than the stage road, but we had the horses to consider. So maybe it would take just as long, arriving in Benson sometime tomorrow morning if the road was all right and if nothing happened.

Well, we left the San Pete mine before eight o'clock and by midnight the first *if* came true.

The trouble was not in following the road, a matter of whether or not the road was "all right." There was just no road to follow. We crossed a shallow arroyo that came down out of the high rocks, and on the other side, where the road should have continued, there was no trace of it.

Wind and rock slides and flash floods had worn the road away or covered it or wiped it clean from the slope. Mendez had no choice. He took the coach down the arroyo, bucking, fighting down through the yellow *palo verdes* that grew along the banks waiting for water, then south again, out into the flat brush country to circle the dry washes and rock formations that extended out from the slopes.

The land lay dead in the heat of the sun, bone dry and thick with greasewood and prickly pear and tall saguaro that looked like fence posts growing wild. Henry Mendez did a good job driving through this, but it took forever. You would look ahead and see an outcropping of rock or a scattering of Joshua trees that looked only a few hundred yards off, but it would take even an hour to reach them and after passing them there would be other marks on the land, like a strangely shaped giant saguaro or more Joshuas or yucca, that would take forever to reach and finally pass. There was nothing to look at, nothing to look forward to.

We stopped to alternate the horses once during the morning, discovering only two waterskins on the back end. We had left one, more than half full, at the San Pete mine.

We stopped again at noon, all of us standing by the coach waiting for the coffee water to boil, Mendez unhitching the teams and feeding them from morrals, Mendez probably waiting for one of the passengers to say this was crazy and why didn't we go back to the stage road? Lose a day, but at least not have to put up with this. But no one said it.

It was strange. There was Mrs. Favor saying it was hot, saying it different ways, but not seeming to mind it. She would glance now and then at the McLaren girl, probably still wondering what the Indians did to her, then look at Braden who had turned quiet today and seemed a different person, as if the effects of whisky had worn off him (though I am not saying he showed any signs of drunkenness the day before). There was the McLaren girl, seeming to be the most patient, aside from Russell (how could it bother him to be out here), and Dr. Favor who watched Mendez, trying to hurry him with his eyes. Nobody asked Mendez if we might get lost or break down. Nobody seemed worried at all. Not even about having left some of our water behind at the San Pete.

We went on, and it was afternoon before we got out of that flat country. Mendez saw the road again up on the slope, a trace of it cutting through the brush, and headed for it. You could see the hills getting bigger and clearer as we approached, shadowed and dark with brush and washes, but up above the peaks looked bare and silent in the sunlight.

We got up to the road and followed it easily for a while, but then it started to climb again, getting higher up into the hills, and finally Mendez pulled in the team.

He leaned down and said, "Everybody takes a nice walk. To the top of the grade."

We got out, all of us looking up, seeing a pretty steep section ahead. Russell was already walking up it, I guess making sure there weren't any washouts we couldn't see from here. The slope wasn't too steep, but Mendez, you could tell, was thinking of the horses.

So we waited until the coach and trailing horses were past us a ways and then started up. Dr. Favor took his wife's arm as if to help her walking, but I think it was so she wouldn't wander off. Frank Braden stood there to make a cigarette, so I fell in with the McLaren girl, thinking hard of something to say. But I didn't have to think for more than a few steps.

She said, "He doesn't look Apache, does he?" as if she'd started right in the middle of her thoughts.

But even that abruptly I knew she was talking about Russell. No question about it. She was squinting a little in the sunlight, looking at him way up on the road.

"You should have seen him a few weeks ago," I said.

She looked at me, waiting for me to explain, and I was a little sorry I'd said it. Still, it was a fact.

"He looked like any other Indian on Army pay."

"Then he *is* Apache?"

"Well, maybe you can't answer that yes or no."

She was frowning a little. "Mr. Mendez said he isn't. That's what I don't understand."

"Well, he wasn't born one. But he's lived with them so long, I mean by his own choice, that maybe he is one by now."

"But why," she said, "would anybody *want* to be one?"

"That's it," I said. "Wanting to be one is just as bad as being one. Maybe worse."

"But wanting to live the way they do," she said.

"You'd have to see things with his eyes to understand that."

"I think I'd be afraid to," she said.

I wanted to say that I didn't think she'd be afraid of anything after what she'd been through, but then thought it best to stay wide of that subject. It could be embarrassing for her. She had talked a little about it in the coach and hadn't seemed embarrassed, but still there could be touchy things. It was like being with a person who has a great big nose or something. You don't want to get caught looking at the nose or even saying the word. (I hope no one reading this who might have a big nose will take offense. I wasn't making fun of noses.)

The trailing horses were still on the grade, but the coach had passed over the crest and stopped. You could only see the top part of it at first. The road leveled into pinyon and a lot of brush, and on the right side, slanting down at the coach, was a steep cutbank about seven or eight feet high.

"I guess we can get in again," the girl said.

I heard her, but I was watching Mendez. He was looking up at the top of the bank.

We walked around the trailing horses and I looked up there too. My first thought was, what is Russell doing sitting up there? And where did he get the rifle?

Then I saw Russell, not on the cutbank but beyond the Favors and up by the teams. Near him, at the banked side of the road, was another man, holding a revolver. I guess the McLaren girl saw them the same time I did, but she didn't let out a peep.

What is there to say, for that matter? You walk up a road out in the middle of nowhere and there are two armed men waiting for you. Even though you know something is wrong, you act as if this happens every day and twice on Sunday. I mean you don't get excited or act surprised. You just hold yourself in and maybe they will go away if you don't admit they are there. You don't think at the time: I am afraid. You are too busy acting natural.

The man on the bank come down to the edge and squatted there holding the rifle (it was a Henry) on us until we were up even with the coach. Then he jumped down to the road, almost falling, and as he stood up I recognized him at once.

It was the one named Lamarr Dean who rode for Mr. Wolgast. And the other one up by Russell, sure enough, was Early. The same two who had been at Delgado's the first time I ever saw John Russell.

What if they recognize him, I thought. Not—what's going on? Or what are they doing here? But—what if they recognize him? I couldn't help thinking that first because I remembered so well how Russell had broken that whisky glass against Lamarr Dean's mouth. Lamarr Dean must have remembered it even better. But he hadn't recognized him. Early hadn't either, else he wouldn't have just been standing there holding that long-barreled revolver.

Mendez, looking down at Lamarr Dean, said, "You better think before you do something."

"Step down off there and don't worry about it," Lamarr Dean said. Mendez climbed down and Lamarr Dean looked over toward us. He waited; I didn't know why until Braden came up past us and Lamarr Dean's eyes followed him. He said, "We like to not made it."

"I kept thinking," Braden said, "they got some catching up to do once they find the way."

"When you didn't come by the main road," Lamarr Dean said, "we went back to Delgado's early this morning. I said to him, 'Are we hearing things or was that a coach passed us last night?' He said, 'You must have been hearing things; there was a coach but it wasn't on the main road.' 'Which way did it go?' I said and that was when he told me you'd taken this other way and I'll tell you we done some riding."

I kept looking at Braden all the time Lamarr Dean was talking. Maybe you aren't surprised now why Braden took the stage in the first place and was so anxious to be on it when we left Sweetmary. It is easy to think back and say I knew it all the time. But I'll tell you I couldn't believe it at first. Braden was not a person you liked, but he was one of us, a passenger like everybody else, and, when he showed himself to be part of this holdup, it must have surprised the others as much as it did me. Though at the time I didn't look to see their reaction. Too much was going on.

Early came over, not saying anything, his face dark with beard growth. He was prodding Russell ahead of him.

Then another man appeared. He looked like a Mexican and wore a straw hat. He was mounted and walked his horse out of the trees, leading two other saddled horses, and stood there in front of the teams. I noticed he wore two .44 revolvers.

Lamarr Dean stood with his hand through the lever of the Henry, his finger on the trigger, but the barrel pointed down and almost touching the ground.

"Old Dr. Favor's pretending he don't see us," Lamarr Dean said.

He moved me aside and motioned the McLaren girl over against the cutbank. "You all spread out so I can see my old friend." Dean was looking directly at Dr. Favor then. "Things start to close in on you?" he asked.

"I'm afraid you're beyond me," Dr. Favor said, though not sounding surprised.

"Ahead of you," Lamarr Dean said. "I've seen this coming for two, three months."

"You've seen what coming?"

"Frank, he's still pretending."

Braden came up beside Lamarr Dean. "He's used to it."

"We're going to Bisbee," Dr. Favor said. "On business. We'll be there two days at most."

"No," Lamarr Dean said. "You'll be there just long enough to get a ride south. You'll hole up in Mexico or else get a boat in Vera Cruz and head out."

"You're sure of that," Dr. Favor said.

"That's how it's done."

"And if I deny it, tell you we're going back in two days?"

"What's the sense?"

"He should be over here with a gun," Braden said.

"No," Lamarr Dean said. "He uses his ink pen. All you do is write down a higher beef tally than what comes in. Pay the trail driver U.S. government scrip for what's delivered and keep the overpayment. Isn't that right, Doctor?"

"Like he never saw you before," Braden said.

Lamarr Dean looked at Mrs. Favor. "You pretending too?"

"I know you," she said, pretty calmly, considering everything. "But I don't remember him," nodding to Braden.

"No, Frank wasn't anywhere near. He was still in Yuma then."

"I guess that's enough," Braden said. "We got things to do."

"I was just trying to understand it," Mrs. Favor said easily. Her eyes shifted to Lamarr Dean who she knew by now was the talker among them. "You were working for the man who had the contract to supply beef."

"Mr. Wolgast."

"And you found out about my husband."

"Audra," Dr. Favor said, sounding unconcerned but hardly taking his eyes from Lamarr Dean or Braden, while the rest of us couldn't help but watch him. (My gosh, the things we were learning all of a sudden!) "Audra," he said, "you know we don't have to talk about our personal business to these people."

Braden moved away. "Let's get to it," he said and nodded to Early who started unhitching the team horses. As he stripped off the harness and brought them out, slapping them and keeping them moving, the Mexican, who was still mounted, bunched the horses and started them along.

The road formed two tracks out across a grassy meadow that was wide, pretty wide across and stetched on at least a mile with slopes rising up on both sides. As soon as the Mexican was off a ways, Early mounted up again and started after him.

Braden was behind the coach now and we saw just part

of him as he yanked down the canvas and started pulling the bags off.

Lamarr Dean started looking us over then, I mean to see if we were armed. He took a revolver from inside Dr. Favor's coat, a small caliber gun that he studied for a minute then threw off into the brush on the other side of the road. He went on to Mendez, passing Mrs. Favor and the McLaren girl, and Mendez opened his coat to show he was unarmed.

"What about up in the boot?" Lamarr Dean asked.

"A shotgun," Mendez said.

"See it stays there and you here," Lamarr Dean said. He came on to me and I opened my coat as Mendez had done.

As Lamarr Dean looked me over Mendez said, "You think it's worth it? You won't be able to show your face again."

"I appreciate it," Lamarr said, "but don't give me no advice please."

"I would bet you're dead or arrested in two weeks," Mendez said.

Lamarr glanced at him now. "You won't have nothing to bet with."

"All right, then remember it," Mendez said. "You already have witnesses."

"I don't see any," Lamarr Dean said. Braden came from behind the coach with a leather satchel. "Frank, you see any witnesses?"

"Not here," Braden said. He knelt down to open the satchel.

Lamarr Dean moved on to Russell. "This one doesn't look like any witness to me. Mister," Lamarr said, "are you a witness?" He pulled Russell's Colt as he said it and flung it backhanded, high up so that it glinted with the sun catching it, and down the road, bouncing and skidding way down it.

But Lamarr Dean wasn't watching the gun. He was staring at Russell, up close to him and squinting, looking right in his face.

"I've seen you somewhere," Lamarr said. The way he said it you knew it bothered him. He waited for Russell to help him, but Russell didn't say a word. They stared at each other and every second you expected Lamarr to remember that day at Delgado's, and you could just imagine him suddenly swinging that Henry rifle up and giving Russell the same thing Russell gave him, or worse.

Or Braden might say something about "the Indian" and then Lamarr Dean would remember. You waited for that to happen too. But, when Braden looked up, the bag open on the ground in front of him, he said, "I'd say it was a good day's pay."

Lamarr Dean looked from Braden over to Dr. Favor. "How much you steal so we won't have to count it?"

Dr. Favor didn't say anything. He was a man in a dark suit and hat standing there watching, with one thumb hooked in a vest pocket and the other hand at his side. The McLaren girl, Mrs. Favor, Mendez, John Russell—all of them in fact just stood there patiently, as if they had stopped by to watch but didn't have anything to do with what was going on.

"He figures he's helped out enough without giving us a tally," Braden said. He rose, handing the satchel to Dean who took it and transferred the currency to his saddlebags.

"About twelve thousand I figured," Lamarr Dean said.

"Somewhere around it," Braden said.

"He did all right," Lamarr Dean said. "But I guess we did better." He saw Braden looking at the two horses that still trailed the coach on a line. "What do you think?" he said then.

"I guess they'll do." Braden looked up at the coach. "And the two saddles."

Lamarr Dean looked at him. "What do you need two for?"

"You'll see," Braden said. He motioned to me. "You get them down."

That's how I come to be up on the coach when they rode out. I threw down Braden's saddle, then Russell's, looking at him as I did.

Russell watched, not saying a word as Braden freed the line and pulled in the horses and slipped the hackamores off them. He put his own saddle on one horse and told Russell to put his on the other.

Right then I thought, they're taking Russell along as a hostage. It made sense; they hadn't bothered us up to now, but they certainly weren't going to be so kind as to just ride off. Which turned out to be right. Only it wasn't Russell they took.

It was Mrs. Favor. Braden brought the horse over to her and said, "I thought you'd come along with us a ways," sounding nice about it.

And just as nice she said, "I'd better not," as if they were discussing it and she had a choice.

Braden held out his hand. "You'll be all right."

"I'll be all right here," Mrs. Favor said.

Braden stared at her. "You're coming, one way or the other." And that was the end of the discussion.

He helped her up, Mrs. Favor holding the skirt to cover her legs as she sat the saddle, and they moved off down the road. Braden stayed close to her and neither of them looked back. We all kept watching, nobody saying anything. Dr. Favor in fact didn't say anything even before, when Braden was forcing his wife to go with him.

Lamarr Dean mounted up then. He sat there cradling the Henry across his arms, looking down at the people there and finally up to me, thinking about something, maybe wanting to be sure he hadn't made any mistakes.

He thought of one thing. "The shotgun," he said. "Open it up and throw it away."

I climbed down to the driver's seat and did as I was told, emptying both shells before heaving the gun off into the brush. Lamarr Dean nodded. He wheeled around and took off after Braden and Mrs. Favor, not hurrying though.

By now Braden and Mrs. Favor were about a hundred yards off, out in the wide-open part of the meadow. Way off beyond them there was just dust to show that Early and the Mexican were up there somewhere driving the horse teams.

I felt the coach shake; I remember that. But I didn't look around till a moment later. When I did, there was John Russell kneeling on the roof right behind me unbuckling the cartridge belt from his blanket roll. He glanced up, keeping an eye on Dean who was taking his time moving away from us. Russell slipped the Spencer out, looking at Lamarr Dean again, and that was when he spoke.

He said, "How do they get that sure of themselves?"

I didn't know what he meant, and certainly couldn't believe he intended to shoot Lamarr Dean. I said, "What?"

"How do they get that sure with the mistakes they make?" Already he was slipping a cartridge into the breech, loading it quick for single fire. I guess I didn't say anything then.

He was busy and it was like he was telling it to himself. "Luck then," he said. "They think they know how to do it, but it's luck." I saw him slip three cartridges from the belt and hold them in his left hand. All of a sudden he held still.

I looked around and saw Dean riding back toward us. Braden and Mrs. Favor, two hundred yards off, had come around and reined in as if to wait for him.

Lamarr Dean had put his rifle in the saddle boot, but now, as he approached us, he drew his Colt.

THREE

Lamarr Dean was close now.

"I pretty near forgot something," he said. Then he noticed Russell up on the roof behind me. "What're you at up there?"

"Getting my things," John Russell said. The Spencer was down between his legs as he knelt there, sitting back on his feet, his hands flat on his thighs.

"Expect you're going somewhere?"

"Well," Russell shrugged, "why sit here, uh?"

"How far you think you'll get?"

"That's something to find out."

Lamarr Dean heeled his horse, moving to the back of the coach. He stood up in the stirrups to reach one of the two water-skins hanging there, unhooked it, and looped the end thong over his saddle horn. Then he came back with the skin hanging round and tight in front of his left leg. He pulled the horse around so he was facing us again.

"You didn't say how far you'd get," Lamarr Dean said.

Russell's shoulders went up and down. "We find that out after a while."

Lamarr Dean raised the revolver, hesitating, making sure we saw what he was going to do. Mendez yelled something. I'm not sure what, maybe just a sound. But as he yelled it, Lamarr Dean pulled the trigger and the waterskin still hanging from the back of the coach burst open. It gushed and then trickled as the bag sagged, all the water wasting itself on that sandy road, and Lamarr Dean just sat there looking at us. He didn't smile or laugh, but you could see he enjoyed it.

He said to Russell, "Now how far?"

There wasn't supposed to be an answer to that. Lamarr Dean took up his reins and started around. Russell waited till that moment.

"Maybe," he said, "as far as Delgado's."

Lamarr Dean held up, taken off-stride and now he was sideways to us, his gun hand on the offside and he had to turn his head around over his shoulder to look up at Russell.

"You said something?"

"Maybe if we get thirsty," Russell said, "we'll go to Delgado's and have *mescal*."

Lamarr Dean didn't move, even with his head turned in that awkward position. He stared up at Russell, and I'm certain that right then something was dawning on him.

He said, "You do that." For a few more seconds he looked up at Russell, then nudged his horse and started off again with his back to us and holding to a walking pace to show that he wasn't afraid of anything.

I kept watching him—thirty, forty, fifty feet away then, about that far when Russell's voice said, "Get down," not suddenly, but calmly and in a quiet tone.

I dropped down on the seat, ducking my head, and Russell said, "All the way *down*—"

And that last word wasn't quiet, still it wasn't yelled or excited. I saw the Spencer suddenly up to his face and I dropped, looking around to see where I was going and catching a glimpse of Lamarr Dean sixty feet out and wheeling his mount and bringing the Colt gun straight out in front of him, thinking he had time to be sure and *bam* the Spencer went off in my ear and Lamarr Dean went out of that saddle like he'd been clubbed in the face, his horse swerving, then running.

Russell must have been sure of his shot, for he was already re-loaded and tracking the horse, and, when he fired, the horse stumbled and rolled and tried to get up. And out past the horse you could see Braden coming in. Coming, then swerving as that Spencer went off again, banging hard close to me and cracking thin out in the open. There was the sound of Braden's revolver twice and I hugged the floor of the boot, looking up to see just the barrel of the Spencer. Russell was full length behind it now, resting the barrel on the front rail, tracking Braden with the sights and not hurrying his fire. Braden swerved again and this time kept going all the way around full circle and back the way he had come toward the small figure way out there that was Mrs. Favor, so you knew Russell had come close. At least Braden didn't want any part of him right then.

I raised up. Russell was loading again, now that there was time taking a loading tube from his blanket and putting seven of the .56-56 slugs in it and shoving the tube up through the stock of the Spencer.

"They'll all come back now," I said. "Won't they?"

"As sure as we have what they want," Russell said.

There was a space there where nothing happened. I saw Dr. Favor and Mendez and the McLaren girl, all three of them in a row, crouched against the cutbank where they'd gone when the shooting started. It was quiet now, but still nobody moved.

Russell was buckling on his cartridge belt, over his left shoulder and down across his chest, working it around so that the full cartridge loops were all in front. While he did this, his eyes never left the two specks way out on the meadow.

We had some time, but I did not think of it then. Braden had to get Early and the Mexican before he came back and they could be a mile off running the stage horses. I kept thinking of how Russell had brought up his Spencer and put it on Lamarr Dean, the way a man might aim at a tin can on a fence, and killed him with one shot. Then he had dropped the horse that was running away with the water bag. He had killed a man, sure of it, and in the same second he had known he must get the horse and he did that too.

The space where nothing happened lasted maybe a minute altogether. Then it was over for good.

Russell moved past me, frontwards, stepping on the wheel and then jumping. He was carrying his Spencer of course, and in the other hand his blanket roll and the canteen he and Mendez had used. (Little things you remember: there was no strap on the canteen, only two metal rings a strap had once been fastened to, and Russell hooked a finger through one of the rings to carry it.)

I don't think he even looked at the others, but started off down the road we had come up, only stopping to pick up his Colt gun and shove it in his holster. Down just past there he left the road and started up the slope, moving pretty quickly through the greasewood and other brush.

Dr. Favor woke up first. He yelled at Russell. Then Mendez was out on the road looking up at Russell, and Dr. Favor had run off into the brush on the other side of the coach.

I started down then, taking the grainsack our provisions were in and my blanket roll. By the time I was on the road, Dr. Favor was coming out of the brush with his little revolver and Mendez's sawed-off shotgun. Mendez and the McLaren girl were still watching Russell.

"He's running," Dr. Favor said. He was not at all calm and at that moment I thought if the shotgun was loaded he would have fired it at Russell.

"We need him," Dr. Favor said then. He knew it right then. He knew it as sure as he thought John Russell was an Apache Indian and we were afoot out in the middle of nowhere.

That's when the rest of us came wide awake. The McLaren girl said, "I wouldn't have any idea where to go. I don't think I even know where we are."

"We're maybe half way," I said. "Maybe more. If we were over on the main road I could tell."

"Then how far's the main road?"

Favor shot a look at her like he was trying to think and she had interrupted him. "Just keep quiet," he said.

It stung her, you could see. "Standing out here in the open," she said, "what good does keeping quiet do?"

Dr. Favor never answered her. He looked at Mendez and said, "Come on," handing him his shotgun, and they hurried out to where Lamarr Dean's horse was, Dr. Favor skirting around Lamarr Dean's body which lay spread-armed like it had been staked out, but Mendez stopped there to take Lamarr Dean's Colt. Then they were both at the dead horse, kneeling there a minute, Favor pulling loose the saddlebags while Mendez got the waterskin. They didn't bother with the Henry rifle, or else it was under the horse and held fast.

While they were at the dead horse, the McLaren girl said, still watching them, "He's not even thinking of his wife. Do you know that?"

"Well, sure he is," I said, not meaning he was actually thinking about her, but at least concerned about her. What did the girl expect him to do? He couldn't just chase after Braden. That wouldn't get his wife back.

"He's forgotten her," the McLaren girl said. "All he's thinking about is the money he stole."

"You can't just say something like that," I said. I meant you couldn't know what somebody was thinking, especially in the jackpot we were in right then. A person *acted*, and thought about it later.

It was getting the things from Lamarr's horse that took time, the reason we were not right behind Russell or had him in sight anymore by the time we got down the road past the cutbank and started up the slope.

Dr. Favor, with the saddlebags over one shoulder, kept ahead of us, following the same direction Russell had taken. The slope was not very difficult at first, a big open sweep that humped up to a bunch of pines along the top; but, as we were hurrying, it wasn't long before our legs started aching and getting so tight you thought something would knot inside and you'd never get it loosened.

We were hurrying because of what was behind us, you can bet all your wages on that. But we were also hurrying to catch Russell, feeling like little kids running home in the dark and scared the house was going to be locked and nobody home. Do you see how we felt? We were worried he had left us to go on his own. In other words knowing we needed Russell if we were going to find our way out of here alive.

When Dr. Favor reached the trees he hesitated, or seemed to, then he was gone. That's when we hurried faster, all worn out by then. You could hear Mendez breathing ten feet away.

But there was no need to hurry. As we reached the top there was Dr. Favor standing just inside the shade of the trees. Russell was just past him. He was sitting down with his blanket open on the ground and his boots off. He was pulling on a pair of curl-toed Apache moccasins, not paying any attention to Dr. Favor who stood there like he had caught Russell and was holding him from getting away, actually pointing his revolver at him. Dr. Favor's chest was moving up and down with his breathing.

Mendez moved in a little closer, watching Russell. "Why didn't you wait for us?" he said. Russell didn't bother to answer. You weren't even sure he heard Mendez.

"He doesn't care what we do," Dr. Favor said. "Long as he gets away."

"Man," Mendez said. "What's the matter with you? We have to think about this and talk it over. What if one of us just ran off? You think that would be a good thing?"

Russell raised his leg to pull a moccasin on. They were the high Apache kind, like leggings which come up past your knees. He began rolling it down, stuffing the pants leg into it and fastening it about calf-high with a strap of something. He didn't look up until he had finished this.

Then he said, "What do you want?"

"What do we want?" Mendez said, surprised. "We want to get out of here."

"What's stopping you?" Russell said.

Mendez kept frowning. "What's the matter with you?"

Russell had both moccasins on now. He took his boots and rolled them inside the blanket. Doing this, not looking at us, he said, "You want to go with me, uh?"

"With you? We all go together. This isn't happening to just one person," Mendez said. "This is happening to all of us."

"But you want me to show you the way," Russell said.

"Sure you show the way. We follow. But we're all together."

"I don't know," Russell said, very slowly, like he was thinking it over. He looked up at Dr. Favor, directly at him. "I can't ride with you. Maybe you can't walk with me . . . uh?"

For a minute, maybe even longer, nobody said a word. Russell finished rolling his blanket and tied it up with a piece of line he'd had inside.

When he stood up, Mendez said—not surprised or excited or frowning now, but so serious his voice wasn't even very loud—he said, "What does that mean?"

Russell looked at him. "It means I can't ride with them and maybe they can't walk with me. Maybe they don't walk the way I walk. You *sabe* that, Mexican?"

"I helped you like you're my own son!" Mendez's voice rose and his eyes opened so that you could see all the whites. But Russell wasn't looking. He was walking off. Mendez kept shouting, "What's the matter with you!"

"Let him go," Dr. Favor said.

We stood there watching Russell move off through the trees.

"What do you expect?" Dr. Favor said. "Do you expect somebody like that to act the way a decent person would?"

"I helped him," Mendez said, as if he couldn't believe what had happened.

"All right, now he'll help us," Dr. Favor said. "He won't have anything to do with us, but we can follow him, can't we?"

Nobody thought to try to answer that question at the time, because it wasn't really a question. I thought about it later, though. I thought about it for the next two or three hours as we tried to keep up with Russell.

It was about 3:30 or 4 o'clock when the holdup took place, with already a lot of shade on this side of the hills. From then on the light kept getting dimmer. I mean right from the time we started following Russell it was hard to keep him in sight, even when he was out in the open.

In daylight the land was spotted with brush and rock, dead and dusty looking, but with some color, light green and dark green and brown and whitish yellow. In the evening it all turned brown and hazy looking, with high peaks all around us once we'd gone on down through the other side of the pines out into open country again.

I say open, but by that I mean only there weren't any trees. I don't mean to say it was easy to travel over.

We moved along with Dr. Favor usually ahead of us. Way up ahead you would see Russell. Then you wouldn't see him. Not because he had hidden, but because of the time of day and just the way that country was, with little dips and rises and wild with all kinds of scrub brush and cactus. The saguaros that were all over didn't look like fence posts now. They were like grave markers in an Indian burial ground, if there is such a place as that. This wasn't what scared you though, it was what was coming behind us and trying to keep up with Russell that did.

He must have known we were following. But he never once ran or tried to hide on us. The McLaren girl wondered out loud why he didn't. I guess he knew he didn't have to.

There was a pass that led through these hills which Russell followed a little ways, then crossed the half mile or so of openness to the other side and headed up through a barranca that rose as a big trough between two ridges. Following him across the openness we kept looking back, but Braden and his men were not close to us yet.

Russell left the barranca, climbing again up to the cover of trees. I think that climb was the hardest part and wore us out the most, all of us hurrying, wasting our strength as we tried to keep him in sight. Once up on this ridge, though, there was no sign of him.

We kept to the trees, moving north because we figured he would. Then after a mile or so there was the end of the trees. This hump of a ridge trailed off into a bare spine and then we were working our way down again into another pass, a darker, more shadowed one, because now it was later. It was here that we sighted Russell again, and here that we almost gave up and said what was the use. He was climbing again, almost up the other side of this pass, way up past the brush to where the slope was steep and rocky, and we knew then that we would never keep up with him.

Dr. Favor claimed he was deliberately trying to lose us. But the McLaren girl said no, he didn't care if we followed or sprouted wings and flew; he was thinking of Braden and his men on horseback and he was making it as hard for them as he could, making them get off their horses and walk if they wanted to follow him.

When she said this and we thought of Braden again, we went on, tired or not, and climbed right up that grade Russell had, skinning ourselves pretty bad because now it was hard to see your footing in the dim light.

It was up on that slope, in trees again, that we rested and ate some of the dried beef and biscuits from the grainsack. Before we were through it was dark, almost as dark as it would get. This rest, which was our longest one, made it hard to get up and we started arguing about going on.

Mendez was for staying. He said going on wasn't worth it. Let Braden catch up for all he cared.

Dr. Favor said we *had* to go on, practically ordering us to.

Braden would have to stop because he couldn't follow our trail in the dark. So we should take advantage of this and keep going.

Keep going, the McLaren girl said. That sounded fine. But which way? How did we know we wouldn't get turned around and walk right back into Braden's hands?

We would head north, Dr. Favor said. And keep heading north. The McLaren girl said she agreed, but which way was it? He pointed off somewhere, but you could tell he wasn't sure. Or he could go on alone, Dr. Favor suggested, watching us to see our reaction. Go on alone and bring back help. He didn't insist on it and let it die when nobody said anything.

Why didn't he mention his wife then? That's when I started thinking about what the McLaren girl had said earlier: that he had forgotten about his wife and only the money was important to him.

Could that be? I tried thinking what I would do if it was my wife. Hole up and ambush them? Try and get her away from them? My gosh, no, I thought then. Just trade them the money for her! Certainly Dr. Favor must have thought of that.

Then why didn't he do it? Or at least talk about it. When you got down to it, though, it was his business. I mean we had no right to remind him of what he should do. That was his business. I don't mean to sound hard or callous; that's just the way it was. We had enough on our minds without worrying about his wife.

We just sat there until Dr. Favor said he was going. When he started off, the McLaren girl started after him, so Mendez and I did too. I guess we had to follow somebody.

From then on I don't know where we were or even what direction we went.

By then there wasn't much talk among us. Once in a while Dr. Favor said something, usually about what way to go. One time though he brought up the subject again of us hiding somewhere and him going on alone.

Mendez said it was all right with him, not caring one way or the other. But neither the McLaren girl nor I would agree to it. I kept picturing Braden somewhere behind us waiting for morning so he could get on our sign and run us down. Who would want to just sit there waiting for him?

The McLaren girl looked at it another way. She said right to Dr. Favor's face, "That money's been stolen enough. Don't worry about one of us trying to take it."

"As if I'd distrust you people," Dr. Favor said. "The things you think about."

"I'd like to know what you think about," the McLaren girl said. "Since it sure isn't your wife."

Dr. Favor didn't say anything and we went on.

If you were to ask me who was the best one, who took it the best and never once complained, who even walked with hardly any trouble, I would say the McLaren girl. If you are surprised, remember she had been held by wild Apaches over a month. She had traveled with them as they kept on the move, keeping up with them else they would have killed her. You looked at her and wondered how something like that could have happened to a young girl and still not see it on her face.

Once she offered to take the grainsack or blanket roll I was carrying, but I wouldn't hear of it.

She even said we should still keep going when finally Dr. Favor led us off into a gully and announced we would camp there. He said if we stopped now we would have a better chance of finding Russell when daylight came. I'm not sure what he meant by that and think it was just an excuse, the real reason for his wanting to stop being his tiredness. The McLaren girl argued we should use the darkness while we had it—it was still a few hours before sunup—but gave in when she saw how tired Mendez was. So tired he could hardly stand up.

We had already eaten some of the biscuits and dried meat from the grainsack. Now there was nothing to do but sleep. I was the only one with a blanket, so I offered it to the McLaren girl. She said no, for me to use it. I did, finally, but all rolled up as a pillow. (Somebody might think this was dumb, but I couldn't cover myself with it being the only one. It would have felt good too, I can tell you that.)

It was only a few hours before sunup when we stopped here; so there wasn't much time to sleep, and it was hard getting to sleep, even as tired as I felt. But finally I did.

In the morning there weren't two words said by anyone. You know how it can be in the morning anyway: on top of having slept no more than two and a half hours on the ground and in the cold after walking almost all night. (Yes, it was cold. Even though during the day it was blistering hot.) And on top of that not knowing where you were and Braden coming after us on horseback.

The only thing we were sure of in the morning was the direction north and that was the way we went, having eaten a little more of the dried beef and biscuits and taken a few swallows of water each.

Going toward the north does not mean we went in a straight line. Unless you wanted to climb steep slopes all the time, and maybe get up there and find no way down, you had to follow the washes and draws that cut through this high country, so that maybe you would walk two, even three miles to get one mile north. You can see nobody talked much. That's the way it was all morning, or until the next part happened which I would judge was an hour or so before noon.

We came out of some trees onto an open meadow, a little graze like that was cupped there in the hills, then crossing the meadow and taking the only way out, we went up a pretty long draw that was deep and lined with thick brush and rocks along both sides, the draw being about sixty feet wide and upwards to three hundred or more feet long, that being a calculation from memory.

We made our way up this draw, looking back across the meadow as we went, finally reached the top and almost dropped everything we carried. Not out of tiredness, out of surprise!

For sitting there with his Spencer across his lap and smoking a cigarette was John Russell.

Mendez yelled his name and ran over to him, Mendez assuming just as I did, I guess, that Russell had changed his mind and gotten the mean feeling out of his system, and now wanted to show us the way out of here.

Mendez scolded him a little, but in a kidding way, that he shouldn't have done what he did. Mendez was too glad to see Russell to be serious or angry at him, telling him how we couldn't keep up with him and how worn out we got trying to.

Russell moved him aside with his arm and motioned all of us back from the crest so we wouldn't be seen from below.

From the way Mendez acted, our troubles were over.

Not so according to Dr. Favor. He said, staring at Russell, "You going to sit there for a while, are you?"

Russell didn't move. "You want to go bad, uh?"

He saw that Russell had no intention of getting up. "Now it comes," Dr. Favor said. "I want to hear how you'll say this."

"You want to go," Russell said, "go on."

Dr. Favor kept looking at him. "What else?"

"Leave the saddlebag and the gun here."

Dr. Favor's big red face almost seemed to relax and smile. "There," he said. "Right out in the open. It took you all night to realize you'd run off and left something behind."

Mendez, not understanding, had that worried look again. "What is it?" he said to Russell.

"It's my money," Dr. Favor said. "He's thinking it looks pretty good. Out here and no law to stop him. But four people against one. Maybe he hasn't thought about that."

Russell drew on the cigarette. "Maybe one is enough," he said.

That was when the McLaren girl stepped in. "Your money," she yelled at Dr. Favor. I mean *yelled* it. "After you stole it! We're supposed to side with you to protect money you stole!" Then her eyes took in Russell too. "You sit here arguing about money and giving Frank Braden all the time he'd ever need."

"Be careful what you say," Dr. Favor said to her. "I think you are talking without thinking. This is my money, in my possession, and it will take more than the word of a dead outlaw to prove it isn't."

"All this talk," Mendez said, like he had just thought of it. "We have to *move*."

Russell looked up at him. "Where do you want to go?"

Mendez said, "Are you crazy? They're coming!"

"Tell me where," Russell said.

"Where? I don't know. Out of here."

"I'll tell you something," Russell said. "There's open country. Maybe it takes you two, three hours to cross it. And while you're there they come with their horses."

"Then hide somewhere," Mendez said, "and wait for dark to cross it."

Russell nodded. "Or do better than that. Wait for them here. Shoot their horses to make it even, uh? Maybe finish it."

"Finish it," I said, understanding him, but I guess not believing what he was asking us to do. "You mean try and kill them?"

"If they get close enough," Russell said, "they're going to kill you."

"But they didn't harm anybody before. Why would they want to now?"

"Do you want to give them your water?"

"They got water."

"Two canteens which they were drinking out of all day yesterday. Do you want to give them yours?"

"No, but—"

"Then they'll kill you for it."

Until then it seemed just a matter of running and getting away or running and being caught and they getting the money after all. But kill them or they would kill us? It was a terrible thing to think about and you couldn't help looking for other ways. Run or hide. Run or hide. Those ways kept popping into your head while Russell just sat there looking down the draw and waiting.

"And if we don't *finish it*," Dr. Favor said, making those last words sound dumb to have ever been thought of. "What then?"

"You don't have a say in this," Russell said, looking up at him. "You can stay or go, but either way you leave the saddlebag."

"You must have kept awake all night," Dr. Favor said.

"It came to me," Russell said back.

"How much you figure I have?"

Russell shrugged. "It doesn't matter."

"Wouldn't take much, would it, to keep you in whisky?"

"You leave the belly gun too," Russell said. And held out his hand for it, turning just a little so that the Spencer in his lap turned with him.

Dr. Favor just stared, not moving. "You're forgetting something," he said. "What if the others decide against you?"

"Then they have you to lead them," Russell answered.

He sat there with his hand still held toward Dr. Favor and you knew he could sit there the rest of his life and never budge. It was his way if we stayed with him. It was either do what he wanted or else go on with Dr. Favor. It was not like choosing between a good thing or a bad thing. Still, one felt to be better than the other and it wasn't much of a hard choice to make.

The McLaren girl was the one who said it out loud, though not very loud. "I would like to go home," she said, hardly glancing at Dr. Favor. "I sure would like to go home. And I know he can't find the way."

Neither Mendez nor I had to say anything. If we'd sided with Dr. Favor, we would have.

With us watching him, I believe, Dr. Favor didn't want to get caught looking awkward or nervous. You had to give him credit for that. He took it calmly, not offering any argument, but I will bet thinking fast all the time. He just shrugged and handed his revolver to Russell.

"Chief make plenty war now," he said. You see how he was passing it off? Like Russell was a bully you had to give in to if you wanted some peace.

Russell didn't pay any attention. He took the gun, then looked at Mendez, noticing Mendez had Lamarr Dean's revolver besides his shotgun.

"You shoot all right?" he asked.

Mendez frowned. "I'm not sure."

"You'll find out," Russell said. "First the shotgun. When they're close. So close you can touch them. Then the other one if you need it."

"I don't know," Mendez said, worried. "Just sit and wait for them like that."

"If there was a better way," Russell said, "we would do it." Just that moment talking to Mendez, Russell's voice was gentle and you remembered they had known each other before and maybe had been friends.

He looked off down the draw, studying the trees over the other side of the meadow. If they were on our sign, he knew, they would come through there and up the draw.

Then he was looking right at me and handing me Dr. Favor's revolver. At first I didn't make any move to take it.

He pushed it out again like telling me, "Come on, take it," and that time I did.

"You have one thing to do," he said and shifted his eyes over to Dr. Favor and back again. "Watch him."

Then it was the McLaren girl's turn. She stood there, her dark nice-looking face very calm, seeing Russell looking at her then.

"You stay with this one," Russell said, meaning me.

"Carl Allen," the McLaren girl said.

It stopped Russell just for a second as if she'd interrupted his thoughts. "You'll have the saddlebag and the water."

"Squaw work," Dr. Favor said. "You ought to like that." He was also saying, "See what you're getting yourself in for?"

It didn't bother her, or else she was so intent on Russell she didn't hear him. She said, "The money and the waterskin, but you carry your own water I see." She meant the canteen that was on the ground next to him. The one he and Mendez had used.

He watched her, getting all the meaning out of her words that she didn't say. "You want it too?"

"Why burden yourself?" she said, and you weren't sure if she was serious or not.

For just a moment there John Russell hesitated, as if handing over the canteen would be giving up his independence. But he did and the McLaren girl took it.

"You and you and you," Russell said, meaning the McLaren girl and Dr. Favor and I, "will be here. You don't stand up. You don't move back away from the edge here and stand up. You sit and don't move." (Like a teacher talking to little children in school!) "Him—"

"Reverend Dr. Favor," the McLaren girl said with that little knife edge in her voice again.

"He can leave up to the time they come," Russell went on. "After that, no." Russell was looking right at me again, but still talking about Dr. Favor.

"If he tries to leave with nothing, shoot him once," Russell said. "If he takes the saddlebag, shoot him twice. If he picks up the water, empty your gun. You understand that?"

(I have thought about those words since then and I am sure Russell was having a little fun with us when he said that. Part serious, part in fun. But can you imagine joking at a time like that? That of course was the reason no one even smiled. He must have thought we were dumb.)

I just nodded, not wanting to say anything with Dr. Favor standing right there.

"I don't know," Mendez said. You could see what had been going on in his mind. "Maybe we should just keep going, try and outrun them."

"You run now," Russell said to him, "they'll catch you and kill you. Believe that more than you believe anything."

Russell told us again to stay where we were, down low. He talked to Mendez, going over it again with him, telling him to wait till they got close and to be sure of hitting something, to shoot first at the men, then at the horses; but watch for the woman. Mendez listened, nodding sometimes, but kept looking over toward us.

After that Russell didn't waste any more talk. He and Mendez crawled out through the brush, working their way about forty feet down the draw, then separating, Mendez staying on the right, Russell crawling way over to the left side so that anybody coming up the draw would pass between them. If one did not have a good shot when the time came, the other probably would.

Both had good cover, for there were sizable rocks that had been washed down the draw, mostly along the sides where they were, and pretty thick brush where there weren't any rocks. Only the middle ground, where water would run off in the spring, was fairly open.

Russell had this timed pretty well, knowing how long it would take them to get on our sign and follow us. He had figured a few other things too. That they wouldn't be as careful by now as they had been yesterday evening and during the first hour or so this morning. There had been good ambush places before this, but nothing had jumped out at them. Why should it now? They would be awake, of course, wide awake coming up something like this draw; but they would tend to keep their eyes on the top and expect it to come from there if it was coming at all.

(It is easy to talk about something like this. It is also interesting to plan and imagine what you would do, but only as long as you aren't there. I wouldn't sit where we were, just waiting there again, no matter what anybody gave me.)

We kept our eyes on the trees that were some kind of pine, big ones, probably ponderosa, across the meadow at the bottom of the draw. Still, when they came, it wasn't sudden at all.

Right at the edge of the trees, in shadow, was a horse and rider and you wondered how long he had been there with you looking right at him. He was awake all right.

He came out of the trees holding to a slow walk and was out in the meadow a ways before the next rider appeared. Then another one came who you knew right away was the Favor woman. (I did not look over at Dr. Favor to see what his face showed. I would have if I had known I was going to write this.) The fourth one was right behind her. That would be Frank Braden, the big sugar of this outfit. He would be the one telling the others what to do, while he stayed with their hostage or whatever Mrs. Favor was.

It was the Mexican rider who dismounted and came first when they reached the bottom of the draw. He seemed to be making sure of our tracks, walking along a little ways with his head down. Then he swung back up and he and Early came on, the Mexican staying a little bit in the lead. They kept looking up at the sides of the draw, being very watchful now. They knew we had come this way and I think they smelled it as a fresh trail. Not so much Early as the Mexican.

You got the feeling he knew by the sign that Russell had passed through here on his own or ahead of us, or maybe Russell had left no tracks at all and the Mexican saw only that the four of us had come up this way. There is nothing to prove this, but I believe he did know. The Mexican seemed so sure of himself, riding right up the middle of the draw first, seeming relaxed but his eyes taking everything in.

Braden, with the Favor woman, kept a good ten lengths back of Early and the Mexican. That was the way they came up, walking right into it.

It was like watching a play. No, it was realer than that. (My gosh, it couldn't get more real!) It gave you a strange feeling to watch it, thinking that in a minute or two you were going to see somebody get killed.

Russell never moved. We could see just part of him. He lay full length as if asleep. His hat was off and his head was down, as if he was listening to them coming up the draw instead of watching them.

Mendez kept looking over to where Russell was, but I doubt he could see him, being on about the same level. Then he would look back up in our direction. You could see he wanted no part of this. Why couldn't he be up where we were? Or the rest of us down there helping him, he was probably thinking. Mendez was nervous. You couldn't blame him for it. Still, it was strange to see him in that state. (In the last two days I had certainly learned a lot about show-nothing, tell-nothing Henry Mendez.)

As Early and the Mexican got up a ways, they started looking up at the top of the draw and studying it. Especially the Mexican. He was closer to Mendez's side of the draw now and about five horselengths ahead of Early. Halfway up, the Mexican drew his right-hand gun and held it ready.

You saw Mendez pressing himself tight against the rock he was behind and not looking around now. He would inch up to sneak a look at the Mexican and then duck down again. You almost knew what he was thinking. You also knew this wasn't something he had done before.

Looking at Russell you couldn't even tell if he was alive, laying there sighting down his carbine now and waiting as if he could wait like that all day, waiting for Early to ride right up to him.

I don't remember what the McLaren girl and Dr. Favor were doing then. I could feel them there. The thing is, the one I really wanted to watch was Russell; then you would see how this was done. But Mendez, the way he was fidgeting, looking up at the Mexican coming and then pressing against the rock, made you nervous and you kept watching him, holding your breath for fear he was going to jump up and start running.

The Mexican was now about a hundred feet away from him, sitting round-shouldered and relaxed, the Colt gun held about chest high and pointed straight up, the sun glinting and moving a little with the motion of the horse and rider.

That was what Mendez saw coming toward him, a man holding a gun that seemed part of his hand, and another gun still holstered; a man you knew was ready, but could still be re- laxed about it and not sit stiff in the saddle or with his shoul- ders hunched.

Maybe if I was Mendez I would have done the same as he did. Which was all of a sudden rise up and fire both barrels of that scatter gun like he couldn't let go fast enough.

At a hundred feet or less, some of the buckshot could have found the Mexican, but Mendez hurried and didn't aim at all. The Mexican straightened and fired three times, faster than I've ever seen a man thumb and fire a Colt revolver, with all three shots zinging off the rocks Mendez had flattened himself be- hind. Then you saw the Mexican twist in the saddle, like some- thing had pushed him, and grab his side right above the belt.

Russell had fired.

He fired again as the Mexican rolled out of the saddle and into cover. He fired again and the Mexican's horse threw up its head, shaking it, and sunk on its forelegs and fell over.

Early was already off and in cover. You saw him reach up to grab his horse's reins as it reared around and started off down the draw. Early missed. Russell didn't though. He fired twice again, quick, and I swear you heard both shots smack into that horse. The horse went down, rolled on its side and got up again and kept going, following Braden and the Favor woman— Braden holding her horse's reins close at the bit ring and lead- ing it as they rode back down the draw, all the way down to the bottom and around the outcrop of rocks into a little patch of scrubby woods. Even after they were out of sight you heard the horses in the thicket. Then everything was quiet.

It was quiet for the longest time. Mendez kept looking over to about where Russell was, not knowing at all what to do and maybe expecting some signal from him.

Russell didn't move. You could see he had learned a lot from the Apaches, a kind of patience few white men could ever command. He lay there sighting, I think, on the place where Early had gone into the brush, waiting for a movement. He lay like that, I swear, for about two hours, all the while this stand-off lasted.

Not much happened during that time. The Mexican started calling out either to Russell or Mendez in Spanish. I didn't know what he was saying, but they were questions, and there was a sound to his voice like the questions were meant to be funny. Not funny, exactly, but like insults or inviting Mendez to step out and show himself, things you wouldn't expect to hear coming out of that draw. You had to give that Mexican something. There was no doubt he had been shot. Still he could yell at Russell and Mendez, trying to draw them out.

Once there was a quick glimpse of Early. He was there and then gone, off behind a scatter of rocks a little farther down the draw. Russell must have been waiting for the Mexican because he didn't fire. We never did see the Mexican squirm out of there and Early only that one time.

Both of them worked their way down though. They stood out in the open for a second, way down at the bottom of the draw. The Mexican, holding his side with one hand, waved to us. Then they were gone into the thicket.

Just for a few minutes we had time to rest, not wondering where they were or worrying about them coming. They would have to think things over and maybe wait until dark to come up that draw again. Though we couldn't count on it. We couldn't sit here for long either. One of them could circle around, even though it would take time, and we wouldn't ever be able to move.

So we had to get out of there. When Russell and Mendez came up, I opened the canteen. Nobody had had any water since this morning. But Russell shook his head. "Tonight," he said. "Not while the sun is out." Meaning, I guess, you would sweat it out right away and be thirsty again before you knew it.

That was all he said, with not one word to Mendez about

shooting too soon and spoiling the ambush. That was over as far as he was concerned; he was not the kind of man who would stew over something finished and past fixing. He just picked up his blanket roll and that meant it was time to go.

Maybe we had showed them it wasn't going to be easy, as Russell had said we might. But look at it another way. We might have finished it in the draw, but we didn't and maybe never would. The only good to come out of the ambush was now they had one less horse—maybe two.

But now they were close. Now they knew where we were. And now there was no doubt they would come with guns out and shoot on sight.

FOUR

We sat there only a few minutes. That's all the longer our rest time lasted, and it was starting again. Only not the way we expected it to. We didn't go right then. We were about to when the McLaren girl said, "Look—" pointing down the draw.

We looked, but we all crouched down at the same time. There, way down at the bottom, was the Mexican again, his straw hat bright in the sunlight so that you knew it was the Mexican and not one of the others. But we could not tell at first what he was carrying. He had to get up a ways—taking his time, his face raised, his one hand holding his side—before we saw it was a stick with something white tied to the end of it.

He seemed careful, but not scared, keeping his eyes on the ridge, not sure we would honor his white truce flag, I guess, and ready to dive for cover it we let go at him. He was armed with both his revolvers.

Nobody said anything. We just watched. He kept coming, almost reaching the place where Mendez had been during the ambush.

Russell stood up holding his carbine in one hand, pointed down, and the Mexican stopped.

Russell said, "You come to give up?"

The Mexican stood at ease, letting his truce flag dip down to the ground. I think he smiled when Russell said that, but I'm not sure.

I know he shook his head. He said, "When you learn to shoot better." He raised his hand from his side and there was blood on it.

"You didn't do so good."

"I tried to do better," Russell said. "I think you moved."

"Moved," the Mexican said. "How do you like them, tied to a tree?"

"On a horse," Russell said. "Like your friend."

The Mexican grinned. "You like to pull the trigger."

"I can do it again for you," Russell said.

"You could," the Mexican agreed, staring up at Russell, studying him and judging the distance between them. "I have to talk to this other one first. This Favor."

He pronounced it Fa-*vor*, like it was a Spanish word.

"He can hear you," Russell said.

"If he can't you tell him," the Mexican said. "This. He gives us the money . . . and some of the water. We give him his wife and everyone goes home. Ask him how he likes that."

"You're out of water?"

"Almost." The Mexican grinned. "That Early. He put whisky in his canteen. He thought it would be easy."

Russell shook his head. "It will get even harder."

"Not if this Fa*vor* gives us the money."

"He doesn't have it," Russell said.

The Mexican grinned again. "Tell me he hid it."

Russell shook his head. "He gave it to me."

The Mexican nodded, looking up at Russell like he was admiring him. "So now you steal the money." He shrugged his shoulders. "All right, we trade with you then."

"She's not my woman," Russell said.

"We give her to you."

"What else?"

"Your life. How's that?"

"Tell Braden how things are now," Russell said.

"What's the difference who has the money?" the Mexican said. "You give it to us or we shoot that woman."

"All right," Russell said. "You shoot her."

The Mexican kept staring at him. "What about the rest of them? What do they say?"

"They say what they want," Russell said. "I say what I want. Do you see that now?"

He didn't see it. He didn't know what to think, so he just stood there, one hand on his side, the other holding that truce flag.

"Tell Braden how it is," Russell said. "Tell him to think some more."

"He'll say the same thing."

"Tell him anyway."

The Mexican hadn't taken his eyes off Russell for a second, sizing him up all the while they talked. "Maybe you and I finish something first," he said. "Maybe you come down here a little."

"I'm thinking," Russell said, "whether to kill you right now or wait till you turn around."

Do you know what the Mexican did? He smiled. Not that unbelieving kind of smile, but like he appreciated Russell or enjoyed him. It was about the strangest thing I ever saw. He smiled and said, "If I didn't believe you, I think you would do it. All right, I talk to Braden."

He turned and walked away dragging the truce flag, not with his shoulders hunched like he expected something, but as calmly as he had walked up.

Russell waited until the Mexican was almost down to the bottom. He got his blanket roll and the saddlebags, just glanced at us, and moved off. He didn't tell us what he had planned. If we wanted to follow him that was up to us.

We didn't expect this. We thought he would talk to them again. But who could be sure what Russell was thinking? We knew we couldn't sit in that draw forever. Sooner or later Braden would try to get at us. But was going on right then the best way? Russell must have thought so, though he wasn't telling us why.

We followed him. What choice had we?

That was a funny thing. I felt closer to Dr. Favor than I did to Russell. Dr. Favor might have stolen government money and left his wife to her own fate; but it was something you had to think about before you realized it. He never admitted either right out.

Russell was something else. He had said to the Mexican, not caring who heard him, "All right, shoot her." Like she was nothing to him, so what did he care? Do you see the difference? Russell was so cold and calm about it, it scared you to death. Also, if he didn't care about her, what did he care about us?

Now it was almost like the whole thing was between Braden and Russell and we were in it only because there wasn't any place else to go. Like it was all Russell's fault and he had dragged us into it.

I would say we walked three miles from the time we left that draw until we stopped again, though we did not gain more than one mile in actual distance. We kept pretty much to ridges, high up as possible in the cover of pinyon pine and scrub, and when we stopped it was because flat country opened up at the end of the canyon not far ahead of us. It was a good two or three miles across the openness before the hills took up again.

Russell didn't say it and nobody asked, but we knew he planned to wait for dark to cross that open part. It was no place to be seen in daylight by three men riding horses. (We did not know then whether Russell had killed one or two of their horses.)

We had climbed a pretty steep grade to reach this place we camped at (high up the way Apaches always camp, whether there is water or not) with thick pinyon on three sides of us and the slope, with some cliffrose and scrub, on the open side.

Russell had made it hard for them to follow. If they came directly on our sign, they would have to come up the open slope. If they came any other way, it would take them hours to work around, and then they would be taking a chance of not finding us. So, we figured, they would come directly when they came. All right, but to come up that open slope they would have to wait until dark. Which was what we would be waiting for to slip off through the trees.

Do you see how Russell figured to stay one jump ahead of them? I estimated we would reach the old San Pete mine some time during the night; Delgado's if we were lucky, some time during the next afternoon or evening. Then home. It didn't seem far when you looked ahead. The trouble was you had to keep looking back.

After the little sleep we had had it was good to lie down again. Everybody picked out a spot. We couldn't make a fire so ate some more of the biscuits, which were pretty hard by now, and the dried strip meat which never was very good.

We did not drink any water though. John Russell had said we would have to wait until night. It was midafternoon now. Imagine not having had a drink since that morning. The salty beef didn't help your thirst any either. But what could we do?

I kept picturing myself sitting on a shady porch with a big pitcher of ice water, sitting there in a clean shirt having just shaved and taken a bath. Boy!

Mendez looked ten years older, his eyes sunken in and his face covered with beard stubble. Dr. Favor's big, broad face, framed by that half-moon-shaped beard, was sweaty looking. The McLaren girl and John Russell were the only ones who didn't look so bad, I mean not as dirty or sweaty as the rest of us. With her hair too short to muss and her dark skin, she looked like she was taking it all right. John Russell was dusty, of course, but had no beard to make his face look dirty. You could tell he had pulled out the stubbles Indian-fashion when he first started to get a beard, years ago, and now he'd never have one.

Russell stayed mostly by the open side, lying down but propped on his elbows and looking down the way we had come up. I guess he was resting and doing his thinking now, taking time to see things clearly. Whatever he saw in his mind, it got him up on his feet after a while.

He brought the saddlebags over to me and dropped them. He didn't say guard them, but that's what his look meant. All he said was he would go have a look at things and he left, taking only the Spencer carbine; no water or anything else. He didn't go straight down the slope but headed off through the pinyon, I guess to keep high up as he scouted the ground we had covered from the draw.

A little while after he was gone, Dr. Favor went over to where the waterskin and canteen and provisions were. He picked up the canteen and was drinking from it before anyone had time to yell stop. It was the McLaren girl who yelled it.

She jumped up, and Dr. Favor held the canteen out to her. "Your turn," he said.

"We're not to drink till tonight. You know that."

"I forget," Dr. Favor said. She could believe him or not; he didn't care.

Mendez, still sitting down, said, "Maybe we should all take one, to keep it even."

"To keep it even!" the McLaren girl said. "What about later when we don't have any. What good does keeping it even do?"

"I'm thinking of now," Mendez said, rising. "You can think of any time you want."

"All right," the girl said. "And what about Russell?"

"Look"—Mendez had this surprised sound to his voice—"if he wants to wait till dark, all right. That's up to him. We drink when we want."

"He doesn't even have to know," Dr. Favor said. He saw

Mendez liked this idea so he put it out there again. "If you're worried about Russell, why would he even have to know?"

"And you think that would be fair," the McLaren girl said.

"It's his rule," Dr. Favor said. "If it's unfair, he brought it on himself."

"Look," Mendez said, making it sound simple, "if you want to wait, you wait. If you want a drink now, then you take it."

That was when he grabbed the canteen from Dr. Favor and took a good drink, more even than Favor had, so that Dr. Favor reached for it and pulled it out of Mendez's mouth.

"You said keep it even."

Then he handed the canteen to the McLaren girl.

She took it, her eyes right on Dr. Favor and hesitating just a little before she put it to her mouth. If this surprises you, look at it this way: they could drink it all while you sat there obeying Russell's rule. All right, if they were going to have some, a person would be dumb not to take his share. That's why I took a drink right after she did. I'm sure she was thinking the same way.

Dr. Favor was still looking at her, more sure of himself than ever now. He said, "If you want to tell him when he gets back, you just go right ahead." He was even smiling then.

What could she say? On the other hand, knowing her, she might have said something at that. But she didn't.

Everybody settled down again. For a little while there was peace. Then Dr. Favor came over to me.

Right away he said, "That's some Indian chief we got," meaning Russell of course.

"Well," I said, "I guess he knows what he's doing."

"He knows what he wants. That much is sure."

If he thought Russell wanted the money, that was his business. But why talk about something you couldn't prove? I just said, "Maybe he's the best chief we got," kind of joking about it.

"Only we're not his braves," Dr. Favor said, and he was serious, his face close to mine and staring right at me.

"If somebody has another idea," I said, "I'll listen."

"I've got one," he said. "We leave right now."

He'd force you right up against a wall like that; then you'd have to try and wiggle out.

"Well, I don't know about that," I said.

"Let me have my gun then."

He said it all of a sudden and I didn't have any idea in the world what to say back. What I finally said was something like, "Well, I don't think I can do that."

"Because he said so?"

"No, not just because of him."

"Because of the others?"

"We're all in this together."

"But not going by his rules anymore."

"Just the water."

"What's more important than that?"

"I'm holding it," I said. "He's the one took it."

"Now that doesn't make much sense, does it?" Dr. Favor said. "What you're doing, you're keeping something that doesn't belong to you."

I couldn't tell the man to his face I thought he was a thief. That's why I had so much trouble thinking of something to say. Even with the gun in my belt, or maybe because it was there, I felt awkward and dumb. He just kept staring at me.

"Maybe I should take it away from you," he said.

When I hesitated, not knowing what to say or do, the Mc-Laren girl got into it. She said, looking at me, "Are you going to let him?"

She pushed up to a sitting position, about ten or twelve feet away from us. "You know what he wants," she said.

"What's mine," Dr. Favor said. "If you think anything else, you're imagining things."

"I know one thing," the McLaren girl said. "I wouldn't give you the gun if I had it. And if you tried to take it, I'd shoot you."

"For hardly more than a little girl," Dr. Favor said, "you certainly have strong opinions."

"When I know I'm right," the McLaren girl said.

Dr. Favor stood up. He lit a cigar and for a while stood there looking out over the slope and smoking. Time crept along. I laid down with one arm on the saddlebags and my head on my arm. I don't think I have ever been so tired, and it was easy to close my eyes and fall asleep. I fought it for a while, dozing, opening my eyes. Once when I opened them, I saw Dr. Favor sitting by Mendez and Mendez was smoking a cigar too.

I heard Dr. Favor say, "You did fine. It took more nerve than most have to lie there waiting for them."

"He shouldn't have made me do it," Mendez said.

"You didn't have to, you know."

"Listen, he makes sense," Mendez said. "Whether you agree with him or not."

"He makes sense even if it kills you," Dr. Favor said. "That's what you're saying."

"It's just I had never shot at a man before," Mendez said. "It isn't an easy thing."

"It seems easy to him," Dr. Favor said. "And if you can kill one person, you can kill four."

"For what reason?"

"My money," Dr. Favor said.

Mendez shook his head. "I know him better than that."

"Where money is concerned," Dr. Favor said, "you don't know anybody."

Within the next quarter of an hour Dr. Favor proved those words.

I should have taken them as a warning, but I had not for a minute thought he would ever use force. By the time I woke up (I mean actually woke up, for I had dozed off again) it was too late. Dr. Favor was standing over me with Mendez's shotgun pointed right at my head.

Mendez sat there with his legs crossed and his shoulders hunched as if he didn't care what was happening—as if Dr. Favor had just taken the gun and Mendez hadn't lifted an eyebrow to stop him.

The McLaren girl was watching too. She had been lying on her side, but now pushed herself up on one arm as Dr. Favor took the revolver from me first and then the saddlebags. He went over to the waterskin next and filled up the two-quart canteen from it, leaving hardly anything in the skin.

That's when the McLaren girl finally spoke. She said, "Maybe you'll leave us your blessing since you're taking everything else."

Dr. Favor was past arguing with anybody. He didn't say a word. He opened the canvas grainsack, looked at the meat and biscuits inside like he was going to take some out, but he pulled the neck closed and swung it over his shoulder with the saddlebags.

He was standing like that, ready to move off, when John Russell appeared out of the pinyon.

They stood facing each other about twenty feet apart, Russell holding the Spencer against his leg and pointed down; Favor holding the sawed-off shotgun the same way.

"You got everything?" Russell said.

"What's mine," Favor answered.

"You better put it down," Russell said. It sounded like he meant the shotgun.

Mendez must have felt funny about Dr. Favor holding it. He said, "He just took it. I closed my eyes and he had it."

Dr. Favor shook his head slowly. "Like I'm against everybody. Like I was running off on my own."

"You sure had us fooled then," the McLaren girl said, her voice dry and sharp enough to pierce right through him.

"Believe what you like," Dr. Favor said. "I was going to get help. One man can travel faster than five. With food and water he could make it out of here in no time and have help back in less than a day."

"So you elected yourself," the McLaren girl said.

"I've tried to reason with you people before," Dr. Favor said. "I decided it was time to do something besides waste my breath."

Russell's eyes never left Dr. Favor. "Put it down or else use it," he said. "You have two ways to go." His tone seemed to say he didn't care which Favor did. One way would be as easy as the other.

"There's no talking to a man who relies only on force," Dr. Favor said. He shrugged, hesitating, holding on by his fingernails for a moment, waiting for Russell to drop his guard for one second. Maybe he could beat Russell, he was probably thinking. But if he didn't beat him, he would be dead. If he tied Russell, he could also be dead.

Maybe that was the way he thought and he didn't like the odds. Maybe if he gave in now he would get a better chance later on. I guess he knew nobody believed his story about getting help, but he didn't care what we thought. Whatever he was thinking, it told him today wasn't the day. He let the shotgun and revolver fall, then lifted off the grainsack and saddlebags.

No, it didn't bother him at all what we thought. He turned his back on us and strolled over by the cliffrose bushes to look down the grade. As if telling us he knew we wouldn't do anything to him, so what did he care what we thought?

But that's where he was wrong. John Russell did not just think things.

As Dr. Favor stood there, Russell said, "Keep going."

All we saw was his back for a minute. Dr. Favor seemed to be waiting for the rest of it: "—if you ever try that again." Or "—if you don't behave yourself." You know.

But there wasn't any rest of it. Russell had said it all.

When Dr. Favor realized this, he turned around to look at Russell. His face had lost a little of its calm cocksureness. Not all, just some. But maybe at that point he half believed Russell might be bluffing.

Maybe, he thought, if he could just pass a little time it would blow over.

He said, "You're betting my money I won't survive all alone."

"You could do it," Russell said. "With some luck."

"If I don't, it's the same as murder."

"Like the way you killed those people at San Carlos."

"This is a new one," Dr. Favor said. "First I'm accused of stealing my own money. Now murder."

"Without enough to eat," Russell said, "people sicken and die. I saw that at Whiteriver and also I heard things, how the agent had money to buy more beef, but he had a way of keeping the money to himself."

"A way," Dr. Favor said. "You figure the way and then prove it."

"That one called Dean said enough."

Dr. Favor seemed to smile. "But you went and killed our witness."

"You think I need one?" Russell said.

We weren't in any court. We were fifty miles out in high desert country, and John Russell was standing there with a .56-56 Spencer in his hand. All he had to do was raise it and Dr. Favor was gone forever.

There wasn't any question, Dr. Favor knew it.

It is hard to try and imagine what was going on in his mind then, because I never did learn much about this Dr. Alexander Favor.

Look at him for a minute. A heavyset man, both in his body and in his opinion of himself. He did what he wanted and did not take much pushing from others. He had been Indian Agent at San Carlos about two years, having come from somewhere in Ohio. The "Doctor" part of his name was not medicine. I have learned that he was a Doctor of the Faith Reform Church. But I had never heard him preaching anything, so you cannot accuse him of not practicing it.

Evidently he got into that profession to make money and for
that reason only, thinking it would be an easy way: the same
reason he applied to the government to become an Indian Agent
and got sent to San Carlos. Though he could have just made up
the divinity title and got the appointment through some friend
in the Interior Department. I would not like to think that he had
ever honestly been a preacher.

He must have started withholding government funds soon
after he got to San Carlos to build up the amount in the saddlebags. About twelve thousand dollars. He probably made some
of it off supply contractors who paid him in order to get the
government business. So you know one thing for sure; he was
dishonest. A thief no matter what he hid behind.

You can also say he was a man who cared more about his
money than his wife. But maybe he always did. I mean maybe
she was just a woman to him. Someone to have around, but not
feeling about her the way most men felt about their wives. I
mean liking them along with having them there.

Maybe he did like her, but she never liked him and didn't
care if he knew it. I think that is the way it was, judging from
the way she didn't pay any attention to him on the stagecoach
and fooled with Frank Braden right in front of him. I think
even then Dr. Favor had finally had enough of her. Leaving her
was a good way to pay her back.

You knew good and well he wasn't thinking about her right
now. I doubt he was even thinking about the money. Right now
he just had his life to worry about. Russell wasn't letting him
take anything else.

There was that little space of silence where he must have
been digging in his mind to say something more to Russell, to
scare him or put him in his place or something. But he must
have thought what was the use? Why waste breath?

He looked at Mendez though, then at the McLaren girl and
said, "You take care of yourselves now. Do everything he tells

you." He was turning then to go. "And remember, don't drink any water till tonight."

We watched him step through the cliffrose bushes and he was gone. Russell went over to the edge, but the McLaren girl and Mendez and I didn't move. Not for a moment anyway. Maybe we were afraid Favor would look back up and see us watching him and laugh or say something else about the water.

When I walked over finally and looked down the grade, he was past the steepest part but having an awful time, skidding and raising dust all the way. We watched him down at the bottom, standing there for a minute, looking up canyon to the flat country that opened up there. He crossed the canyon to the other side and started up a little wash (he had learned something from Russell) and after a minute you couldn't see him for the brush and the steepness of the cutbank.

Nobody said a word.

Without Russell I know we could never have sat there in that place until dark. It was too easy to imagine them sneaking up on you, knowing they were out there somewhere and drawing closer all the time. Russell sat watching the slope. Then he'd move off into the trees for a time. He never said anything. He smoked a little, maybe twice. Most of the time though he sat watching; watching and I think listening. But all that time there was no sign of them.

As it started to get dark in the trees, we ate again and Russell held up the canteen and handed it to the McLaren girl.

"Finally, uh?" he said.

She didn't look at him. She took a drink and passed the canteen to me. Mendez was next. Then Russell took his turn. The McLaren girl watched him drink, holding the water in his mouth before swallowing it, and I kept thinking: She's going to tell him.

Russell lowered the canteen.

Now, I thought, waiting for her to speak.

Russell pushed the cork in tight. She watched him. I think right then she almost told, so near to doing it the words were formed in her mouth. But she didn't say it.

She said instead, "Maybe we should have let him take some." Meaning Dr. Favor.

Russell looked at her.

"I mean just some," the McLaren girl said.

I thought of something then. All of a sudden. "We left a waterskin at the San Pete! Remember that?"

The McLaren girl looked at me. "Will he remember it?"

"I don't know," I said, "I just started thinking, Braden knows about it too."

We did not go down the slope we had come up but went off through the trees, following Russell and not asking any questions.

I remember we crept down through a gully that was very thick with brush and near the bottom of it Russell held up. The open part was next and it was not dark enough to cross it.

When I think of all the waiting we did. It made being out there all the worse because it gave you time to imagine things. We kept quiet because Russell did. I have never seen a man so patient. He would sit with his legs crossed and fool with a stick or something, drawing with it in the sand, making circles and different signs and then smoothing out the sand and doing it all over again. What did a man like that think about? That's what I wondered about every time I looked at him.

From this gully you could not see anything but sky and the dark hump of the slope above us. I kept thinking that if I was back in Sweetmary I would have finished my supper and would be reading or going to visit somebody; seeing the main street then and the lanterns shining through the windows of the saloons; seeing lights way off in the adobes that were situated out from town.

There were some sounds around us, night sounds, which I took as a good sign; nothing was moving nearby. I heard the clicking sound of the McLaren girl's rosary beads, which I had not heard since the first evening in the stagecoach. It was funny, I had forgotten all about making conversation in order to get to know her. If I did not know her after this, I never would. It was something the way she never complained. But maybe she spoke out a little too quickly; even when she was right. That was something I never could do.

When the time came it was like always, coming after you had got tired of waiting for it and wondering when it ever would. There was Russell standing up again, like he knew or felt the exact moment we should leave, and within a few minutes we were down out of the gully with dark, wide-open country stretching out on three sides of us.

We did what Russell did. He didn't tell us. He kept in the lead and we followed with our eyes pretty much of the time. When he stopped, we stopped, which was often, though you could never guess when it was going to be. Or you could listen till your head ached and never know what made him stop.

All of us together made some noise moving through the brush clumps and kicking stones and things, which couldn't be helped. Just grit your teeth and hope nobody else heard it. Yet when Russell moved off from us to scout a little, which he did a few times, he never made a sound going or coming. His Apache-type moccasins had something to do with it, but it was also the way he walked, a way I never learned.

You know how it is outside at night as far as seeing things, shapes and the sky and all. It is never as dark as indoors, in a cellar or in a closed room without a window. We would see a dark patch and it would turn out to be a brush thicket or some Joshua trees. There were those saguaros, but not as many as had been in the higher country. There was greasewood and prickly pear and other bushes I never knew the names of, most of them low to the ground so that you still felt yourself out in the open and unprotected.

I mentioned that Russell would stop and then we would,

listening hard to make out some sound. We never heard any-thing except twice.

The first time, we were maybe halfway across, though it is hard to judge. I remember I was looking down at the ground, then up and I stopped all of a sudden seeing Russell standing still. He had turned and was facing us with his head raised a little.

Then we all heard it, thin and faraway but unmistakable, the sound of a gunshot.

We waited. A few minutes later it came again and seemed a little closer, though I could have imagined that. About ten sec-onds passed. A third gunshot sounded faintly, off in another direction, way off in the darkness.

Russell moved on, faster now, knowing they were still be-hind and not somewhere up ahead waiting. I was sure then that the gunshots were signals. Say they had split up to poke through that area where we had hid. Say one group found a sign of us (probably the Mexican) and signaled the others with a shot, then with another one when they did not answer at first. The third shot was when they did answer.

The McLaren girl thought differently. Right after the shots, as we went on, she said to me, "They've killed him."

I had forgotten about Dr. Favor until she said that. I ex-plained what I thought about the signals.

"Maybe," she said. "But if they haven't killed him he'll die of thirst or starvation. He doesn't have any chance at all."

I said, "He sure didn't worry about us."

"Because he would do such a thing," the McLaren girl said, "should we?"

How do you answer a question like that? Anyway it wasn't us that did it, it was Russell. She certainly worried a lot without showing it on her face. I will say that for the McLaren girl.

The second time we heard a sound was a little later. This time it was a horse, sounding close, but far enough out so we couldn't see it. We went down flat and stayed that way for some time. We heard the horse again, never running or galloping, but walking, his shoes clinking against stones. It never came so close you could see it, but there was no doubting what it meant. They were out in the open now looking for us.

When Russell moved off finally it was at his careful, stopping, listening pace again. Nothing could hurry him, not even feeling them out here. He moved along with the Spencer down-pointed in one hand and the saddlebags over the other shoulder, like there wasn't anything in the world could make him hurry. Add that to what you know about his patience.

We saw the shape of the high ground ahead of us by the time we were halfway across. That's what made going slow so hard. There was cover staring right at you, but Russell chose to walk to it.

Finally he led us into some trees that was like going into a house and locking the door, and right away (which surprised nobody) we were climbing again. All the way up to the top of a ridge and along it instead of taking the pass that led into these hills. This part wasn't hard; it was even ground, grassy and with a lot of trees. But when we came to a higher ridge and Russell started climbing again, Mendez complained.

I don't think Russell even looked at him. He went on climbing and the rest of us followed: up through rocks and places you had to grab hold of roots and branches to pull yourself up. Then along a path that was probably a game trail, and finally on up to the top.

A couple of hundred yards along this ridge Russell stopped. There, down below us, was the San Pete mine works.

We had approached it the back way, from up above the shafts and crushing mill and all, which were on this side of the canyon. Way over on the other side you could make out the company buildings, even the one we had eaten breakfast in two days ago.

I think I would have bought John Russell a drink of liquor right then had there been any to buy. The McLaren girl and Mendez just stared; you could see the relief on their faces. That's what seeing something familiar did, letting you forget Braden for a minute and look ahead and start to see a little daylight.

At that point there was the sure feeling with all of us that we would make it to Delgado's without Braden ever getting close again. Except that just a little later on there was another familiar sight. One we had not counted on.

I am referring to Dr. Favor.

But I will get to that in a minute.

It was still dark as we came down the ridge toward the mine works. We didn't go down all the way, only about fifty or sixty feet to a level place where the open mine shafts and a shack were.

Farther along this shelf there was a shute built on scaffolding that went down to the big crushing mill located about forty or fifty yards down the grade. Ore tailings, which were slides of rock and sand and stuff that had been taken out of the shafts and dumped, formed long humps down on the other side of the crushing mill. Everything was quiet and there wasn't even a breeze moving.

As I have said, it was still dark, but you could make out the shapes of things down below: the crushing mill and ore tailings to the left of where we were; the company buildings about two hundred yards away, directly across the canyon from us.

We stood there for a few minutes, Russell looking over the works and I guess, thinking. Finally, when he spoke he said, "This is a good place." Meaning the shack up here on the shelf.

"There's more water for us down there." Mendez said, meaning the waterskin we'd left in that company building the day before yesterday.

Russell shook his head. "If we stay here all day, you want tracks leading up and down?"

"Stay!" Mendez said. The waiting was worrying his nerves. "Man, we're so close now!"

"If you go," Russell said, without any feeling at all, "you go back the way we came."

Mendez looked at him with those solemn eyes of his. He

didn't say any more. We went inside the shack which was empty except for a couple of bats which we shooed out. On the two side walls were shelves that held bags of concentrate. (Evidently they had used this shack to test ore samples in.) We just stretched out on the dusty floor and used some of these bags as pillows.

Russell left the door part way open and laid down his head near the opening. I laid down over by one of the windows. There were two of them in front, with board shutters you couldn't close.

Just one small thing: Russell did not offer his blanket to the McLaren girl, but used it himself. I offered mine to her again, as I had done the night before, and this time she took it. Figure that one out.

It was a few hours later, say between six and seven in the morning, after we had slept some and eaten and had our day's water, that we saw Dr. Favor again. The McLaren girl, by the right-hand window at the time, saw him first.

He was already down out of the south pass that approached the mine from the direction of that open country we had crossed. He was moving slow; dead tired you could see, his clothes messier and dirtier looking than before. He walked straight down the middle of the canyon in the sunlight and in the dead silence of those rickety buildings, looking up at the crushing mill for the longest time, then over at the line of company buildings.

Watching him, nobody said a word, waiting to see if he remembered the waterskin.

Alongside one of the buildings was a trough with a hand pump at one end of it. When Dr. Favor saw it, he ran over and started pumping. He fell on his knees and kept on pumping, his shoulders and arms moving up and down, up and down, keeping at it even when he must have known he wasn't going to get any water. After a few minutes he was pumping slower and slower. Finally he fell over the pump and held on there, not moving.

Inside the shack it was quiet as could be.

I remember when the McLaren girl spoke it was hardly above a whisper. I was by the other window with Mendez; Russell was by the door; but we all heard her. "He doesn't remember it," she said.

None of the others spoke.

"We have to tell him," she said then, calm and quiet about it, stating a fact, not just giving in to pity at the sight of him.

"We don't do anything," Russell said from the door. He kept his gaze on Dr. Favor who had sat down now, one arm still on the pump handle.

"You can look at that man," the McLaren girl said, "and not want to help him?" She was staring at Russell now.

"He'll move off," Russell said. "Then you won't have to look at him."

"But he's dying of thirst. You can *see* he is!"

"What did you think would happen?" Russell said. He looked at her then. "You didn't think you'd see him again. So yesterday was all right, uh?"

"If I didn't speak up yesterday," the McLaren girl said, "I was wrong."

"You'd feel better if he had run off with the water?"

"That has nothing to do with him down there now."

"But if you were down there," Russell said, "and he was up here."

"You just don't understand, do you?" the McLaren girl said.

Russell kept staring at her. "What do you want to do?"

"I want to help him!" She raised her voice a little, like she was running out of patience.

It didn't seem to bother Russell any. He said, "You want to go down to him? Make tracks on that slope that hasn't been touched in five years? You want to make signs pointing up where we are?"

"The man's dying of thirst!" She screamed it at Russell. She had run clean out of patience and threw the words right at him.

I don't mean she screamed so loud Dr. Favor heard her. He had now got up from the pump and was moving along the front of the company buildings, reaching the one we had stopped at the day before yesterday and looking up at it.

I held my breath again. Maybe he'd remembered the water-skin. But no, he went on by.

The next thing I knew the McLaren girl was out the window and running down the slope. Russell was out the door but too late to stop her. He stood there in front of the shack, Mendez and I by the window, and watched her raising little dust trails down the grade, seeing her getting smaller and smaller.

Near the bottom the McLaren girl called out. We saw Dr. Favor stop and look around. (He must have been surprised out of his shoes.) He started toward her, but she was yelling something at him now, motioning to the company building.

He stood there a second, then was almost running in his hurry to get to the building, the McLaren girl waiting now to see if he'd find the waterskin.

We were watching all this. We saw him reach the front of the place, just out from the shade formed by the veranda, and that's where he stopped. Right away he started backing off, like edging away. Next thing he had turned and was running toward the McLaren girl who didn't know what was going on anymore than we did and stood there watching him.

As he got close he must have said something. The McLaren girl started up the grade, looking back at the company building as she did.

About then was when he appeared. It was Early. He came out of the veranda shade, to the edge of it, and stood there with a Colt gun in one hand and a canteen in the other—evidently the canteen with whisky in it which the Mexican had mentioned to John Russell, for I think Early was drunk or close to it. The way he stood, his boots wide apart, looked like he was steadying himself. I won't swear to it because there wasn't time to get a good look at him.

He started firing his Colt, waving it toward us or at the McLaren girl and Dr. Favor as they came up the grade, causing Mendez and me to duck down, and firing until his gun was empty. He started yelling then, but we couldn't make out any of it.

I kept waiting for Braden and the others to appear, but they didn't. Not right then. Evidently Early had been sent on ahead, Braden figuring we would come this way.

I was still there at the window when the McLaren girl and Dr. Favor reached the shack. She came inside and went out again with the canteen and gave it to Dr. Favor who drank until she yanked it away from his mouth. He yanked back, held onto it and handed it to Russell. I think he could tell from looking at Russell that saving him had been just the McLaren girl's idea. He seemed to be smiling some, like the joke was on Russell.

"You will learn something about white people," he said to Russell. "They stick together."

"They better," Mendez said. "We all better."

Just for a second there was the old tell-nothing Henry Mendez talking. It sounded good after seeing the other side of him for two days. He wasn't looking at Dr. Favor. I noticed then Russell was looking off down the slope too.

Like they had been following Dr. Favor (and no doubt they had), there came the Mexican on foot, Frank Braden and the Favor woman each on a horse, this little procession coming down out of the south pass, keeping close to the other side and in no hurry at all. The Mexican raised his arm up and waved.

We were all back together again. Right back where we had started. Except now we were up on that shelf of rock, looking down and seeing them moving up canyon and dismounting in front of the company building that was straight across from us and drawing their rifles.

You think about an awful lot of things at once. That we should be doing something; getting out of there or doing *some-*

thing. That this never should have happened. That if it wasn't for the McLaren girl and her act of kindness to a man who didn't deserve it, they never would have found us; they would have looked up at that bare unmarked slope and gone right on. Maybe you would like to have said something to the McLaren girl. It was a temptation. But only Mendez did.

He said, "You see?" looking at Dr. Favor and then at the McLaren girl in the doorway. "You see?" he said again, wanting to say more, but just shaking his head as he thought of everything at once.

The McLaren girl had been quiet, but I think Mendez made her mad. She said, "I'd do it again. Knowing they were there I'd do it again. What do you think of that!"

"He's not worth it!" Mendez said, keeping his teeth together so he wouldn't scream it at her. Still it was loud.

"Who are you to say who's worth it!" When she got mad, she spoke out, as you have seen.

Dr. Favor didn't get into it. He was running his tongue over his swollen lips, I think still tasting the water.

And Russell. Russell, still outside squatted down, sitting back on his heels. He was smoking a cigarette, gazing over across the canyon. Russell didn't look at the McLaren girl (not then) or say anything to anybody. Russell was Russell.

He just smoked the cigarette as he watched Braden and the others over in front of the company building, watching them take the two horses into the shade of the built-up, second-storey veranda, watching the Mexican come out again in the sunlight and walk up and down in a show-offy way, his hands on his hips and looking up toward where we were.

That's when Russell came inside the shack. Next thing I knew he was at the other window with the Spencer at his shoulder. I doubt the Mexican saw him. I'm sure he didn't else he would have done something before Russell fired.

With the sound of the shot and dust kicking up in front of

him, the Mexican stopped dead. Russell fired again and this time the Mexican jumped back into the veranda shade. Russell was not taking anything off that Mexican.

"What do you start that for?" Mendez said, sounding pained.

Russell must have thought there was an awful lot of dumb questions asked. He said to Mendez, "So they'd see us."

Nobody down there returned the fire, but we kept expecting it. Everybody was inside by then. Russell was already piling those bags of concentrate on his window sill. I started building up the other one then, the McLaren girl helping. Mendez brought a few over to Russell, but Dr. Favor didn't lift a hand. He was doing his thinking now, I guess, and eying the saddlebags. Since Russell didn't say anything to him, I didn't either. Hell.

Next Russell pulled the loading tube out of his Spencer and stuck two more cartridges in it from his belt. I kept by the other window wondering if this little revolver I had would do any good.

The minutes went by but the awful nervous feeling I had and tried not to show didn't ease up any. I remember wondering if Russell was scared. He had taken his hat off and I could see the side of his face good. As I have said before, he looked so much younger with his hat off and his hair pressed down on his forehead. He would swallow or scratch his nose, things everybody did, and he didn't seem any different than the rest of us.

Only he was different. As Braden was about to learn first hand.

Frank Braden's idea was to let us worry some, I suppose. About a half hour passed before we heard from him. Then it came all of a sudden.

He yelled out from across the way, "You hear me!" He waited. "I'm coming up to talk! You hold your fire!" He waited and yelled again. Maybe a minute passed.

Then Braden appeared at the edge of the veranda shade. Early and the Mexican were behind him. They waited there as Braden moved out from them carrying a Winchester rifle and a white cloth or something tied to the end of it. Frank Braden's idea of a truce flag.

Russell watched him. As Braden came across the open, out in the sunlight and without any cover close by, Russell raised the Spencer and eared back the hammer.

"He wants to talk," Mendez said. "You heard him. It's no trick. He's got something to say to us!"

Russell didn't bother with Mendez or even look up. He steadied the Spencer on the ore-sample bags and put the front sight on Braden.

FIVE

Frank Braden had nerve. You can put that under his name big. A man does not hold up stagecoaches without nerve, or walk up an open grade in plain sight of people he knows are armed.

If he was afraid at all, he never showed it. The way his hat was funneled and tipped forward over his eyes he had to raise his head to look up. He kept watching, but it did not make him hesitate. He came across the open from the company building like nothing in the world bothered him, the Winchester raised a little and the white truce flag tied to the end of it.

He was putting his faith in that truce flag and the fact that the Mexican had done the same thing yesterday without drawing fire. It showed he still didn't know John Russell very well.

Russell was letting him come. He never took the Spencer away from his shoulder, but the barrel kept lowering a hair at a time as Braden came closer. Anyone else might have been covering Braden; but somehow you knew Russell meant to fire on him, else he never would have raised the gun. The question was how close Braden would get.

"Listen—he just wants to talk," Mendez said, moving toward Russell as you would approach a bronc with your hand out to gentle it. "You can see it's no trick. The man is coming to *talk*. Can't you see that? You want to start something when there's no need to?

"Look at me!"

Russell's head raised up a little, interrupted from what he was concentrating on. But he kept his eyes on Braden who had now reached some ore-cart tracks that came across from the crushing mill and past a little shack on out into the open a ways. On this side of the tracks Braden was less than a hundred yards off. He kept coming.

"Just see what he wants," Mendez said. "You don't have to talk to him. You don't want to, one of us will." Mendez looked outside, seeing Braden on the grade now and starting up.

"You don't know what he wants. Man, you got to find out what he wants," Mendez kept saying. "Listen to him. He trusts us . . . we have to trust him and see what he wants. Doesn't that make sense to you?" Mendez said it all fast. If it didn't convince Russell, it bothered him enough so he couldn't concentrate on Braden.

By that time Braden was part way up the grade. He stopped there and yelled out, "Anybody home?"

Mendez saw the opportunity looking at him and he grabbed a hold of it. "We hear you!" he yelled back.

"Come on out of that boar's nest," Braden called. "We'll talk some."

"Say what you want," Mendez answered.

"I thought maybe you'd like to go home."

"Say something," Mendez said.

"It's looking at you," Braden said back. "We can sit here long as we want. I can send a man for more water and chuck, but you people can't move. You only move if we let you. You see that?"

"What else?"

"There doesn't have to be much else."

"All right, what do you want?"

"You leave the money, we leave the woman."

"And everybody goes home?"

"Everybody goes home."

"We'll have to talk about it."

"You do that." Braden held the Winchester cradled over one arm, the truce flag hanging limp. He stood with his feet spread some, posing, it looked like, confident he knew what he was doing.

"We'll let you look at the woman while you talk," Braden said. "Then when you're ready you bring the money down and take the woman."

"We'll talk about it," Mendez said again. He glanced over at Dr. Favor who was at the other window, then down at Braden again.

"What if," he said "—well, what if nobody wants this woman?"

"Wait a while," Braden answered, "before you think anything like that."

"I just want to make sure what you mean, that's all."

"You just have to be sure of one thing," Braden said. "You don't leave here with the money. You see that?"

Mendez didn't answer. Frank Braden waited a minute then started to go.

"Hey," Russell called out to him and Braden stopped, half way around so that he was looking back over his shoulder.

"I got a question," Russell said.

Braden was squinting to make out Russell in the window. "Ask it," he said.

"How you going to get down that hill?"

Braden knew what he meant. He stood there a moment, then came around slowly to face the shack again, showing us he wasn't afraid.

"Look, I come up here to tell you how things are. I'm making it easy on you."

"We didn't ask you," Russell said. "You walk up here yourself. You come and say we're not leaving with the money . . . uh?"

"You heard what I said." Braden was tenser, you could tell.

"We give you the money or you kill us."

"I said you wouldn't leave here."

"But it's the same thing, uh? . . . Maybe we give up the money and you still kill us."

"You better talk to your friends."

"I think," Russell kept on, "you want to leave dead people who can't tell things."

"If that was so, we'd have killed you at the stagecoach."

"You tried to," Russell said, "taking the water. But it came back to us."

"You think what you want," Braden said, meaning to end it.

Russell nodded. He nodded up and down very slowly two or three times. "I've already thought," he said in that mild way, so calm you did not suspect what he meant until he raised the Spencer. Then there was no doubt what he meant.

"You hold on, boy!" Braden said. "I'm walking down the same way I come up." But he was backing off, keeping his gaze fixed on the window.

Russell had the Spencer at his shoulder, but his head up as he watched Braden.

"You hear me!" Braden yelled. "You hold on!"

It was like Russell was letting out rope, giving Braden a little slack before he yanked it tight. It was coming. We knew it and Braden, still backing away, knew it. But only Russell knew when. That's what finally spooked Braden. He might have had seven miles of nerve inside of him, but all of a sudden he found it all let out and there was only one thing left to do.

He started running, starting so fast across the slope toward the crushing mill that he fell within four or five steps, falling just as Russell pressed his face to that Spencer and fired. Maybe that fall saved Braden's life; for certain it hurried Russell's second shot, trying to get Braden while he was down, but that one kicked sand right in front of Braden who was lunging to his feet, running again, getting some distance as Russell took his time and aimed and when he fired again Braden twisted and rolled a ways down the slope. That's when the gunfire opened up from the company building as the Mexican and Early woke up and started giving Braden some cover. Braden was crawling, then up on his feet and running again, limping-running, favoring one leg—and *bam*, the Spencer went off and Braden was knocked down again, down on his hands and knees, but somehow kept going, clawing the ground and half running half crawling, the Winchester truce flag behind him now and forgotten. Russell fired again, hurrying it because Braden was close to the crushing mill by then and that was Russell's last one; Braden made it, reaching the corner of the building, about forty yards over from us, as the sound of Russell's shot sang off down canyon.

It was the Mexican who got Braden out of there. He came up over on the other side of the crushing mill and brought Braden down the same way, keeping the crushing mill between us and them so they wouldn't get shot at.

Early came out of the veranda shade to help the Mexican take Braden inside: Early looking back like he was afraid Russell would open up again, and Braden walking but dragging his legs and leaning on the two men. He had been shot up good.

Mr. Braden, I thought to myself. Meet John Russell.

But was our situation any better?

Maybe. Depending on Braden. If he was hurt bad enough, they would have to get him to a bed or a doctor. So for a while we watched with that hope. But the hope kept getting smaller and smaller as time passed and nobody rode out from the company building.

When there was no doubt but they were staying, Henry Mendez started on Russell again. Why did you have to do that? Why didn't you let things just happen? he kept saying. It would be worse for us now, Mendez was sure. And it was Russell's fault.

"Nothing is different," Russell said. In other words, they could be mad or shot up or hungry or drunk, they'd still try to kill us. When you thought about it, you knew it was true.

While Mendez and Russell were together I brought up the idea of getting out the way we'd come in.

They'd shoot us off the wall as we climbed up, was Mendez's answer. "Not when it's dark," Russell said; you saw he was thinking of ways.

So far, you will notice, no one had said Russell should give them the money in exchange for Mrs. Favor: do what Braden wanted and *see* what would happen, not just guess. Maybe because it would be wasting breath to mention it to Russell. Or maybe because no one was thinking of Mrs. Favor at that time.

Well, that changed as soon as the Mexican brought her out. Maybe an hour had passed from the time Braden was shot. (It's hard to remember now the different spaces of time.) It had been so quiet over there. Then the Mexican was coming out across the open with Mrs. Favor in front of him. Her hands were tied and there was a length of rope, like a dog leash, tied around her neck with the Mexican holding the other end.

He brought her all the way out to the ore-cart tracks that came down from the crushing mill and made her sit down there. Kneeling, he tied the leash to one of the rails, keeping Mrs. Favor in front of him as he did. He drew his left-hand Colt then, holding his right elbow tight against his side, and ran to a little shed that was just above and over a few yards.

He surprised us then. Instead of going back, keeping the shed in line with us as a cover, he made a run all the way across a pretty open stretch to the crushing mill.

Picture him about forty yards down and over to our left; Mrs. Favor straight down, looking small sitting there and staring up at the shack, about eighty yards away.

It was while the Mexican was making his run that Early came out carrying a rifle and moved off toward the south pass on foot. I did not have to think about it long. Early was circling around to get behind us, closing the back door whether we wanted to use it or not.

That's what Russell said too. He was still at the window watching the corner of the crushing mill where the Mexican was. The McLaren girl asked him where Early was going and Russell said, "Behind us," not taking his eyes off the crushing mill; the Mexican had not shown himself yet.

Dr. Favor, at this time, was at the other window looking down at his wife. It was a strange thing, while he was there no one else went out to the window, as if letting him be alone with her. But he did not stay too long; he walked away and lit up a cigar and sat down, I guess to think some more.

The McLaren girl and Mendez and I finally found ourselves at that window, where we stayed just about all the rest of the time we were there. Of course we kept looking at Mrs. Favor.

Remember Braden saying, "We'll let you look at the woman while you talk?" He knew what he was doing.

She sat there between the ore-cart tracks looking up this way most of the time. We soon learned that she could not stand up straight; the rope tied to her neck was not long enough. She could get in a bent-over position, but that was all. For a time she tried to undo the rope end tied to the track, but evidently the Mexican had tied it too tight.

So she just sat there out in the open with the sun getting higher all the time, sometimes brushing her hair out of her face or picking things off her skirt. The way she would look up—my gosh—you knew what she was thinking. But she certainly was calm about it, not even crying once. It was not till a little later we found out they had not given her any water.

It was after the Mexican started on Russell.

He yelled out from the corner of the crushing mill, just showing part of his head for a second, "Hey, *hombre*! How do you like that woman? . . . You want her? . . . We give her to you!" Things like that.

John Russell did not answer. Except he put his face against the stock of the Spencer and the front sight on the corner of the crushing mill.

The Mexican waited a while. Then he yelled, "If you want that, *hombre,* you better hurry! Maybe there won't be nothing left in the sun!"

It was about 10 o'clock by then, maybe a little earlier.

Then the Mexican yelled, "Man, why don't you come out and give her a drink of water? She hasn't had none . . . not since yesterday morning!"

There he was, just a little part of him at the corner, and *bam* the Spencer went off and you saw the wood splinter right where the Mexican's face had been.

It was quiet right after, long enough for us to wonder if Russell had got him. Long enough for the McLaren girl to say, "That woman hasn't had any water." Then to Russell: "Did you hear what he said? She hasn't had water since yesterday."

Russell was watching the corner still. The McLaren girl kept staring at him. "Is that why you want to kill him?" she said then. "To shut him up? So you won't have to hear about her?"

I touched her arm to calm her, but she jerked away. "It won't help to get fighting among ourselves," I said.

"Are we all on the same side?" she said. "Do you really think that?"

"Well, we're all sitting here."

She was looking at Russell again. "He's sitting here with twelve thousand dollars of somebody else's money and that woman is tied like an animal out there in the sun." She looked at me like somebody should do something.

"Well, what do you want him to do?"

The McLaren girl never answered. The Mexican yelled out again, letting us know he was still alive. "Hey, *hombre!*" he called out. "You got wood in my eyes! . . . Come down here and help me get it out!" Honest to gosh, like he thought it was funny to be shot at.

He kept it up, yelling at Russell from time to time, trying to get him outside. We heard from Early a few times too. Rocks coming down on the roof from above: Early still feeling his whisky and being playful, or else just letting us know he was up there and not to try anything.

The McLaren girl was quiet for a while. I guess she had calmed down. The sole of one of her shoes was loose and she kept fooling with it, trying to twist it off, even when she was looking at Mrs. Favor who sat with her shoulders hunched over now and her head down. The McLaren girl could not look at her too long, or fool with that shoe forever.

She started looking at Russell and finally went over and kneeled down next to him. Russell was smoking, sitting back on his feet, the Spencer resting on the ore bags lining the window sill.

"We have to give them the money," she said, very quietly, "I think you know that."

He looked at her, not just glancing but taking his time to look at her dark sun-browned face good.

"Like you had to give that one water," Russell said. Meaning Dr. Favor.

"That's over with." She bristled up a little.

"You think he would have done it for you?"

"Somebody would have."

"How do you know that?"

"I just know. People help other people."

"People kill other people too."

"I've seen that."

"You're going to see some more."

"If you want to say it's my fault we're stuck here, go ahead," the McLaren girl said. "It might make you feel better, but it won't change anything."

Russell shook his head. "The thing I want to know is why you helped."

"Because he *needed* help! I didn't ask if he deserved it!"

She let her temper calm down and said, half as loud, "Like that woman needs to live. It's not up to us to decide if she deserves it."

"We only help her, uh?"

"Do we have another choice?"

Russell nodded. "Not help her."

"Just let her die." The McLaren girl kept staring at him.

"That's up to Braden," Russell said. "We have another thing to look at. If we don't give him the money, he has to come get it."

The McLaren girl almost let go of her temper then. "You'd sacrifice a human life for that money. That's what you're saying."

Russell started making a cigarette, looking out the window at the crushing mill as he shaped it, then at the McLaren girl again. "Go ask that woman what she thinks of human life. Ask her what a human life is worth at San Carlos when they run out of meat."

"That isn't any fault of hers."

"She said those dirty Indians eat dogs. You remember that? She couldn't eat a dog no matter how hungry she was." Everybody was watching him. He lit his cigarette and blew out smoke. "Go ask her if she'd eat a dog now."

"That's why!" the McLaren girl said, like it was all clear to her now. "She insulted the poor hungry miserable Indians and you'd let her die for that!"

Russell shook his head. "We were talking about human life."

"Even if there was no money, nothing to be gained, you'd let her die!" All the McLaren girl's temper was showing now, and she was just letting it come. "Because she thinks Indians are dirty and no better than animals you'd sit there and let her die!"

Russell held the cigarette close to his mouth, watching her. "It makes you angry, why talk about it?"

"I want to talk about it," she shot back. "I would like you to

ask me what I think a human life is worth . . . a dirty human
Apache life. Go on, ask me. Ask me about the ones that took
me from my home and kept me past a month. Ask me about the
dirty things they did, what the women did when the men
weren't around and what the men did when we weren't running
but were hiding somewhere and there was time to waste. I dare
you to ask me!"

She knelt there tensed, like she was to spring on him if he
moved, though it was just she was so intent on telling him what
she'd just said.

It was all out of her system then. I think everybody wasn't
so tense anymore. She sank back to a sitting position, taking
her eyes off Russell, looking down at that loose sole on her
shoe and fooling with it as she thought something over.

Next thing, she was saying, "I haven't seen my folks in almost two months . . . or my little brother. Just he and I were
home and he ran and I don't know what happened to him,
whether they caught him or what."

She looked up at Russell again, all the softness gone out of
her that quick, like it was starting all over again. "What do they
think of an eight-year-old human life?" she said. "Do they just
kill little boys who can't defend themselves?"

Russell had not taken his eyes off her, still holding the cigarette up near his face. "If they don't want them," he said, and
kept looking right at her.

That ended it. For a thin little seventeen-year-old girl she
was tougher than most men and I think you know that by now.
But she had to give some time. I thought she was going to cut
at Russell again, but the words didn't come. Her eyes filled up
first. She sat there trying to keep her chin from quivering or
crying so we'd hear her, still looking right at Russell even with
her eyes wet, daring him to say something else.

Right at that time (and it was almost welcome) the Mexican
started again. He yelled out, "Hey man, you hear me!" Russell
turned and looked down the barrel of the Spencer. The Mexi-

can wasn't showing himself now and his voice sounded a little farther away. You knew he was there though.

"Come on down here," the Mexican yelled out, "I got something for you!"

Russell had something for him too if he showed even part of his face.

"Man!" the Mexican yelled then. "We both come out—talk to each other!"

He waited.

"You bring that piece of iron you got. I bring one, uh?"

Every word he yelled echoed up canyon and came back again.

"Hey, *hombre,* whatever your name is—you hear me!"

After that he said some things I had better not put down here, terrible words that were embarrassing to hear with the McLaren girl in the same room. He was trying to get Russell out by insulting him, but he could have been yelling at a tree stump for all the good it did. Russell sat there waiting for the Mexican to show himself; which he never did.

Something Russell had said to the McLaren girl bothered me, so I asked him about it: about them having to come up here if they wanted the money. Why couldn't they just outwait us? Our water would run out (there was about a quart and a half left) then what would we do?

Theirs would run out too, Russell said. But, I said, they can go get more.

All the way to Delgado's? Russell said. Who would go, the one up behind us? The Mexican? Then who would watch us? No, Russell said. Some time they have to come up here. They know it.

I said that may be, but the Favor woman would be dead by then. Russell didn't answer.

About two o'clock in the afternoon the Favor woman started screaming.

It could not get any hotter than it was then. There was no breeze, no clouds; the sun was bright, boiling hot and you would not even dare look up to see where it was.

The Favor woman sat down there near the bottom of the grade, no hat or anything to cover her head, no shade to crawl into. As I have said, there was a little shack near where she was, but the rope tied to her neck would not even let her stand up straight much less get over to the shack. She had given up trying to undo the rope.

For the longest time she sat hunched over, her face buried in her arm resting on her raised knees. Now she was looking up toward us, as she had done when the Mexican first put her there, and now every once in a while she would scream out to her husband, calling his name at first.

"Alex!" she would call, but drawn out and faint sounding, not sharp and loud as you would imagine a real scream.

"Alex . . . help me!" Sounding far away almost, like hearing only an echo of the words. She had not had water since yesterday. It was something that she could call out at all.

Dr. Favor raised up when she started and looked down at her for a while. I don't know what he was thinking. I don't even know if he felt sorry for her, because his expression never changed; he was just looking at something. He didn't call back to her or say a word.

Some people can hide their feelings very well, so I had better not pass judgment on Dr. Favor. I remember picturing him and his wife alone and wondering what they ever talked about and if they had ever got along well together. (I couldn't help having that feeling she had been just a woman to him. You know what I mean, just a woman to have around.) I tried to imagine her calling him Alex when they were alone. But it didn't sound right. He was not the kind of man you thought of as having a first name. Especially not a name like Alex or Alexander.

There it was though, faintly, coming from out of that big open canyon, "Alex . . ." And he just sat there looking down at her, not moving much other than to feel his beard, to rub it gently under his chin with the back of his fingers.

Once she stood up, as far as she could, and yelled his name louder than she ever did before. "Alex!" And this time it was sharp and clear enough and with an echo coming back to give you goose pimples at the sound of it.

And then again, which I will hear every day of my life.

"Alex . . . please help me!" The words all alone outside, echoing and fading to nothing.

It was strange to be in a room with four people and not hear one sound. Everybody sat there holding still, waiting for the Favor woman to cry out again. Maybe a couple of minutes passed; maybe more than that, it seemed longer. It was so quiet that when the sound came—the sound of a match scraping and popping aflame—everybody looked up and right at John Russell.

He lit his cigarette, shook the match out and threw it up past his shoulder, out the window.

The McLaren girl, closer to the window where Mendez and I still were, kept staring at Russell. Do you see how his calm rubbed her? I think any of the rest of us could have lit a cigarette at that time and it would have been all right. But not Russell. Lighting that match touched it off again. Just the way she was looking at him you could see it coming, so I tried to head it off.

I said, "I've been thinking"—though I hadn't, it just came to me then—"when it gets dark, why can't a couple of us sneak down and get her? Maybe we could get her up here without them even seeing us."

"But if they heard you—" Mendez said.

"By dark she'll be dead," the McLaren girl said.

"You don't *know* that," I said.

"Do you want to wait and find out?"

"I was thinking something else," I said. "Braden's watching her too. What if he sees it's not working or he feels sorry for her or something and has that Mexican bring her back in?"

"You just think nice things, don't you?" the McLaren girl said.

"It could happen."

"The day he changes into a human being." She looked at Russell smoking his cigarette. "Or the day *he* does. That's the only thing will save her."

Russell was watching her, but just then the Mexican yelled out from the crushing mill, and Russell's head turned to look down the barrel of the Spencer.

"Hey, *hombre!*" the Mexican yelled, followed by a string of words some of which were in Spanish and were probably as obscene as the English ones mixed in. "Come on down and see me!"

Russell kept looking down the Spencer for at least a minute. When he turned to us again, he drew on his cigarette and dropped it out the window. The hand came down on the saddle-bags next to him. He lifted them up, feeling the weight of them, then let them swing a little and threw them so they fell out in the middle of the floor.

"You want to save her?" Russell said. He looked at Mendez and me and then over to Dr. Favor sitting with his back to the wall a few feet from me. "Somebody want to walk down there and save her?"

Nobody answered.

"Somebody wants to, go ahead," Russell said. "But I'll tell you one thing first. You walk down there you won't walk back. Leave that bag and start to take the woman and they'll kill both of you."

The McLaren girl was watching him, leaning forward a little. "You're saying that so nobody will take the money and try it."

"They'll kill both of you," Russell said. "That's why I'm saying it." He looked over at Dr. Favor before the McLaren girl could say anything else.

"That woman's your wife," Russell said to him. "You want to go untie her?"

Dr. Favor, his head down a little, had his eyes on Russell, but he didn't say one word.

Russell took his time, making it awful embarrassing, so you wouldn't dare look over at Dr. Favor. Finally Russell turned to us again.

"Mr. Mendez," he said, "you want to save her? . . . Or Mr. Carl Allen, I think your name is, you want to walk down there? This man won't. It's his wife, but he won't do it. He doesn't care about his own woman, but maybe someone else does, uh? That's what I want to know."

He was looking right at the McLaren girl then and said, "I don't think I know your name. We live together some, uh? But I don't know your name."

"Kathleen McLaren," she said. He must have surprised her, caught her without anything else ready to say.

"All right, Kathleen McLaren," Russell said. "How would you like to walk down there and untie her and start up again and get shot in the back? Or in the front if that one by the mill does it. In the back or in the front, but one way or the other."

She kept looking at him but didn't say a word.

"There it is," Russell said, nodding to the saddlebags. "Take it. You worry more about his wife than he does. You say I'm not sure or I'm not telling the truth—all right, you go find out what happens."

Russell did a strange thing then. He took off his Apache moccasins and threw them over to the McLaren girl.

"Wear those," he said. "You run faster when they start shooting."

He opened up his blanket and took out his boots and pulled them on. While he did, the McLaren girl kept staring at him; but she never spoke. And when he looked up at her again, her eyes held only for a second before looking away.

It was one thing to know a woman would die if she didn't get help. It was another thing to say you'd die helping her.

I kept thinking of what Russell had said right to me ". . . do you want to walk down there?"

No, I didn't, and I will admit that right here. I believed Braden would shoot anybody who went down there with the money. I think everybody believed it by then. Yes, even the McLaren girl.

The best thing to do, I decided, was just sit there and wait and see what happened. That sounds like a terrible thing to say when a woman's life is at stake, Mrs. Favor's; but I will tell you now it's easier to think of your own life than someone else's. I don't care how brave a person is.

I will admit, too, that Dr. Favor being there made it easier on your conscience. If anybody should go down there it was him. He wasn't going though; that was certain.

Some more time passed. The Mexican, who was patient and had as much time as we did, yelled out at Russell once in a while. Russell stayed with his face pressed to that Spencer longer every time the Mexican insulted him or tried to draw him out. You could see Russell was anxious to get the Mexican. After quite a while passed and the Mexican did not yell at him again, Russell turned around to lean against the wall and make a cigarette. I noticed he threw the tobacco sack away after. It was his last one. He did not light it though; not yet.

Time passed as we sat there and nobody said a word. Russell was thinking, working something out and picturing how it would be; I was sure of that.

About four o'clock the Favor woman started screaming for her husband again; the sounds coming not so loud as before, but it was an awful thing to hear. She would call his name, then say something else which was never clear but like she was pleading with him to help her.

Sitting there in the shack you heard it faintly out in the canyon, "Alex"—the name drawn out, then again maybe and the rest of the words coming like a long moan.

It was quiet when Russell stood up. He looked out the window, not long, just a minute or so, then went over and picked up the grainsack, emptying out what meat and bread and coffee were left, and brought it back to the window. He took one of the ore bags from the sill and put it in the sack. Nobody else moved, all of us watching him. That was when he lit his last cigarette. He drew on it very slowly, very carefully. We kept watching him, maybe not trusting him either, knowing he was about to do something.

"I need somebody," Russell said, looking right at me. Not knowing what he meant I just sat there. "Right here," he said, nodding to the window.

I went over, not in any hurry, staring at him to show I didn't understand. But he didn't explain until he'd motioned again and I was kneeling there with the stock of his Spencer between us. Russell put his hand on it.

"You know how to shoot this?"

"I'm not sure." Frowning at him.

"Push the trigger guard down with your thumb. That ejects and loads . . . uh? Right now it's ready and maybe you only need the one." He added, almost under his breath, "Man, I hope you only need one."

I said, "I'm going to shoot at them?"

"The one by the mill." Russell looked out the window. "He'll come across and walk past that shack by the woman and stand with his back to you, up this way from the shack a little. Then, be sure then, you keep the front sight on him."

"I don't understand what you mean," I said.

"What's there to understand?" There was just a little surprise in his voice, mostly it was quiet and patient. "If he touches his gun, you shoot him."

"But," I said, "in the *back*?"

"I'll ask him if he'll turn around," Russell said.

"Look," I said, "I just don't understand what's going to happen. That's what I'm talking about."

"You'll see it," Russell said. He thought a minute. "Maybe you have to see something else. The money—that it gets up to San Carlos."

"Look, if you'd just explain—"

He touched my arm. "Maybe it's you who has to take it up to San Carlos after. That's easy, uh?"

I kept staring at him. "You never were keeping it for yourself, were you?"

He just looked at me—like he was tired—or like what was the use explaining now?

He put his hat on, straight and pulled down a little over his eyes. He picked up the grainsack, swinging it up over his left shoulder. All of us were watching him, the McLaren girl never moving.

She kept staring and said, "You're going." Just those two words.

Russell made a little shrugging motion. "Maybe try something."

"What if they don't think you've got the money in there?"

"They come out and see," Russell answered.

"They might," the McLaren girl nodded. "They just might."

"They have to," Russell said.

The McLaren girl kept staring at him, wanting to ask why he was doing it, I think. But Russell was looking at Mendez then. "You'll watch this Dr. Favor. Good this time?" he said.

Mendez said something in Spanish and Russell answered also in Spanish, shrugging his shoulders. Mendez appeared like he was afraid to breathe. Russell turned to Dr. Favor. He had something for everybody.

"All that trouble you went to, uh?"

Dr. Favor didn't answer, not caring what anybody said or thought about him now. He sat there staring up at Russell, his big face pale-looking with that reddish hair around it and with hardly any expression. He probably thought this John Russell was the biggest fool God ever made.

We were watching him, every one of us; perhaps still not certain he was going down there and having to see it to believe it.

He was at the door when the McLaren girl picked up his

moccasins and threw them over to him. "Wear those," she said. "You run faster when they start shooting."

Do you see what she was doing? Giving it right back to him. Using the same words even that he had used before. Saying it calmly and watching to see his reaction.

And seeing his smile then; a smile you were sure he meant. Even with his hat on, at that moment he looked young and like anybody else.

Russell stood with his hand on the door, looking over his shoulder at the McLaren girl, at her only.

"Maybe we should talk more sometime," he said.

"Maybe," the McLaren girl answered. She was looking at him the same way, intently, like seeing something in him that was not there before. "When things calm down," she said.

I had the feeling she wanted to say more than that, but she didn't.

Russell nodded, his strange light-blue-colored eyes not moving from the girl's. "When things calm down," he said back.

He pulled the door open and stepped outside with the grainsack over his shoulder. The next time I was close enough to John Russell to see his face, he was dead.

Not long ago I was talking to a man from Benson who said they were playing a song now about Frank Braden and the woman he stole for reasons of love, and that I would appreciate it. I said are they playing a song about John Russell? He said who is John Russell?

What took place that afternoon at the San Pete mine has been written many times and different ways. (Including the song now.) Maybe you have read some of them. All I want to say is the account that appeared in the *Florence Enterprise* is a true one, even to the number of shots that were fired. Except even that account does not tell enough. (Which is what caused me to write this.) It describes a man named John Russell; but you still do not know John Russell after you have read it.

I am not saying anything against the *Florence Enterprise*.

Their account was written in one hour or so, just telling what
happened. I have been writing this for three months trying to
tell you about John Russell as he was, so you will understand
him. Yet, after three months of writing and thinking and all, I
can't truthfully say I understand him myself. I only feel I know
why he walked down that slope.

I watched him from the window. I was also keeping an eye
out for the Mexican. The Mexican must have seen Russell as he
started down, but he did not come out from the crushing mill
until Russell was about half way.

That was when Russell held up the grainsack. "Hey!" He
yelled out, the same way the Mexican had been yelling at him,
"I got something for you!"

The Mexican was being careful as he moved across the
grade, keeping his eyes on Russell all the time. By then the Favor woman had seen him; sitting stooped over, her hair hanging
and straggly, she was watching him come.

Russell did not look at the Mexican, though he must have
known the Mexican was moving down and across the grade as
if to head him off. By then you could see part of the Mexican's
back. I got down lower and, as Russell had instructed, put the
front sight of the Spencer square on him, getting an awful feeling as I did.

At that moment, Early, up above us on the ridge, was probably putting his sights on Russell.

I kept expecting the Mexican to do something; but as he got
over more by that little shack he slowed up so that he was
hardly moving; not taking his eyes from Russell for a second,
his right elbow bent and the elbow pressed against where he
had been shot, his left hand hanging free. That was the hand I
had watched, feeling the trigger of the Spencer and ready to
pull it if the hand went to the Colt gun along side it.

The Mexican stopped.

He was almost in line but a little to the left; so that from here you would look down past his right side to Russell who was nearing the Favor woman. She did not call out or appear to have said a word; she just kept staring at him, maybe not believing what she saw.

It was as Russell reached her that Frank Braden showed himself.

Braden came out of the veranda shade. He was limping some, I think trying not to show it, though he kept his left hand on his thigh, gripping it with his fingers spread.

The Mexican had not moved. I kept sighting on him, trying to watch Braden and Russell at the same time. Russell was kneeling by the woman, not paying any attention to Braden who kept coming. Braden called something, but Russell did not look up.

Braden called out again, slowing up and ready, you could tell.

Russell rose to his feet, helping the Favor woman as he did and you saw she was untied now. You also saw the grainsack lying over on the other side of the ore-cart tracks.

Russell and the Favor woman had taken only a few steps when Braden called out again. This time Russell stopped, though he motioned the Favor woman to keep going. She did, but looking back as Russell stood there watching Braden. She got up as high as the Mexican. He paid no attention to her. She was walking kind of sideways, coming up but looking back all the time.

The next thing I knew the front of the Spencer was on her. She had wandered just enough, looking back and not watching where she was going, to get behind the Mexican. I looked up, about to yell at her, but didn't. The Mexican would hear it too.

All I could do was keep telling her to get out of the way in my mind. Please hurry up and get out of the way.

Braden had reached the grainsack. He stood by it saying something to Russell who was about ten feet from him. Russell answered him. (What this was about, no one knows. Braden could have said to open the sack, show him the money. Russell would have told him to look in it himself if he doubted it was there.)

The Favor woman looked up at where we were. I stood up and waved my arm, but as I did she was looking back the other way again.

Even standing and sighting down with the Spencer against the side frame, the Favor woman was still in the way. I could only see part of the Mexican.

In my mind I kept telling her over and over again to get out of the way, to please, for the Lord's sake move one way or the other and to *hurry*! Now, right now, just move or look up here again or sit down or do *something*!

She stood there. She turned around to watch what was happening below and did not move from the spot.

Braden, his left hand still holding his thigh, straightened the grainsack with his boot toe so that the open end was toward him. Russell watched.

Braden went down to one knee, his right one, and now the hand came away from his thigh and unloosened the opening of the grainsack. Russell watched.

Braden straightened up, still kneeling. He said something to Russell. What? Warning him? Telling him not to try anything because the Mexican was behind him?

I saw Braden's hand reach inside the grainsack.

Move! I thought. Get somewhere else!

If there was time—

Just move! I actually heard it in my mind, and I was to the door and out the door, running along the shelf, seven, eight, ten yards to be sure of the angle, to be sure of not hitting the woman.

But I had not even brought up the gun to aim when Braden's hand came out of the grainsack. He was rising, trying to get out his revolver, but was already too late. Russell drew and fired twice with his Colt extended and aimed . . . his other arm coming up as he fired the second round and he was stumbling forward as if kicked in the back. The Mexican had pulled his long-barreled .44 and fired three shots in the time Russell had hit Braden twice and Braden and Russell both went down, Russell to his hands and knees, but turning with his revolver already raised and he fired as the Mexican fired again, fired as the Mexican stumbled forward, fired as the Mexican staggered and dropped to his knees and fell facedown with his arms spread. There were three more shots at that time, exactly three, because I can hear them every time I picture what took place; the shots coming from the ridge above us, from Early who was up there. I turned, aiming the Spencer almost straight up, but there was no sign of him. (There was no sign of him ever again that I know of.) When I turned back again, I saw Russell lying facedown between the ore-cart tracks. In the quiet that followed, all of us went down there.

Frank Braden had been shot twice in the chest; there was also the wound in his left thigh and a bullet crease across the shin of his left boot which had not touched him. Frank Braden was dead.

The Mexican had been hit in the chest twice and once in the stomach; plus the wound in his side that looked awful enough to have killed him. He lived another hour or so, but never told us his name, though he asked what Russell's was.

John Russell had been shot three times low in the back. We turned him over and saw he had been hit twice again, through the neck and chest. He was dead.

I was the one rode to Delgado's, running the horse most of the way, and ruining it, not intending to but not caring either. Delgado sent one of his boys to Sweetmary for the deputy. Delgado and I rode back to the San Pete in a wagon and got there in the dark of early morning. You could hear the crickets in the old buildings. Down in the open the McLaren girl and Henry Mendez and Dr. Favor and his wife were by a fire they'd kept going. Only Mrs. Favor had slept. Mendez had dug two graves.

Delgado and I sat with them and by the time it started to get light the Sweetmary deputy, J. R. Lyons, arrived.

He looked at the bodies, Braden's and the Mexican's by the graves, Russell's in the wagon. Dig a hole for him too, J. R. Lyons said. What's the difference? He's dead. The McLaren girl said look all you want, but keep your opinions; we were taking Russell to Sweetmary for proper burial with a Mass and all and if Mr. J. R. Lyons didn't like it he didn't have to attend.

J. R. Lyons said of course he would. Once Dr. Favor and the stolen government money were handed over to a United States marshal.

(Which was done. Dr. Favor was tried in the District Court at Florence about a month later and sentenced to seven years in a Yuma prison. Mrs. Favor was not at the trial.)

John Russell was buried at Sweetmary. It was strange that neither the McLaren girl nor Henry Mendez nor I said much about him until after the funeral, and when we did talk found there wasn't much to be said.

You can look at something for a long time and not see it until it has moved or run off. That was how we had looked at Russell. Now, nobody questioned why he had walked down that slope. What we asked ourselves was why we ever thought he wouldn't.

Maybe he was showing off a little bit when he asked each of us if we wanted to walk down to the Favor woman, knowing nobody would but himself.

Maybe he let us think a lot of things about him that weren't true. But as Russell would say, that was up to us. He let people do or think what they wanted while he smoked a cigarette and thought it out calmly, without his feelings getting mixed up in it. Russell never changed the whole time, though I think everyone else did in some way. He did what he felt had to be done. Even if it meant dying. So maybe you don't have to understand him. You just know him.

"Take a good look at Russell. You will never see another one like him as long as you live." That first day, at Delgado's, Henry Mendez said it all.